THE HOLLOW SUNDAY

THE HOLLOW
SUNDAY

*

ROBERT HARLING

THE COMPANION BOOK CLUB
LONDON

*Made and printed in Great Britain
for the Companion Book Club (Odhams Books Ltd.)
by Odhams (Watford) Limited
Watford, Herts.*
S.468.UAO.

Word of any Fleet Street project comes in whispers of proof and gusts of rumour.

No whisper is heard for longer than a few hours or beyond a few streets. No gust for longer than a week or beyond the Seven Seas. Yet neither somehow dies.

Soon the whole thing is like an isobar map: minute areas of low-pressure fact encompassed by monstrous shapes of high-pressure fiction. And even those few facts are soon distorted by rumour, some still bearing a semblance of truth, others plainly false but too good to let die.

New Sunday was no different from all this.

Spurway rang me out of the blue.

After a few sparring felicities, he said, in his gravelly twentieth-century television voice: 'They tell me you're taking a sabbatical year.'

'Then they lie, whoever they are. I was *given* a sabbatical year.'

He laughed. 'What's the difference?'

'For my kind you get paid.'

'Sounds wonderful. Is it?'

'Mixed,' I said and meant.

'How did it start?'

'It's a long story. Let's forget it.'

'I can't forget it. When I heard I couldn't believe it. Sounds so academic. Fleet Street going all Ph.D. Wish it could happen to me, but I'm not the donnish type, as you may remember. Forgive the probing and all that, but there's one or two questions I'd like to ask.'

'You can ask two more. Then the day's done and I ring off.'

'Are you still working?'

'Occasionally.'

'What on?'

'A book of sorts.'

'What about the paper?'

'The occasional piece.'

'How occasional?'

'When I feel like it. When I'm sufficiently interested in something. When they're desperate. I don't want to be tied.'

'That's the kind of lingo I like to hear. Wish I could talk it. So you're untied?'

'Not exactly. Neither tied nor untied. I've got a retainer. You could say I'm part-tied.'

'It all sounds very subtle and umbilical. I'll try sorting it out.'

It was time to break up the banter. I said: 'You've had your share of questions. Now one from me: Why ring me? Not to ask after my health, or my ideas of freedom, that's certain. I haven't seen you in months. What is it?'

'Actually I'm ringing to ask if you're enjoying your new-found freedom. Now I find it's not even freedom. Do you enjoy it, by the way?' He laughed. 'Don't sound like it to me.'

'I enjoy getting up late. I enjoy spending more time at the B.M. The rest I'm not sure about.'

I was also enjoying hearing myself say the truths aloud, so I went on: 'Like most scribblers I need to be told what to do. A touch of the lash. Not too hard, not too light.'

'The silken lash. Sounds most diverting and perverting.'

'Whatever it is, I need it.'

'Humiliating discovery. I made it years ago. Why don't we lunch sometime?'

'Why don't we? But what's all this in aid of? The sudden solicitude, the sudden queries?'

'Me, principally,' Spurway said, laughing again.

The reply was unexpected enough for me to laugh, too. I said: 'I never thought of you as needing aid of any kind.'

'I do, y'know. I've got an idea. I want to talk to you about it.'

'I wouldn't be interested. In any case my retainer puts me under an obligation.'

'An obligation's scarcely a contract. And what are you

6

obligated not to do? Not to write? Not to talk? Not to listen? Not to what?'

'After I've finished writing there's damn-all left.'

'O.K., O.K., but is keeping up to date with the Fleet Street grapevine barred?'

'Dead cunning.'

He laughed and said quickly: 'Good. It's a date then. What about next Thursday?'

'All right,' I said, grudgingly, knowing damn well I'd been caught by curiosity crossed with blarney. I knew it, even as I agreed, but I still didn't like it.

'Good. Savoy. One o'clock. Meet you in the foyer.'

We talked about nothing for another minute or so before I rang off with lacklustre farewell noises.

I went out into the kitchen. Going through the living-room I noticed the skeleton clock said ten-fifteen. It was slow by ten minutes. I put it right. In the kitchen I picked up a tea-cloth and began to dry a breakfast cup.

Mrs Harry Cowell—Molly—my daily, firmly took both cup and cloth from me.

'No need to do that,' she said. 'You're not very good at it and it's dry, anyway. You only do it when you're fussed and then you usually break something. What's upset you, the phone call?'

I nodded absently. 'Only mildly.'

'The missus again?'

'Not this time.'

'Shall I make some more coffee?'

'Not a bad idea.'

'And then what?'

'I'm going out.'

'Straightaway?'

'Not if you've any other ideas.'

She said she had.

3

This narrative probably needs a break here if I'm concerned with truth, as I tell myself I am. Or even with my own version of the truth.

As I see it, then, if I'm to put down something of the Spurway-Frensham Baker story, I need to put down something of my own. Not that they're invincibly interlocked, but for me they have a snarled-up kind of link and that's all that matters in this kind of record.

Mrs Harry Cowell, then, was my daily and also my bit on the side. Nowadays she's neither. Things have changed.

She came to work for me after my marriage got bitched up. She was (and presumably still is) handsome, wide-hipped, brassy, blonde, uneducated, uncomplicated. She was thus everything my education, training, tastes and all the rest of the environmental hotch-potch should have dismissed on the instant. What a hope! Molly Cowell reeked of sex the way the kitchen reeked of burnt cheese when she did what she called one of her 'super-duper welsh rabbits'.

She lived near by, with her husband and small son, in one of those chilling Victorian charity blocks in Cale Street, behind the King's Road. Each morning she took her eight-year-old boy, Gary, to school, *en route* to my flat in Swan Court.

Molly's husband—Harryboy, as she called him—was a long-distance lorry-driver. He worked punitive hours, was usually half-drunk or half-asleep, and she didn't get enough of it. Or so she had confessed or heartily implied fairly early on. So we organized that side of things in the inevitable double-talk, cross-talk way these things get fixed, and the results showed in her better pay-packet and my better moods. Once, in a blushing outburst, she confessed she enjoyed the contrasting favours and techniques of her part-time Harryboy and part-time employer. She also made no bones about enjoying the extra lolly.

Sordid? Squalid? Immoral? Amoral? I suppose it might seem all those things to a canon or even a curate, but I'm neither. I enjoyed this sensual entanglement without strings. I enjoyed my daily's casual lust and sprawling limbs, first explored, she once explained, by a fitter on a waste lot behind her wartime aircraft components factory in Ponders End. That's where, she said, she found she was ready-made for the job.

8

So much for that. The rest of my domestic set-up is typical of half the broken marriages I know. I see my wife, Helen, about twice a week. Occasionally I take her out to dinner. From time to time I even stay with her, sleep with her. All very handy, randy, modern, practical and hopeless. She lives with our ten-year-old daughter, Marion, on the other side of King's Road in the small house in Milner Street we once shared.

All in all, a good all-round Royal Borough of Chelsea triangle or, possibly, quadrangle.

Helen is tall and slim, with fine bones, fine eyes and the most captivating chestnut hair in Christendom. She's a sharp dresser, a sound and economical manager and a mother in ten thousand. She's also well-read and what is known as well-informed, which means, I suppose, that she reads *Vogue*, *The Queen* and the *Daily Telegraph*. I admire her a great deal. But admiration is not enough.

What went wrong then?

Who can answer that kind of question? Bed was almost all right. We had almost enough money. Up to a point we had almost the same kind of interests. We both adored Marion. Finally, I suspect, ours was just another case of what might be called marital fatigue. Although there might have been a modicum of love in the match at the beginning, there was damn-all left after a couple of years. Merely the substitute of formal unmoving tenderness.

After ten years we'd turned it in.

I read somewhere that fifty per cent of all broken marriages last at least ten years. And that ninety per cent of all marriages last until death do us part. But not for Helen in Milner Street, in our onetime small and pretty house, or for me in a two-room flat in Swan Court. What a way to run a marriage! But there it was and there it still is.

We met, as I've said, once or twice a week. Each time we took up, in a listless, nagging kind of way, where we left off. I usually stayed overnight at Milner Street when we dined out.

There were other men in Helen's life, but she was discreet

9

about them. None ever stayed in the house. She had no yearning for divorce or remarriage. Neither had I. We just drifted. Until Molly Cowell came along there had been other women in my life, but not many and one at a time. Basically, I imagine, I'm a two-woman man, as, I suspect, are most of my fellow-men.

Perhaps we both hoped that one day we'd grow up and get together again and discover the secret of the beautiful monotony of happy marriage. In more self-truthful moments I knew we never would. We hadn't got the answer. We weren't the types. As I see it, all men and most women are selfish. The great secret, I believe, is to marry somebody whose ideas of selfishness dovetail with your own on a positive-negative basis. If you've got a self-willed, pathological urge to make decisions, get there first, be boss, then marry somebody with a spineless but selfish urge to sit back, look on and have decisions made for her (or him). And so on and on. I've no other thoughts to offer on the subject. Like death it's too big, too diffuse and has no answers this side of the crematorium. All I know is that our effort didn't work from about square three onwards and upwards.

I see that this has become a digression, even a dirge. But it has a place in the record, all the same. Any man setting out to tell a tale of another man is, in part, telling his own tale, too. This, then, is partly mine as well as Spurway's, Baker's and Gregory's. More will doubtless come out *en route*.

Meantime, back to Spurway.

4

I'd known Spurway on and off—mostly off—for fifteen years. I'd met him first at Oxford. He came up when I was in my last disastrous year. He started the way he meant to go on, by causing trouble to his seniors and would-be helpers and avoiding due retribution by moments and inches.

He had grown up somewhere in the Midlands, attended a Black Country grammar school, won an Open Scholarship.

He had, apparently, known where he was going from about the age of ten. This was merely the beginning.

At Oxford he didn't give a damn for anyone. He carefully kept his flat Midland accent and made no friends. He quickly saw that academic success didn't mean a thing at Oxford or anywhere else unless you had ambitions to be a don or any other kind of pundit on a dais, pulpit or rostrum. And as his ambitions were of a strictly non-academic order he set about making a noise about Michael Sydney Spurway. He also played rugger extremely well, only just missing a blue. That helped, of course.

He'd got a First in Geography, a cold piece of self-reckoning, he told me long afterwards. 'I needed a First, but I haven't got a first-class brain. It's a speedy piece of mechanism but not profound. Not by any standards. So I opted for Geography. The experts know it's a soft option, but the outside world—where I knew I was going—don't. A First is a First to the unversed masses. It worked.'

By the time he came down he was already fairly well known. On the strength of his *Isis* performance he'd got a job as assistant features editor on the old *Sunday Graphic* before Kemsley closed it down. After a year he'd moved, first into steam radio, then into television.

A BBC top man later told me that Spurway could do any minion's job—from cutting to projecting—as well as his own jobs of writing, directing, producing. He'd learned the lot, despite the spies and tank-traps of the manifold unions he dealt with.

His interim ambition was to be a programme boss. And that he was at twenty-eight. He had been given his own programme, which he called *History is Men,* and had thereupon set about seeking to prove that reasonable thesis by dealing with men still living, not with those long dead. He got perilously near the legal edge sometimes, of course, but he was always saved by careful documentation. Defiant homosexuals, pompous warriors, impecunious poets, importuning politicos, were all hypnotized on to his programme in that extraordinary way the television camera lures mankind into its diminishing images and half-truths.

11

He followed *History is Men* with *Memories of my Dead Youth,* in which he got an eminent dozen, men and women, with under-privileged beginnings to retrace their steps around the Gorbals, Spitalfields, Tiger Bay and other sombre settings. They told their scarifying tales of early hunger, poverty and worse, against a background that was still there, despite the Welfare State. It was quite a programme, and, as usual, made Spurway few friends and a lot of Establishment enemies.

There were other programmes where that one came from: he produced them, directed them, forced them through.

But finally—after three years as a petty chieftain—he'd fallen out with the BBC top brass. The fall-out was inevitable. Some said he'd calculated the timing to a day. He moved over to ITV and had stayed there for two years, mainly on programmes of his own devising, all controversial, all somehow touched by a twisted rancour against mammon and success, the very touchstones of his own ambition. The rancour came out in everything he said and did.

'What are you after?' I once asked him.

'Power.'

'So are a lot of other people. It always eludes.'

'That's a truism usually voiced by the unambitious.'

'You may be right. But what *kind* of power do you want?'

'No particular kind. It's quantity I'm after first. Not quality. I'll sort out the quality later. A local vicar has power of a kind but I wouldn't be interested in power that size.'

'But isn't it true that the only kind of power worth having is specialized power?' I asked. 'The vicar has a kind of specialized power. So has a good Housing Minister, a kingpin physicist or brain surgeon.'

'What if your sphere happens to be this great new bogus science called communications?' he countered.

'Which segment of the sphere? Newspapers, radio, telly, Early Bird or what?'

'The lot!' he said simply but grandiloquently.

'How are you training yourself for the top job?' I asked, tongue in cheek.

He was in no mood for that kind of pleasantry and ignored the jibe. 'Supposing I make myself the best-trained, most versatile, most knowledgeable goon on all forms of communications in this country? Supposing, by my early forties, there's a major crisis of some kind—not necessarily war but a catastrophic industrial blow-up or economic collapse—and they have to call in the best man for the job, the way the British people had to call in Churchill in nineteen-forty because he'd prepared himself to be the only man for the job, what then?'

'You're not underplaying your comparisons.'

'Why should I? Who cares? This whole bloody business of communications is still in its infancy. Inside ten years I aim to know more about every facet of the subject than any other man in Britain.'

That had been three years before. He had kept to his programme. Hence, presumably, his call to me.

5

He was there first, the way he probably set himself to be first for any appointment, I thought tetchily, going through the swing doors, seeing him standing foursquare to the door.

He was well above middle height with thick hair, once black, now streaked iron-grey. His flushed, heavy-featured face was still handsome, but good living was beginning to sew thin threads in nose and cheeks. Yet the grey eyes, although bloodshot, were still steely; the butt of jaw still belligerent. He was putting on weight, but the extra kilos seemed to have been loaded on to his torso rather than his belly, giving him more the air of a latterday pouter pigeon than the eaglet of yesteryear.

His dark-blue two-piece lightweight suit was well made, but he wore it with the swagger of a sailor just ashore; the unbuttoned jacket flapped like an out-of-hand jib. Like many hard-drinking, hard-case, hardening-artery youngish men, he was alive with go-getting vitality and unquestioning self-assertion. From his quick steps to the set of his shoulders he was brimful of bounce.

The voice was still the same. Or almost. The flat vowels, deliberately retained from early days in that well-publicized mining village, were now touched by a slight drawl, cultivated no doubt from transatlantic trips and sound tracks. The sounds still grated aggressively, but quicksilver asides still enlivened the harsh inflections. A slightly fruitier and more self-appreciative voice, I thought, but basically the same.

At the table he took out a pair of horn-rimmed spectacles with heavy black frames, the kind that Churchill and Spaak made famous and fashionable. He took the menu with one hand, opened the spectacles with the other, frowning, pre-occupied. The gesture was plainly part of the act—if you have to wear 'em make 'em do a job of work for you. So here they were, further demonstration of authority: symbols not of myopia or incipient middle-age but a man at ease with himself and his likely destiny.

He already knew what he wanted. He put the menu down and lit a cigarette. I declined.

'Afraid I'm a creature of habit,' he said. 'Always the same. And I have to watch the calories. Smoked salmon, poussin or minute steak, green salad. Poussin today. What about you?'

'Suits me,' I said, wishing I had the contrariness to order contrariwise, but the meal seemed what I needed.

The waiter scribbled and went. Spurway said, 'How's things?'

'I told you.'

'What are you working at?'

'A book I've been working at for twenty years.'

'What about?'

'Sarah, Duchess of Marlborough.'

'God Almighty. You're not serious?'

'I'll send you a copy one day. Say ten years' time.'

The wine waiter came. Spurway took the list.

'What'll you drink?'

'Pimms.'

'Two Pimms. Number two,' he said, returning the list. The waiter went.

Spurway opened with a sighting shot. 'Let's see. Must be over a year since we met.'

'All of that. Nearer two.'

'A lot happens in a year in Fleet Street these days. Whole place is like a damn powder keg.'

'Are you on one?'

'I've always been on one.' He came to the point: 'Why did you try to resign?'

'How did you know?'

'My spies tell me you're all set for a change.'

'Well, I'm not. Your spies need a shake-up.'

'I think they're pretty good. And I'll prove it. I'm told that although filthy lucre mightn't tempt you, a brand new serious feature might.'

'Sly spy, I see, but I doubt whether anything on your wonder sheet could tempt me.'

'We'll come to that later.'

'No, let's come to it now. Will it ever get off the ground? Will it ever be more than a multi-millionaire-printer-publisher's pipe dream?'

'It's nearer than you think.'

Drinks came. Then the smoked salmon. Spurway drank, then began to eat, but still managed to talk. He did the manifold job swiftly and, up to a point, efficiently.

'What are you on it?' I asked. 'Editor? Rumour says you are.'

'As usual, rumour's only about ninety-eight per cent right. I *wasn't* editor but I *am* now. West brought me in to be editorial adviser. King-pin, in fact. A kind of one-man brains trust to spark off new features. I could have been editor from the word "go", but I made Robbins editor-designate, gave him more backing than any editor-designate's ever had. Budget like an oil-man's ransom. But a week ago, after we'd had a great bash-around with the dummies, and he was all lined up to make a pre-publication presentation, he went to pieces. In front of half a dozen of us.'

'You wept for him, no doubt?'

'No doubt.'

'What exactly d'you mean by "went to pieces"?'

'Showed he didn't know what kind of paper I had in mind. Not by a million miles.'

'And what kind of paper had you in mind?'

'The best in the land. News as good as the Telegraph's, features as off-beat as the Observer's, the whole thing as readable and up-to-the-minute as the Sunday Times, arts features as good as Country Life's or Apollo's—and all in colour tabloid form.'

'A tall order.'

'It's got to be.'

'Do you and West see eye-to-eye?'

'On this, at least. Why d'you think I joined the outfit?'

'To learn more about newspapers if I remember correctly. You once told me that was one of the few chinks in your armour.'

'Elephantine memory, I see. Well, it's true. Or was. This past year I've learned enough to stack me up for the next five years.'

'And now West's asked you to take over?'

'It was the inevitable choice. It was also his intention from the word "go". And mine—neither of us wanted to be precipitate. We wanted to size things up first.'

'And when is D-Day?'

'Two months from now.'

'Cutting things fine, isn't it?'

He shook his head. 'My original time-table.'

I doubted that, but I said, 'What's your print order going to be?'

'Around half a million. Maybe more. We'll see on the day.'

'Why so few?'

'West wants to see where he's going.'

'Look. I'm in the business. In this game you either print at least a million and a half or you're out. Preferably two million. If you're offering colour right through the paper you could sell two millions the first day.'

He was suddenly defensive. 'That's rather my view. West thinks otherwise. He's the boss. Maybe we shall. We'll see.'

'What's against it?'

'Nothing so far as I know. But West is the business man. I leave all that to him. It's his decision. As he sees it, he'd rather have the first half-dozen issues in short supply and at a premium than get left with half a million unsolds. He wants everybody asking for it, newsagents clamouring for it. That way it's non-obtainability becomes a positive selling-point. That's West's reasoning. He's had a lot of experience in promotion. He may be right.'

'You should call it Dream Sunday.'

He laughed, then said: 'Anyway, I'm not here to talk about our print order or likely sales. Whatever they are, the paper's going to be a winner. I'm not interested in failures.'

'How much has West spent on his machines? I hear they're terrific.'

'Three millions. They are.'

'Web-fed offset job, isn't it?'

'It is.'

'So he's got to make a success of things?'

'Up to a point.'

'Which means?' I persisted.

'That there's a lot more millions where those came from. He's got nerve.'

'He can afford to have nerve. He's always had successes so far.'

'This is a new kind of venture for him.'

'That's true. What's *your* nerve like these days?'

'Not bad. In my own meagre way I've got every bit as much at stake as West. My reputation. My future. That's my lot.'

'You've announced that it's going to be the paper for Tomorrow's Top Brass and Today's Young Turks. Is it?'

He winced as I repeated the slogans. 'I like our slogans. They're good, but I prefer 'em read rather than said.'

'And how are you going after tomorrow's top brass?'

'How would you?' he countered.

'I'd get hold of some of the young writers who're stirring up the theatre here and in the provincial reps. I'd buy a political reporter from Transport House. Or from the Bow Group. Or both. I'd get hold of some of these young camera zanies on the glossies and give them their head. I'd get my layout men from the advertising agencies or the glossies. They know what it's all about.'

'Go on.'

'Why should I go on? It's your beat,' but I went on: 'I'd get some talent from the world you came from, the telly world of movement, and see what they could make of newspaper pictures. With such men and colour you could do a lot.'

'I've done a lot. You'd be surprised. What else?'

'Nobody over forty would get anywhere near it and nobody who hadn't a maestro's knowledge of his subject or an obsession with it, whether news or films, politics or sport, would stand a chance.'

'Well, on your estimate I might be in. I'm thirty-five. How old are you?'

'Thirty-eight.'

'Pretty near your own cliff-edge.'

'I chose forty as a symbol-figure. Some seventy-year-olds never get to forty. The Beaver never did. Cocteau never did. Beecham never did. Picasso never will. Sargent never did. Britten never will.'

'West never will.'

'Phoney loyalty will get you nowhere. T. J. West is as old as Mount Sinai. I've seen him. He was born that way. He'll die that way. He was never young.'

'When did you meet him?' Spurway demanded. Sharply, I thought.

'I interviewed him once for Mason. A profile piece. West didn't like it.'

Spurway grinned. 'Of course. I remember. No, he didn't like it. He mentioned it when I said I wanted you. I'd forgotten.'

I ignored that and went on with West. 'He didn't like it because I said he was hypnotically convinced he could do anything, buy anything with his millions. Like any other man who comes to a foreign country and makes a quick

18

million, he's got a built-in contempt for the people who let him do it.'

'He's got a lot more millions now.'

'And a lot more contempt for Britain and the British.'

'I don't think so. In fact, I'd say West is more English than any native I know,' Spurway said, apparently enjoying himself.

'His clothes maybe. His mind is still a cold Hungarian goulash.'

'Rumanian,' Spurway corrected, grinning.

'How d'you get on with him?'

'As I said, we usually see eye to eye. Finally.'

'And when you don't?'

'He's still Mr Big. He's the money-bags. But he's slowing down a bit. With luck I'll see him off and be king-pin of the whole bloody shooting-match.'

'Would you settle for the West empire rather than communications overlord of Great Britain?'

Spurway chuckled. 'I'd toss a coin,' he said. 'But we're digressing. Let's keep to New Sunday, shall we? And that means you.'

'I doubt it. But you're the one with the big ideas. Why not spill 'em?'

'All right. I'm weak on writers. You suspect it. I know it. Not critics. They're two a penny. And I'm not having regular critics, anyway. Not for books, theatre, films or anything else. I've watched 'em elsewhere growing old and fat and pompous, writing the same old cock week after week, and I'm not having any of them or it.'

'You've got a point there. What's your bright idea?'

'I've got a rota of young men and women who've done the job themselves. Written novels, made films, acted, produced. They're the only people fit to criticize other people's creative work—not these fat-arsed, sterile nits who've never done a creative stint in all the drivelling days of their hoary old lives.'

I laughed. 'Hysteria now,' I said.

'You can laugh, but you know it's true. I'm all right on my critical team, but I'm weak on writers who've got something to say about the world we live in. That's why I rang you. I like what you write. A lot of it fits in with my own notions.'

'Such as?'

'I want first-rate text. Features in depth.'

'Oh Christ!' I groaned. 'Not that in depth stuff. Please.'

'My notions may not be as upstage and long-haired as your own,' Spurway said, smiling thinly, 'but they're pretty clear-cut. "In depth" is my phrase for today, buster.'

'What else have you—or West—got?'

'The first machines in England that will print the best part of a top-class Sunday newspaper in colour. Not just colour supplements, but pretty well the whole damn job. And up to three million copies. And more if wanted.'

'That's dreamland, the future. What's he got now?'

'He's got to take his chance like any other innovator.'

'Meantime, look at his magazines. Junk. A load of money-making, semi-literate, semi-technical trade magazines full of ads and information that wouldn't get anybody an "O" Level.'

'Let's keep to New Sunday, shall we? He's given me the go-ahead to put out the best brand-new Sunday newspaper this country's ever seen. And he's going to get it. Talent's a purchaseable commodity, and I've bought some of it.'

'And he bought you?'

'Yes, he bought me and I've bought some others. I like what I've got. But I need more. You, for instance.'

'Very flattering and all that, but not my line,' I said, flicking the offer aside in the best moment of the lunch. 'I like newsprint and I like black-and-white. I'm not made for colour.'

He exploded. 'And you have the audacity to talk about Robbins and others being down on their mental uppers!' he scoffed. 'You make me sick!' He mimicked my words: ' "I'm not made for colour." Well, let me tell you, buster, colour's made for a few million other people. They seem to like it. The supplements show that. Colour's here to stay.'

I laughed, loudly and genuinely, but I still shook my head. 'My job's words,' I said. 'The day you prove they're easier to read in red or yellow ink, I'm your man. Meantime, I'll stick to old-fashioned black. Comes off on the hands but stays in the mind—sometimes.'

'Of course your sacred, beautiful, twenty-four carat golden prose would be printed in black ink,' he barked back, '—but what about pictures? Don't you ever want to see the pictures for your lousy features in colour?'

'Never,' I lied.

'Balls!' he said. 'And now, Paul, flattery apart, what about it?'

'Not interested.'

The waiter came to the table. For a moment greed drove out Spurway's curiosity, but with poussin and salad before him he was at ease again. 'Why have you never wanted to edit?' he asked in a tangential switch.

Like most other journalists I'd thought about that particular matter too often to hesitate for words. 'A good editor enjoys making decisions. I don't. A good editor tells other people what to write. I prefer to write. A good editor is ambitious. I'm not. At least not in that way. I'd like to be, but I'm not. Any more? I could give you another dozen.'

'You've sold me the idea,' Spurway said, sliding a minute slice of poussin on his fork, stretching across to spike a leaf of lettuce in a glutton's competent gesture. 'Frankly, I never saw you in the rôle. I was flying a kite.'

It's one thing to denigrate one's own talents: another when somebody else essays the job. I didn't like Spurway's laconic words. 'And how did you see me?' I asked, nettled.

'I see I've upset you, by agreeing with you,' he said without apology. 'It's a hard world. I can't win. I agree with you and you don't like it. Yet what I'm offering you and what you've turned down before hearing me out, is, I suspect, all you've ever wanted, tailored personally to *your* measurements. But vanity's vanity anywhere. You're so bloody pleased with your job on *the* great Liberal newspaper that you'd already decided to turn down whatever I offered you.'

'Cut the cackle,' I said, still ruffled. 'What's the great and glorious temptation?'

21

'What I'm offering you is a couple of pages every week to fill any way you damn well like. As editor-in-chief all I want to see is the final page proof. We're large tabloid, by the way. It's all yours. No strings. You can use colour or you can stay black-and-white. I've even got a title for it: Faces and Places, preferably with an ampersand. I want it to be the best thing of its kind. Better than Atticus, Hickey and the rest of the gabby gang. If you want the whole bloody feature to write about an unknown female sculptor who makes phallic symbols out of wire and wickerwork one week and the fifteen members of the Harlequins the next week it's all yours.'

'Your two weaknesses,' I said. 'Your phallus and the rugger field.'

He grinned. 'That elephantine memory again.' He went on: 'As a sideline I could also do with some immediate and dispassionate editorial advice. You seem made for that job, too. There's still some areas of this bloody Fleet Street jungle with booby-traps I don't spot quite soon enough. You would. I'd like you around. Now what d'you think?'

Of course I was interested. He had touched on the weakness that wears away at the vanity of any journalist: his very own feature with no strings, no directives, no petty, intervening, interfering bosses.

'Well, what about it? Temptation or not?' Spurway asked after a pause.

'Of course it is,' I growled. I was down for a count of nine and groggy.

'It was meant to be. And I'd do my best to see it wasn't too much of a risk. Contract-wise and all that, Paul.'

'I'll have to talk it over with Mason. And by this time tomorrow I shall have second thoughts.'

'Before that, if I know you one tiny bit.'

'I have obligations.'

'Don't overdo that obligations line. Loyalty will get you nowhere, as you said just now.'

'I said phoney loyalty.'

'D'you think old-fashioned loyalty is part of Mason's creed?'

'It's my idea of loyalty that matters, not Mason's.'

Spurway lowered his head in mock deference. 'Forgive me. These philosophical subtleties sometimes elude me.' He lit another cigarette.

'When d'you have to have an answer?'

'Every day's important to me now. Today's Thursday. What about Saturday?'

'Too soon.'

'Next Tuesday, then, at the latest. I'll put all this in a letter when I get back this afternoon.'

'What else is there to put?'

'Terms and so forth.'

'I'd forgotten that. What's your idea there?'

'In view of the extra work, the risk to your reputation and present security, twelve hundred a year more than you're getting, plus three hundred expenses more than you're getting, plus car and usual perks, and a two-year contract.'

'Sounds reasonable enough. But no contract. I've never had one.'

'This time you get one, Paul. You may need it. Send me a note of the figures involved. Talk it over with your wife and tell her the figures, too—if you dare. I'll work it out your way. West says he'll pay for talent so he'd better live up to his boast.'

'Tell me more about West.'

'Wish I could. He's still a mystery man to me. Even now. Came here nearly sixty years ago as a boy of ten or so. Christened, I've been told, Tadeusz Johann Weitzmann. He's at least kept his initials. Started work at twelve in a Manchester paper mill. By the time he was twenty he owned the mill. As a Rumanian he was an ally in the Kaiser's war, escaped conscription and cleaned up. Next he had a couple of warehouses. Before Hitler's war he had turned that little lot into the rudiments of the empire he's got now: forests in Nova Scotia, forests in Finland and the Congo; paper mills in Toronto and Kent; publishing offices in London and Birmingham; printing offices in Bristol, Leeds, Edinburgh, Glasgow and God knows where else. All this in addition to the headquarters outfit he's built down at Ludgate Circus. You've seen it, no doubt. That's quite a palace as office blocks go.'

We went on talking until a quarter-to-three, but the rest was padding; the real work had been done. I knew that when he called for the cigar tray, chose one lovingly, lit up, sat back. His afternoon stint was beginning.

6

The most pleasurable part of my sabbatical year, especially during that early summer, was meeting my daughter, Marion, from the Lycée most afternoons.

I met her that afternoon, after the lunch with Spurway.

As usual, she came out promptly from the school doors, a slight, slim figure with an unfashionable but beguiling pigtail. She looked around expectantly and then came towards me, swinging her satchel from hand to hand.

'What did you do today?' I asked as we turned towards South Kensington station.

'French, French and more French.'

'Dis-moi en Français tous les noms des rois et les reines d'Angleterre,' I asked absently, still brooding over Spurway's proposition. 'Et, pour commencer, le premier roi des deux pays.'

'Guillaume le Conquereur,' Marion said uncertainly.

'Le Vainqueur. I wonder whether he was called that in France. He can't have been.'

'Parles en Français, papa.'

'Ah, oui. Pardonnes-moi. Et le nom du roi qui suivit Guillaume?'

'Edouard le Confesseur.'

'Non. Non. Il précède Harold et Harold précède Guillaume.'

'I know, I know,' Marion said, dancing at my side in excitement. 'I always make that mistake to begin with. C'est Guillaume le Second, et alors Henri le Premier et alors Stephen, et alors les Plantagenets, Henri le Second, Richard le Premier. . . .'

'Bon! Bon!' I said, trying to stay the flood. 'Je te donne huit marques pour dix. Et maintenant, dis-moi les noms des villes capitales des pays de l'Europe. Quel est la ville principale de Suède?'

'Oslo.'

'Non.'

'Stockholm.'

'C'est inevitable.'

We walked steadily towards the King's Road. Soon Marion tired.

'C'est tout. What's for tea? Mummy said anchovy toast.'

'I see no reason why not.'

'What did you do today?'

'Had lunch.'

'Not all day?'

'Most of the day.'

'What did you eat?'

'Saumon fumé, le poussin, les petit pois, les pommes de terre rôtis, la salade laitue, le fromage de Camembert, le café noir,' I recited in recollected pleasure.

'No wonder you took all day.'

We talked about going to Brittany until we got back to Milner Street.

I stayed for tea. I had nothing else to do. I talked vaguely about nothing to Erika, the pretty *au pair*. An hour later Helen came in. I asked if she had a date. She said no. I suggested dinner. She said yes. A curious bloody way to run a marriage, I thought, but there it was. We'd made our curious bed and it seemed only just that occasionally we should lie in it.

7

We dined at the 'Popote' and talked spasmodically about this and that: Marion, Erika, my book, my life, Helen's life, holidays, Spurway, his proposition, the cat at Milner Street. But not Molly Cowell. I kept mum about her. I never even committed myself to referring to her as my daily. I thought I might guffaw.

Later, sometime after midnight, Helen, sitting at her dressing-table, brushing her dark abundant hair, said, be tween the strokes: 'Tell me more about Spurway. Wasn't he the chap who was in all the papers, resigning from the BBC—or was it ITV? a year or so ago?'

'It's his technique. He kicks up hell in his jobs, gets sacked, gets in all the headlines, gets himself a bigger and better job and then goes to earth while he learns all the new expertise. When he wants to move on he comes back into the headlines with some kind of explosion. The whole process starts all over again. And each time he's one more rung up his own particular ladder.'

'I rather like the sound of Mr Spurway.'

'Why?'

'For one thing, I like the sound of these tough eggs in a tough world. I'm so mushy myself. For another thing he has a high opinion of your talents. Best of all he proves it by offering you a job. Of course I like the sound of Mr Spurway.'

'I wish I took the same simple view.'

'Describe him.'

I described him.

'He sounds like a self-made Roman senator running to seed.'

'I wish my description had been half as good. He does rather look like that. Yet I enjoyed seeing him. I enjoyed the meal.'

'So you should. He offered you a plum job.'

'But I've got a plum job.'

'Now you're playing hard to get.'

I'd had enough. Starting at random I began to count the brush-strokes. 'Three hundred and forty-nine . . . three hundred and fifty . . . three hundred and fifty-one. . . . . Come to bed for Christ's sake.'

'Control yourself.'

'It's not only that: it's the damnable rhythm of that brushing movement. It gets to be a mesmeric agony.'

'Big words, eh? You say you like my hair. "Lustrous." That used to be your word for it.'

'It still is, but I'm no hair fetishist. My nerves can stand so much lustrousness and no more.'

She put down the brush and began to gather her hair into its habitual bedtime chignon. She said quietly: 'What did Spurway offer you?'

'Enough. More than I need, even after supporting you.'

'Am I so expensive?'

'Not all that, judging by other tales I hear.'

'And will you take the job?'

'Dunno.'

'On account of Mason?'

'I suppose so. That and the sabbatical year.'

'The sabbatical year is important, but is Mason so important?'

'He's paying me. It's mainly due to him that I'm doing no hack scribbling at this precise bloody minute, merely waiting for you to come to bed.'

'I'm also interested in coming to bed, but I'm also curious about Spurway and all this lolly. I wish I could sort out what he really wants you to do.'

'What I've told you. What I've always wanted. My own feature. To write how I like about what I like, who I like.'

'But what do you think you'll do, involved as you are with your outsize conscience?'

'Come to bed and I'll tell you.'

'That sounds like bribery or corruption,' she said, standing up, 'but I'll play your pimping game.'

'Thank God you've kept your figure,' I said in heartfelt gratitude for this rare miracle in ten years of marriage, motherhood, crack-up, parting and occasional reconciliation. I was also, as usual, excited by her slenderness after the voluptuousness of Molly. Why should Molly have all the pleasures of contrast in concupiscence? And Helen? Did she also have her own secret contrasts? I wondered. Perhaps this was part of the trouble. I could discuss these things with my inarticulate daily, could never discuss them with my highly articulate wife.

'You've kept yours, too,' Helen said, slipping into bed. 'Nice for both of us.'

'You should have seen Spurway. In five years' time he'll have a belly like a football.'

'Apart from your conceit, must we talk about Spurway's belly or footballs? If we must, I'll get out and go on with my hair. Now tell me what you were going to tell me.'

I laughed. 'I've forgotten. I've other things to discuss.'

'Let's discuss other things, then,' she said, switching off the light.

8

Other aspects of living-together-and-apart were so ludicrous that when I reflected upon them I grinned. Sheepishly maybe, but outright. Yet so resilient are we that I took the extravagant oddments of my perennial existence in my stride.

The following morning, for instance:

I got up early, walked round to Swan Court, shaved, picked up my post and, having promised to walk Marion to the Lycée, walked back to Milner Street for breakfast. What a way to run a broken marriage!

9

Walking back to Milner Street I read Spurway's letter, dated June 20th, headed, curiously enough: *Confidential*. I wondered whether his spy had advised such thoughtfulness.

Dear Paul: Following our luncheon I saw Mr West and he is in full agreement with the proposals I made to you. Briefly, we should both like you to take over the projected feature, *Faces & Places*, which we discussed and I should also like you to act as a special editorial adviser to myself, chiefly on matters concerning the commissioning of special features and so on, and would like to think that we could call upon you for the occasional major profile or an industrial piece. I wouldn't wish to overload you, of course, but I do want to get into the paper some real flesh-and-blood writing.

As I said, we would be prepared to offer you substantially more than you are now getting. I outlined my general proposals, but would be very willing to discuss these afresh once I have the actual figures from you.

I hope we can meet soon and get going as soon as possible after that meeting. I look forward enormously to a partnership which I hope will be of considerable interest and profit to us both.

Yours sincerely

He had scrawled 'Mike' above the typed 'Michael S Spurway'.

I handed the letter to Helen, across the breakfast table.

'What will you do?' Helen asked, slowly folding the sheet and handing it back.

'See Mason.'

'Must you, Paul? Couldn't you just write, thank him and tell him you're going to do this?'

'No. I've got to see him.'

'Then there's only one answer.'

'Which is?'

'He'll appeal to your conscience and you'll stay. Bang goes my new summer coat.'

'But you're getting a new coat.'

'I mean a better one.'

'How much better?'

She laughed. 'Not a tiny bit. The one I'm buying is just what I want. Wouldn't change it for any other. But I sometimes wonder how these really ambitious alimony wives go to work. Why not tell Spurway to stuff his job?'

'Aren't you now overdoing the loyal little onetime wife line?'

'Not really, Paul. I like having you here, even on your own occasional terms. I like you taking and fetching Marion to and from school.'

'Just a hewer, taker and fetcher and all that?'

'Especially all that.'

But still the marriage didn't work, despite the pretty words.

10

I went on brooding over the offer during the morning walk to the Lycée and throughout the rest of the day.

I was still brooding when I met Marion from the Lycée. Again I talked rather absent-mindedly.

At the door of the house she asked whether I was coming in for tea.

I said no. I couldn't start making a habit of domesticity again, I thought.

Would I come for breakfast the next morning, then?

I said I would. Would she tell her mother?

I kissed her goodbye and wandered on.

<h1 style="text-align:center">11</h1>

So I went to breakfast.

'I think I'll go and see Mason this morning,' I said to Helen, spooning honey from a jar.

'But it's Saturday.'

'Good God, I'd forgotten. The way one forgets.'

'Perhaps you could see him at home?'

'Perhaps, but it's a bit of a bore for him listening to my soul-searchings on his day off.'

'He mightn't listen.'

I laughed. 'You're probably right. I'll go in and see him tomorrow afternoon.'

'I'm taking Marion down to see the Bilstons at Plaxtol tomorrow. Why not take us?'

'That delays the decision another day.'

'But you like delaying decisions.'

'Don't rub it in. It also looks as if some decisions are being delayed for me.'

'Some of the best decisions make themselves by strategic delay.'

'No reputable historian would agree with you.'

'Our old history mistress used to say historians only remake history.'

'She had a point.'

'What will you do this afternoon?'

'Nothing.'

'But it's going to be a gorgeous day.'

'What are you doing? You plainly have a plan.'

'Driving Marion down to Brighton. Why not come, too? I'll make a picnic.'

'Please,' Marion pleaded, standing by the door in her nightdress.

'It's a put-up-job,' I said, and went to Brighton that afternoon.

I also went to see the Bilstons on the Sunday.

12

I went to see Mason on Monday, the last day of June.

His room was on the first floor of the corner block, overlooking Fleet Street and Fetter Lane.

Passing bus-tops were almost level with his desk. The scurrying masses, at which he hurled his urgent morning headlines, were no more than thirty feet below him. Recent technical developments in double-glazing, air-conditioning, space-heating and acoustical engineering had made his room into a kind of twentieth-century fortress, insulated against this outer world. Inside his fortress he was accustomed to make his one-man evaluation of the world's events. Was one woman's death on a London doorstep worth more than ten thousand deaths in an Indian flood? Was a second-rate English politician's bombast worth more than a Caribbean hurricane? Which one ranked the lead?

Despite his aggressive, didactic liberalism, I sometimes thought that daily dealings with these human sums had made Mason into something of a dictator. He frequently acted as if he controlled events rather than reported them. But all editors incline to this behaviour sooner or later.

I always had to steel myself before entering his room, my apprehensions deriving partly from the size of the room, the fitted carpet and mahogany panelling, but mainly, no doubt, from Mason's personality.

He was a short, dark, thick-set Midlander of about forty-five, with iron-grey hair *en brosse*, spade-shaped nose, thin lips, pointed chin and hard, grey eyes. With his stocky body, bowed legs and excessively wide shoulders he had something of the air of a one-time forward who, at a pinch, could still step into the second row and hold his own in a mauling scrum. Despite his whiter-than-white shirtings he seemed better fitted to a track suit than a natty City suit. Fierce energy was implicit in all that he did—or didn't, for even when sitting at a desk he seemed ready to leap up at a split-second's notice to engage in some new enterprise.

As I crossed the room he said: 'I was damn glad when you rang, Paul. I hope this means you're coming back. You've been away too long.'

Mason's method was always to put the newcomer, the suppliant, the assistant, the employee, into the position of reasserting himself. But that day I said, 'Not today, Jimmy. I've something else to talk about.'

'A new series? That's what we really want.'

'Not even that.'

'Too bad. All right, what is it?'

'I've been offered a new kind of job.'

He took the comment in his stride. 'Why not? Talent's as scarce in the newspaper business as in any other. What is it? And how much? Perhaps we can better it.'

I was invariably astonished by the ease with which Mason overrode factors I thought worth momentary enquiry. His calm acceptance of my own disloyalty in getting another job whilst on extended leave from a generous employer shook me. So did his assumption that jobs meant money and nothing else.

'You don't seem very surprised,' I said.

'Why should I be surprised? You're one of the best of your sort in the country. Word gets around.'

'But you don't even seem surprised that I should go off and get another job while I'm on a decent retainer from you.'

'Why not? Every man for himself. You'd never take a contract here. It was to our benefit to try and keep our hooks on you when you got a bit unsettled. Anyway, you didn't go after the job. That's out of character. The job came looking for you. Am I right? And you haven't gone yet. I'm prepared to pay out good money to hold a good man.'

'You pay me well enough, as it is.'

'Apparently not. But you haven't told me who it is.'

'It's the New Sunday.'

'I thought it might be. I'm surprised Spurway waited so long. It makes sense for them. Not much sense for you. I don't think they'll last the course, despite West's millions.'

'I've got my doubts, too, but I'm still prepared to go.'

'What have they offered you, apart from more money?'

'Basically, my own feature. A gossip page along egghead lines, I suppose one could call it.'

I explained more about *Faces & Places*. Mason heard me out and then said briefly: 'Sounds interesting.'

'I think it could be. I'll never have a better chance to put myself on the map.'

'I think you're right. Perhaps we could try to match it,' Mason mused.

'You could try, but you wouldn't give it the space it needs.'

'Not wouldn't. Couldn't. But we might, once a week, if you make a go of it there,' Mason said, grinning broadly. 'That's what I'll do. The usual Fleet Street line. Let you work out all the growing pains there, let them bill you and build you up, then buy you back as a household name in a year's time or when it folds.'

'You'll scarcely have to buy me back if it does fold.'

'I take it the money's O.K.?'

'Very O.K.' I told him the figures.

'That's quite a rise. I can't match that.'

'Anyway, it was mainly the job itself.'

'I see that. Whose idea was it: Spurway's?'

'He says so. D'you know him?'

'I've met him. A good brain, but a bit of a swine, I've always thought. But he's chosen well this time. Think you'll be able to stand the pace?'

'The pace!' I said, astonished. 'A Sunday after a daily! Are you mad?'

'I'm not expecting you to crack up. Not physically, anyway. I imagine you're as half-fit as most men of forty or so.'

'I'm thirty-eight.'

'All right. Don't be so pedantic. I mean the strain of dealing with West and Spurway when things aren't going their way. Ever been in at the beginning of a newspaper?'

'No.'

'Well, I have. Sheer bloody cut-throat hell. Everybody walking around with two daggers instead of the usual one. Of course, it's all very matey on the first day, but after a week—if the thing hasn't been a sell-out—everybody's looking for a scapegoat.'

'This one could be a sell-out if they produce anything like a paper. Their machines are fantastic, I gather.'

'Men make newspapers,' Mason said. 'Machines help, that's all. You know that. Spurway may have been a hell of a telly whizz-kid, but I've got my doubts about his newspaper genius.'

'What about West?'

'He's always dealt in publishing hardware—and all in the lowest common denominators. How can he hope to make a go of a serious paper?'

'Not all serious papers have been published by serious men.'

'That's true, but just because the Sunday Times and the Observer got in on this vast, new, affluent, teen-age, tech-educated public, West and Spurway think they can clean up merely by getting hold of some brand-new machines and a few good writers: it's not enough.'

'But what Spurway's offered me has the right sound, wouldn't you agree?'

'Of course it has, but it's not new. It's Atticus and Pendennis written in three words instead of one, and in colour—that's all.'

'You can't expect me to agree with that definition.'

'Of course I can't,' Mason said on the instant, grinning. 'I'm talking emotionally. Sheer bloody envy probably. They may make a go of it yet. The Times isn't stuffed with dons even though it reads like it and the Sunday Times isn't above taking its staff from the Express—and vice versa, of course.'

'That's better,' I said, smiling.

'Make yourself a big name and then come back here when it folds. Of course you've got to go on with it, Paul.

And I want to hear what happens. Keep in touch.'

'When shall I start work here again?'

He laughed. 'Any time you want. That car strike last week needed your touch. I almost rang you. We haven't had a decent human-interest-industrial-profile piece since you left. But I'd still rather you came back here after you've had a bashing from this Spurway lark. If you came back now you'd feel thwarted or something. You're a free man as far as I'm concerned, Paul, and I wish you well.'

He walked with me to the door. As if to test his man and flex his power muscles, he said casually, 'If you feel inclined to let me have a shortish piece—say twelve hundred words— by tomorrow, on the background to this latest engineering wage claim, and the characters involved, it would help me out. Call it your swan-song.'

'Nothing I'd like better. There's two sides to it, you know.'

'That's why I want you to do it. Two-faced Mortimer.' He laughed again. Thanks a lot, Paul. Ring me. I'll send down for the copy, or you can put it in a taxi as usual.'

He walked me out of his room to the lift. Standing there, he said: 'And, by the way, get a contract. You've always refused to have one here. This New Sunday thing is different. It's sheer bloody Indian territory, Paul.'

'Spurway says he insists, too. I'll think about it.'

'Meantime don't forget that Mortimer piece for me.'

'I'll ring.'

I went down in the lift and out into Fleet Street, interest already engaged.

13

Helen rang me that evening, asking how my interview with Mason had gone, indulging her taste for communication by telephone.

'He sounds far less of a whiplash than you've sometimes implied,' she said after I'd outlined the give-and-take of the afternoon.

'Almost noble, you'd say?'

'Very noble,' she said defiantly.

'Even though he's got me to write this last piece?'

'I see his point.'

'Perhaps it's all part of what Spurway calls the silken lash.'

Helen laughed. 'It's a good description of the whole Fleet Street racket.'

I laughed. 'Despite Mason's apparent nobility, I almost got the impression at one point that he was infiltrating me into the other outfit as his secret agent.'

'Perhaps he is. Wouldn't it be rather amusing?'

'No, it wouldn't,' I said firmly. 'I don't see journalism in terms of 007 and all that.'

'Perish the thought, then. Be honest. Aren't you as relieved your sabbatical's coming to an end as you were when your marriage came to an end?'

I denied both accusations, but wondered how much truth lay in her barbs and banter. I asked after Marion. She was well. We rang off after appropriate *aux revoirs*.

Always, after these telephone conversations, I went through a gruesome five minutes of despair and doleful hope, yearning to try again, knowing the impossibility of success. If only some marriages could be conducted exclusively over the telephone, they might work out. With these comforting thoughts I went across to my workroom and began the task of ousting marital pessimism in assembling my views on the engineering wage-claim deadlock.

Pen in hand, I was apt to become a man of decision, forthright and unwavering. My views upon this and similar controversial subjects were fluent, persuasive and lucid. So, at least, I often thought, rising from my desk. So did others reading them, to judge from the paper's post-bag. Yet as soon as I had screwed the cap on my fountain pen or replaced the lid on the typewriter, I was caught once again into the appalling dilemmas facing the men I had been writing about, their policies so bitterly opposed, their ways of life a century apart. I thanked my household gods that I had never been involved in the task of being a flesh-and-blood negotiator, agitator, mediator. Far easier this pen-and-ink dissecting.

I worked on the story half-way through the night and finished the summarizing paragraphs at half-past four the following morning, Tuesday. At nine I woke, re-read the piece, made one or two minor corrections, went out into King's Road and gave the envelope to a taxi-driver to take to Fleet Street, C.O.D. By the time I got back to Swan Court Molly was already there, making coffee.

'Out and about early,' she called from the kitchen.

'I had to work half the night. I'll have coffee and go back to bed.'

Now I was free to return to my personal worries, but I decided to postpone decisions on those until after breakfast.

We went back to bed.

Afterwards, waking, I could hear Molly moving about the flat, Hoovering, humming. I looked at my watch: just after eleven. Now, indeed, I was beset by conflicting views of the way ahead. In a half-dozing daydream I saw myself telling Spurway the whole thing was no good, the job couldn't be done within the context of all that he and West stood for. Hearing this, Spurway obligingly fell into panic and rushed off to tell West. And so on and so on. What a hope! I thought, coming awake. I had some more coffee.

Spurway had his own crystal ball. He rang soon after midday. 'Hello, buster. We talked of today as the day of decision. Remember?'

'I remember.'

'Well, made any decision?'

'I'd like to see some of those new dummies you talked about. Does that seem reasonable?'

'It seems like a classical tactic, a delaying-action gambit, but also a reasonable and logical request. It may seem a bit presumptuous, but I've also got an appointment laid on for you to see West this afternoon. I was hoping to take you in with your name on the dotted line and all that, but perhaps you'll come out that way. Four's the best time for West. Any good for you?'

'Suits me.'

'Good. See you then.'

'Don't forget the dummy.'

'Dummy singular? Don't be daft. We've got fifty. You can see the latest half-dozen. And I'll show you a copy from last Sunday's dummy run.'

'Good. See you then.' I rang off.

15

The West House commissionaire sent me straight up. 'Fifteenth floor,' he said in pride-by-proxy.

I went up in one of those swift and silent lifts commonplace in New York, still mildly surprising to find in London.

Spurway met me outside the lift: we entered another lift, went another five floors up to the uppermost floor and padded our way along a corridor deep-carpeted in dark brown pile. Halfway along the corridor Spurway opened a door into a small office.

Looking more like marionettes than secretaries, three young women with headphones were typing at small desks as if they were the opening scene in curtains-up to a modern ballet. They glanced up as we entered, but showed no undue interest. Spurway passed through the room into another office. I followed.

A tall, young woman in her early thirties, dark, handsome, red-lipped, black-eyed, black-suited, sat at a large L-shaped desk. Her typewriter was on the side-desk. Onwards and upwards in the status league, I thought. Her main armament seemed to be three telephones, two black, one red, and her own dictaphone. She stood up as we entered and crossed to a second door.

'Mr. Spurway, Mr Mortimer,' she said, and a quiet voice said, 'Ah.'

We went through into a large room, about thirty feet square, I judged. The continuous carpet was still underfoot, even deeper now.

To my surprise the room was as modern as the hour: an enormous black leather-topped desk; black-leather, chrome-legged armchairs and a couple of Barcelona chairs. Plus one wall of open shelves crowded with books of all sizes, shapes and colours. Facing the bookshelves was the window: a vast clear frame for St Paul's, which looked a yard away, its dome almost on speaking terms with West. How could anyone get on with any job with such a vista? But West stared straight ahead—at me.

He didn't get up from his desk, didn't offer to shake hands. He held, balanced by its tip, the long ivory blade of a paper-knife with a silver handle. He stabbed remotely at the armchairs.

'Sit where you like,' he said in a curiously high-pitched voice.

I took it that he meant the pair of us. So did Spurway who made to sit down with his back to the window, but West said thinly, 'I was wondering, Mike, if it might not be a good idea if you left Mr Mortimer and myself alone. Then, perhaps, we'll be able to make up our minds about each other, uninfluenced by your own forceful personality.'

I thought the remark a gratuitous insult, calculated from the word 'go'. So did Spurway. He was lowering himself into his armchair as West spoke. Dignified recovery from such a posture, especially for a big man, was difficult, but Spurway made it. 'Good idea,' he said, lumbering up. My sympathies were with him and I gave him full marks, despite a split-second's malevolent satisfaction at the discomfiture of this prince of professional discomforters.

'After all, Mr Mortimer might easily think it was unfair; two against one and so on,' West said, as an unnecessary touch.

Spurway crossed to the far door without another word and went.

West was still smiling. He said: 'Do you smoke, Mr Mortimer?'

I had been too interested in watching the oneupmanship to take a chair. Now I crossed to the desk, took a cigarette from the large ebony box, lit up with my own lighter, crossed to one of the leather armchairs.

'I don't myself,' West said. His thin, high-pitched voice was quiet, even gentle, with the faintest sibilance.

In that useful moment of first drawing at my cigarette I examined the man I had first and last seen four years before, and then across a crowded meeting.

My first impression was surprise that such a bland, round, almost avuncular face could conceal the ambition, ruthlessness and purpose he had shown in more than half a century's operations. Straight, thin strands of rather lank grey hair were brushed back over a yellowed cranium, slightly paler than his olive skin. His nose was aquiline; the eyes brown and watchful; the full lips almost pouting; the chin, above the dewlap, pointed like an avocado pear. The skin was wrinkled and dry. All in all he looked more like a well-tailored, cunning old Oriental carpet-bagger than a conventional occidental millionaire, but I knew my view to be inexact and superficial, based on face value rather than expert inside knowledge and I let it fade. The curious thing was that I had no idea of his height. In two encounters he had so far stayed seated.

In his soft insistent voice, West broke into these ruminations. 'Usually, I am told, would-be employers ask for credentials from prospective employees, but in this particular case, Mr Mortimer, I feel that the reverse is probably called for. I am asking a group of talented men to undertake such a formidable task that I feel I should try to establish my own bona-fides.'

Not bad, I thought, and wondered why. 'But why?' I asked.

His eyes were half-closed as he went on: 'Until now, although I publish more magazines than I can number, I have spent most of my life providing the materials for other men's printed words. Machines, paper, ink and so forth. Now I am proposing to launch what I regard as the most potent of all forms of the printed word: a great newspaper. It is a large and, some say, pretentious project for me, of all people, to underwrite.'

'Fortunately, it's a free country and you're risking your own money,' I said. 'Presumably, you weighed all the pros and cons as you have in your other businesses.'

He still balanced the paper-knife. I wondered what came

next. He'd plainly been through all this before. The ploy was too smooth to be an off-the-cuff job. He looked up. The heavy-lidded brown eyes opened; they were conciliatory, almost confiding. I didn't trust them a flicker. He said: 'First, I think it would be difficult to start this kind of newspaper without a very strong conviction about its necessity. Would you agree?'

'Wholeheartedly, but I've often found that tycoons are apt to make their own necessities. What makes your project so necessary?'

He countered with another question: 'Do you think we have a surfeit of serious newspapers in this country?'

'You've answered me,' I said.

He laughed gently. His dewlap shook. 'I am glad you say so. I might have had this day-dream and left it at that.'

'It would have been understandable. The task is immense. Is it logical for your kind of business to start a newspaper, Mr West?'

'Isn't it logical for a newsprint business to be interested in the finished product?' he countered gently. 'Most oil producers are oil distributors. Most paper manufacturers are in the packaging business. I am myself.'

'A newspaper is something more than a packaged product.'

'Looking round at our newspapers today, I doubt that, Mr Mortimer.'

I laughed.

'I hope to do better,' he said and went on: 'I have watched the rise and comparative success of the colour magazine supplements. I have also watched the comparative success of local newspapers printed in colour. It seemed to me logical to combine the two on a national superlative scale. I am happy to think that my one-man hunch was confirmed by two years of research and three marketing groups. I hope that my four-colour machines will confirm these findings.'

The play on numbers rolled out smoothly. He had played that one before, too.

'Did your hunch or researches tell you what kind of newspaper was required?' I asked, trying to keep the sarcasm out of the words.

I wasn't all that successful, but West went on: 'I have now lived long enough, Mr Mortimer, to know that one man can't do everything. It is a hard lesson for someone like myself to learn. The answer to your question is, frankly, no. I had a vague idea of the paper I needed—a paper of the highest standards, influenced pictorially by Life Magazine and Paris-Match, and with the highest writing standards comparable with those existing in the Observer and Sunday Times. The rest is up to the editor and the men he has chosen.'

It was a big-hearted statement. Made at an N.U.J. dinner as a proprietorial statement it would have brought the house down. Yet it left me unmoved. Basically, I didn't believe in West, I decided. Or was I being too determined not to get caught? Was I a front-row member of a music-hall audience, resisting the wiles of the stage hypnotist whose skill has been too wildly publicized?

I reconsidered West, still finding it difficult to relate this quiet, explaining man to the ruthless legend. But the facts and figures, mergers and takeovers were there in the record books in Somerset House and the Companies Office in City Road.

'Well, there it is,' West was saying. 'As you have implied, many people think that I am suffering from paranoia on the grand scale and advise me to keep to my paper mills, to my printing and publishing interests. Yet a group of hard-headed men of proven journalistic skills support me. What shall I do?'

The question was flattering, no doubt, but I said: 'You need advice from no man, Mr West. I think you're determined to go ahead.'

He lowered his head in assent. But I had a few more queries, too. 'Supposing the demand just isn't there?' I heard myself asking.'

'Such a possibility is not in my plans,' he said quietly. 'In this nation of fifty million people I think there is a place for a newspaper of this kind. The task is to fit a paper to the need.'

'How important do you rate colour?'

'Very, very high. The Sunday colour supplements have shown that the public will respond very enthusiastically—and profitably—to colour.'

'The Sunday colour supplements are adjuncts,' I said. 'Super sales gimmicks if you like. Nobody knows how many —or how few—they'd sell if they were out on their own. Nobody's made the test. The Sunday Times was selling a million before it started a colour supplement. Now it's on the way to a million and a half. What is that to you?'

He smiled thinly and, in a curious way, I thought, appreciatively. 'I follow your implications clearly, Mr Mortimer. There is much realism in what you say. Yet colour is here to stay, and has greater possibilities in publishing than anyone has yet envisaged. I think I am the man to point the way. It is, I think, as simple and as big as that.' With these prophetic phrases he seemed to dismiss all the problems awaiting his newspaper. He went on: 'Meanwhile, what of yourself? Are you coming in with us, despite your pessimism?'

'I find it all intensely interesting . . .' I began.

He cut across that. For a moment the steel glinted beneath the velvet as he said: 'Come, now, Mr Mortimer . . .'

He had a point there and I said: 'I will join you to do the job that Mike Spurway has asked me to do.'

'Good. I am glad.'

He stood up. About five-feet-six, I judged. The interview was at an end. I stood up, too. He had gained his point, but I still had one or two more queries. 'May I be more personal for a moment or so, Mr West?'

He seemed momentarily surprised, even nonplussed.

'By all means,' he said hesitantly. He sat down again. So did I.

'Finance, for example. Am I to understand that side of things presents no problems at all? We've both seen many newspapers and magazines fold since the end of the war because even the richest proprietors couldn't stand the strain of money running down the drain. Hulton, Kemsley, the Cadburys—they've all closed down worthwhile newspapers and magazines.'

'It is a reasonable question, but you need have no fears. I have formed a separate company for this venture—as you may confirm at Somerset House, although those details will tell you little enough, as you well know. Between these four walls I am prepared to invest several million pounds in the future of the New Sunday. I am not a poor man, neither am I a young man. Time is not on my side. I mean this to be a success. I shall back it to the limit.'

'But do you know what that limit might mean? I know your record. You've made vast profits. But I doubt whether your Board has ever been trained to see money going out the way it will go out once the rotaries start to roll. Of course I'm talking portentously, but what I'm getting at is that it could be an alarming experience for men who've so far only seen money coming in.'

He still held the paper-knife. He stabbed at the air as he said: 'A great deal of money went out in the early days of this business, Mr Mortimer. And still does. One does not replant a forest or build a paper mill with threepenny pieces.'

'But your markets were assured once your trees had matured and your mills were built.'

'One could only hope so.'

'This is utterly different,' I persisted. 'A far more hazardous world.'

'New worlds are for conquering. And perhaps the project is not quite as hazardous as you think.' Again he smiled that thin secret smile. 'We shall see. And my board is well-trained. And, finally, it is mostly my own money.'

I still hadn't done.

'What about advertising support?' I asked.

'It is promising,' West said. For a moment he stared out of the great window, but scarcely to reflect, I thought, on the problems that Wren had met and vanquished in building that dome. He was too busy with his own. 'We have a good team working on that side of things. And we have other sources of support. I have other interests apart from newsprint. I am what has been termed a considerable diversifier.'

44

'So I've heard,' I said. He nodded.

'I am Chairman of the British National Stores Group. I have arranged that their advertising appropriation will substantially contribute towards New Sunday's running expenses.'

I nodded my obsequious notice of his business acumen.

'It is a sensible move for such a group,' he said, as if musing aloud. 'We are anxious to get at the top million families in this country. New Sunday will help us do that. Respectability works downward in this country.'

'It all seems very logical,' I said dutifully.

'I think so, too.'

He seemed prepared to go on talking, but I was probably over-staying my allotted span of the great man's time. But I wanted to get one thing clear.

I said: 'Shall we see how we get on for six months? Does that seem reasonable?'

'Eminently reasonable, but nothing is certain in this life and for your own protection I advise you to take a two-year contract.'

He replaced the paper-knife on his desk, gravely considered me for a long moment, and then stood up and moved towards the door. Slowly I followed him. For the first time in the hour he was suddenly an ageing man. He said: 'I am very glad you have seen things this way, Mr Mortimer. I have enjoyed our discussion. Few journalists are interested in the economics of the papers they help to produce. Let us meet again. Perhaps you will dine with me sometime soon?'

I made suitable noises.

'I will send you a note,' he said.

He had pressed a buzzer somewhere, for the tall, dark, young woman opened the door. West smiled. Like many men accustomed to the belief that their charm works magically on their behalf he switched off the smile a fraction of a split-second too soon. The efficiency expert took over. He said: 'Spurway will arrange all the details. Perhaps you will take Mr Mortimer down, Miss Moore.'

And that was that.

I followed the tall Miss Moore from the room, absently watching her long legs and shapely ankles. We waited in silence by the lift doors. The lift came. We went down five floors. She left me at the door to Spurway's office.

He was sitting at his desk, brooding. The office was more like a chartroom in a small warship than an office. And as shipshape. Nothing disturbed the serenity of the desk-top. No galley proofs, no page proofs, no typescripts. Nothing. From one efficiency expert to another, I thought.

'He's just rung down. I gather things went his way,' Spurway half sneered.

The taste of that curt dismissal obviously still rankled, but I didn't rise. 'Let's hope it's my way, too,' I said mildly.

'Let's get down to brass tacks, shall we, and see how much you're going to cost the old bastard?'

So we got down to brass tacks.

I would join *New Sunday* nominally on Friday the first of August, but actually on Tuesday, the fifth. This was later than Spurway wanted, but, as I pointed out, I had promised Helen and Marion that I would take them both to Brittany. Spurway grudgingly saw my side.

'Anyway, you'll be better for a rest. It's going to be a pretty hectic shambles here for the first six months. You won't even have time to come up for air before Christmas.'

'What about your own holiday?' as asked.

'Don't need one. My holiday starts once the paper starts. The grind is now.'

16

Our precipitated holiday meant some inconvenience and Continental telephoning and cabling, but we made it. Marion got a week lopped off her term and added to her holidays, but made no objection to that part of the programme.

So a fortnight later, I went off to Cartearet in Normandy with Helen and Marion. There, in a small hotel overlooking the dunes and the sands, we lived *en famille* for ten days. The weather was kind and the days floated away in a golden haze of sun and sea, rose-tinted by a general disbelief, on my part, that any place as improbable as Fleet Street could co-exist on the same planet with this peaceful holiday resort.

In our determination to make Marion's holiday a happy memory, Helen and myself were carefully considerate of each other at every moment of the day. So considerate it hurt. We were like two dancers, engaged in a formal *pas de deux*. Neither partner was allowed the slightest lapse lest the whole damn thing collapse, back-cloth, flats, the lot, in a scene of irreparable despair.

Since that holiday I have often wondered how much of its phoney façade Marion took in. I have always worked on the belief that children over the age of five, especially daughters of breaking or broken marriages, are wholly aware of every evasive nuance in the unnatural routines of marital pretence and evasion. One day, I tell myself, I shall ask her.

One never does, of course.

But we all agreed it had been a terrific holiday.

17

We got back on Tuesday, the twenty-second of July. Spurway rang the next morning. Could I lunch? I agreed. 'Savoy one o'clock,' he said briefly, and rang off.

He felt, he said, as we began to eat, like a fly in a well-corked bottle. In all his previous jobs he had been planning a new venture with an old one still operating. This was all bloody planning. And all on paper. 'I'm not all that good at blueprints,' he said. 'I need action.'

Now that I was signed up he talked more openly, easily, forcefully. He plainly needed a confidant.

'Why did you ever decide on a tabloid format?' I asked at one point during the meal.

'Because it's got to be tabloid. It was my idea from the beginning and West has kept to it. Otherwise I'd have resigned two years ago. It's the only possible size for a modern newspaper. That's why the machines are the way they are, although they can be adjusted, of course. Tabloid's the ideal size to combine the best from the world's best: text as taut as Time, pictures as good as Paris-Match, features as good as the best of the glossies.' I wondered who was plagiarizing whose words: West or Spurway. 'I shan't use this colour just for pictures. I want to use it for explanation. Diagrams, drawings, maps, graphs, the lot. We live in a graphic age. I come from a graphic job.'

'What about the poor old written word?'

'Don't be a clot. What d'you think I've lived by and with and to and from all my life? But the text in New Sunday has got to be easy—to read and to understand.'

'What about all that "in depth" stuff?'

'You never relent, do you?'

'Not with that kind of cliché.'

'O.K., O.K. All I want is natural, hard-hitting prose. No flannel and no cotton-wool. But I also want all the facts dug out. Is that too much to ask? People these days can wake up and find themselves in the middle of a major crisis in the Far East, in the City, in the docks or on the railways and know nothing about situations which the newspapers should have explained. The politicians don't try to explain. Sometimes they don't even want to explain. If they can't or won't, then it becomes our job. I aim to do just that.'

'A tall order.'

'Not with the men and machines I've got.'

We went on arguing and discussing. Occasionally I was convinced and even began to feel that his intelligence, vitality and force might yet win out. I'd thrown in my lot with him and the only sensible course to do was to back him to the limit, go along with him all the way. And in a curious inexplicable manner my attitude towards him was changing. I was beginning to be not only amused by many of the things he said, but impressed by the sincerity and intensity behind the words. Like so many prideful cynics he had himself to blame if others stayed dubious when he did become sincere. I also found that I was beginning to like him, to sense that beneath the tremendous self-assertion was, inevitably, a good deal of self-doubt.

'Are you married?' I asked him during that lunch. 'You never mention a wife.'

'Why should I? I'm part of a merciless classical set-up. I hate my wife and she hates me. It's as simple as that. None of this modern love-hate stuff. This is hate all the way. If I could kill her or get her killed—not necessarily painlessly, but tracelessly, as you might call it—I would. Willingly. I'd pay five thousand quid in pound notes to the joker who'd do it? Any offers?'

I laughed, mildly chilled. 'But why not leave her?' I said. 'Shaw contended that most murders could be avoided by one of the parties taking a bus-ride. Why not ride out one day?'

'I will one day, but I'm afraid the day's a long way off.'

'Any children?'

'Two boys.'

'Is that why you stay?'

'Not necessarily. I like seeing 'em, but in the best tradition of self-made grammar schoolboys I've sent 'em to Harrow. One's there, the other's on the way. So I don't see much of 'em. And if you've been bitten by the success-bug as badly as I have, your children aren't all that important in your life. The fact is, buster, I'm a Spurway Number One man through and through. I've not much time for anything or anyone else. Remember that. It's a tip worth bearing in mind in a crisis. Never bank on any altruistic thoughtfulness from me. I'm a fulltime Spurway man. I'll be the one with the lifebelt.'

'I'm not quite certain you're quite as ghoulish as you make out.'

'Bank on the fact that I am. Anything less will be sheer profit,' he said, grinning.

'Noted. But what about the contract you made me sign for my protection?'

'That's T.J.'s money,' he said simply.

I enjoyed that meal. We were down to brass tacks.

18

Two days later, on the Friday, he rang again, interrupting Molly's housework. So to speak.

'You ought to come along and see these machines at work tomorrow.'

Coitus interruptus ousted all charitable thoughts and technical inclinations. 'If I have to know all about your hardware in order to be able to write my stuff, you can have the job back,' I said tetchily.

'Forget I ever asked you.'

'Machines aren't my line. I don't care if we print on a hand-press so long as it's the kind of newspaper I like. I'll come in later next week. I've far too much to do here before I start getting cluttered up with machines.'

'Maybe you're right,' Spurway conceded. 'A pity. I needed some moral support. See you next week. Let's have lunch soon. What about next Wednesday?'

I agreed.

He rang off. I felt mildly conscience-stricken, but soon revived in the activity of the work I had on hand, as I had so persuasively told myself.

19

But Spurway struck again, before the following week.

I was in our small onetime sitting-room, now Helen's sitting-room, that same evening, Friday. Helen was upstairs, urging the reluctant Marion into bed. We had all been early dining *au Père de Nico* in our first meeting since returning from Normandy on the previous Tuesday. It had been a treat for Marion which had momentarily upset domestic discipline.

I was well out of that, having bestowed my goodnight kiss half an hour previously, although I knew I would be needed upstairs within ten minutes for a further-postponing post-goodnight kiss.

Meanwhile, I was relaxing with a large whisky of Helen's

mixing. Her blendings were encouragement to reflection, conversation and dreams of doughty action. All her friends said so.

I was reflecting on my new job, now ten days away, taking to pieces every statement West and Spurway had made, analysing their words, searching for hidden meanings, looking for snags and traps. Then I moved on to my own replies to their questions, and queries to their answers, taking those to pieces, too, seeking for truths I might have evaded or subdued, deprecating my own enthusiasm for a venture which sometimes seemed too bold and already destined for disaster.

Helen came downstairs. 'Marion is expecting you. Why so thoughtful? New Sunday, I suppose.'

'What else?'

'The state of our marriage, your daughter's future education, whether you're staying the night, whether you're proposing to see your wife and daughter during the weekend.'

'Those oddments will take care of themselves. In the Biblical phrase, I need to take thought about other things.'

'What's biting you about that?'

'Only my basic disbelief in the stated intentions of any tycoon.'

'But his plans for the paper make sense, don't they?'

'Not entirely. I know there's a snag somewhere and I can't get to it.'

'What kind of snag?'

'It's all out of character. All his life he's been a supplier of specialized goods and, to a lesser degree, specialized services. He's never been a creator of anything new or big. He doesn't think that way. He's a raider, a manipulator, a buyer-upper. His whole life's been a series of take-overs of other men's notions or businesses, making fifty quid flower where a penny flowered before.'

'Perhaps he feels the creative urge.'

'No man starts being creative at that age, certainly not an industrialist. Seventy's the age for bowing out or, at most, for consolidation. Even the diversification programme he's so proud of is only another word for another set of take-overs.'

'But this New Sunday thing fits in with your own ideas.'

'Perhaps that's the snag. It fits in too well. I'm always suspicious if any journalistic idea of mine turns out to be commercially sound.'

'What about Spurway, then?'

'The whole thing's different for him. It's just another rung in his upward climb.'

Helen poured herself a gin and Dubonnet, me another whisky.

'But you've made some kind of name for yourself as a journalist, Paul, however much you may scoff at the suggestion. You must know something about the world you're in.'

'I'm a writer. A journalistic pawn. I don't know a damn thing about the finances of journalism. I don't know the cost of newsprint, comps' wages, the cost of metal, how a rotary works, still less how web-fed offset works. I know damn-all about what makes the set-up tick.'

'Presumably West does.'

'That's what makes me wonder. Three millions is a figure that gets bandied about. Three millions on machines. Three millions to launch the damn thing. I don't see West investing six millions in an idea. I can see that he would invest that in another business, another take-over, but not in a journalistic idea. Somewhere there's a snag.'

The telephone rang. Helen answered, cupping the receiver. 'For you,' she said. 'Talk of the devil.'

Spurway was at the other end. 'Your answering service told me to ring this number,' he said defensively.

'Why not? It's what I pay 'em for.'

'But it's a bit late.'

'That's what I've been trying to persuade my daughter. Being a daughter she disagrees. What is it, anyway?'

'Ten past ten.'

I laughed. 'Why the call, then, if you're so guilty about the time?'

'One or two things I'd like to talk about before we go

through our usual Saturday dummy run again tomorrow. I suppose you're not coming in?'

'I'm not on the pay-roll for another fortnight.'

'Ten days.'

'All right, ten days. Where are you speaking from now?'

'Savoy. Where else is there?'

I laughed again, relenting. 'Why don't you bring your drink over here?'

'It's an idea. Where's here?'

I told him.

'Sounds pleasant. All right. Thanks I will. Be with you in ten minutes.'

'What've you done now?' Helen said.

'Taken you at your word. You said you'd be interested to meet Spurway. He's on his way.'

'Well, I suppose I asked for it. And you pay the rent. Do I have to change?'

'I shan't.'

'Very funny as a non-answer.'

'You look very pretty as you. I always like you in that coral colour. Wonderful foil for your hair and my clerical grey.'

'I'm changing all the same. Just in case. You can get out the drinks.'

She went upstairs.

In a muzzy kind of way I was enjoying myself. The Santenay at the restaurant and now the whisky were slowly exorcising my demons of discontent and self-examination.

Downstairs again Helen handed me another drink. I said: 'How come you do everything so well, Helen? You put Marion to bed without a whimper. You change in less than a minute. You look like a Vogue model. You even know the exact ratio of whisky to water. Where d'you learn it all?'

'As an *au pair* girl in Basutoland. You're drunk.'

'I certainly am not. Mellow maybe, drunk never. You're a clever woman, Helen, a mother in a million, an excellent wife. Why can't we make a go of it?'

'Takes two. A woman can't do everything. If you're not drunk you're maudlin.'

I could see she wished she hadn't said it. The door-bell

rang. Spurway was outside. I ushered him through the narrow hallway and into the sitting-room, made the introductions, offered drinks, poured drinks, all in a sustained major-domo sequence. Helen sat down in an armchair and swept out the skirt of her black dress in an ostentatious swirl.

'Have you eaten?' she confidently asked our plainly well-fed, well-wined guest.

'I've eaten enough to run a fair-sized holiday camp,' Spurway said.

We drifted into chitter-chat about summer holidays. Helen talked about the holiday in Brittany we'd managed to sandwich between jobs. Spurway expressed doubts whether he'd be able to take a holiday, even if he wanted one. 'That's another curious thing about this New Sunday of ours. West was adamant about starting it now, right in the middle or, at best, tail-end of the holiday season. The end of August—one of the worst times to start any kind of magazine or newspaper. We always tried to give a new telly programme a good send-off with high Tam ratings at the beginning of the autumn, say late September. Why d'you think he did it, Paul?'

'Because he's boss. Maybe his marketing boffins told him late summer's a good time to get new people into his National Stores Group. Perhaps that's when they're most likely to take up new spending patterns or whatever the jargon is.'

'You make the New Sunday sound like an advertisers' hand-out.'

'I've always worked on old-fashioned going concerns,' I said. 'I never bothered to ask whether they started in June, eighteen-sixty, or October, nineteen hundred and six.'

'Very funny,' Spurway said. 'Did he say one original thing about newspapers the other afternoon?'

'I'd have to be a lot clearer-headed than I am now to answer that question. He seemed to talk some horse sense.'

'Because he agreed with your own ideas, I daresay,' Spurway said. His words were half-genuine question, half-scoffing irritant.

'Possibly.'

But Spurway wasn't to be deterred. 'I'll tell you this, Paul, I've listened to him at fifty or more meetings and I haven't yet heard him say one original thing about newspapers.'

'His subject's money. He's done some original things with that. Perhaps he's leaving all the original thinking about newspapers to you.'

Spurway grinned. 'All right, perhaps he is. But why? And if so, why does he poke his nose in from time to time in irrelevant, crazy, unexpected ways? Why?'

'He probably thinks he's keeping you on your toes.'

'But it's always *my* paper . . . *my* plans for the future . . . *my* decision . . .'

'These are the statements all chairmen make. You'll at least admit he's got a genius for building and running one of the largest financial outfits of its kind in the world.'

'Have another drink, Mr Spurway,' Helen said, getting up.

'Aren't these pretty potent, Mrs Mortimer?'

'I sometimes think so,' I said.

'Very unbuttoning drinks, indeed. Take it from me. I know. I'd love another.'

'Why do you feel so strongly about Mr West?' Helen asked, getting the drinks. 'After all, he's given you a wonderful chance, hasn't he?'

'You're absolutely right, Mrs Mortimer. He has. And what I'm saying is mean-gutted. Intolerable. In a way I suppose I envy him. I'd like some of those millions. I want this to be my newspaper and it's going to be his. Old-fashioned sour grapes. I do a job and he does a job, but he seems to do his with other people's lives.'

'All jobs are lives,' I put in.

'Nuts,' Spurway said curtly. 'Sorry, Mrs Mortimer. Anyway, my relationship with him is changing. Before—two years ago—when all this started, I was his white-haired boy. Now, as D-Day gets nearer, I'm at loggerheads with him. All the way. God knows what the situation will be like by the year's end.'

'But isn't this all part of the tremendous strains and

stresses you're all subject to at this stage?' Helen asked. 'Mr West must be worrying about all the money he's venturing and you've got dozens of your own kind of worries, I'm sure.'

'You can say that again,' Spurway said.

He grinned. 'I've had my say, Mrs Mortimer. These drinks are too civilizing by half. I really came here to try and persuade Paul to come in tomorrow.'

'We had all that out this morning. What's so special about tomorrow?'

'It's a day or rather a week nearer D-Day, that's all. We all learn something from these trial-run sessions. I hope you'll be in two out of every three Saturdays, even if it's only to add your moral support to the editor.'

'You know I'll be there most Saturdays,' I said. 'I'll also come down tomorrow.'

'Good,' Spurway said hastily. 'We'll have lunch with one or two of the others. You ought to meet them. Thanks a lot, Paul.'

The evening's exercise was over. Ten minutes later and he had gone.

20

I went down to West House the next day and Spurway showed me over the place, but, generally speaking, it wasn't my day.

As far as testing out my likely worth to *New Sunday* was concerned, it was a dead loss, but I enjoyed watching the others playing at newspapers the way sixth-formers play at school magazines.

For them it was plainly a far more promising and profitable day. A day to get all the technicians geared up. A day to see how the subs subbed and comps comped; how the machines were running; how the telephones were tinkling; how the copy and pictures were coming in from the agencies and the staff men. And so on and on.

The disposition of offices and services followed American practice, with executive offices on upper floors, and the composing-room immediately above the machine-room and not on the top floor, the illogical practice in most British newspaper buildings.

West and his administrative staff had their office on the penultimate floor—the twentieth storey. Above that was the penthouse. Here West entertained his V.I.P.s from the four corners of the earth. On four floors below, the marketing and clerical staffs were housed. The editorial staff of *New Sunday* was on the fifteenth floor. Other floors were devoted to various divisions of the West industrial empire. Five were sub-let on short tenancies, Spurway said. The old man was always needing floorspace, following his various take-overs.

The composing-rooms of *New Sunday* were, as I've said, on the first floor. The machine-rooms occupied a vast, open, double-storey complex made up of the basement and ground floor. Apart from the reception hall, the ground floor was an enormous glazed peepshow along the street: London's perambulators would be able to view West's new venture at work. Even when quiescent the machine-room looked efficient and impressive. On Saturdays, with the machines running, and quires of *New Sunday*, mechanically bundled and tied, going up the chutes to the waiting vans, the place promised to be a tourist's delight.

The only drawback, as far as I could see, was that if West kept to his current launching figures, the machines would be only employed for a fractional working week: five hours at most. I wondered how long a round-the-clock tycoon like West would be willing to keep them thus dormant.

On Saturdays, Spurway explained, subs and reporters would move down to the news-room, a large open-plan floor above the composing-rooms, more like an aircraft hangar than a newspaper office, he added. The wire-rooms, telephone reporters' kiosks, photographic dark-rooms were also on this floor.

West had certainly spared no shekels in providing his staff with model quarters. That Saturday the news-room was vibrant with movement as if *New Sunday* were already on its way.

For *Faces & Places* I had written a dummy piece on Sarah, Duchess of Marlborough, treating her as if she were a twentieth-century story. The translation in time and treatment had proved an entertaining exercise *in vacuo* and Spurway liked the result. Secretly, I had been astonished by the extra kick my paragraphs seemed to get with the aid of colour reproductions of paintings of Sarah and the Duke, Queen Anne and Blenheim, Vanbrugh and the rest.

That Saturday morning, Spurway again praised the feature, perhaps in thanks for my visit. I was equally fulsome.

'I take back all I said about colour,' I said. 'I'm converted, ruined for black-and-white for evermore.'

'A handsome retraction, buster. Now let's eat.'

'Weren't we supposed to be eating with some colleagues?'

'Let 'em eat cake in the canteen. I want to talk.'

Over lunch—needless to say at the Savoy—I posed my question about the five or six quiescent days facing the colour machines. What would West do about that little problem?'

'Sell the printing capacity, no doubt,' Spurway said. 'There's more than one major daily would like to have the colour without the colossal capital expenditure on colour machines.'

'Would any such daily want a Sunday colour newspaper buzzing around, stealing its thunder?'

'Let's get this New Sunday running first,' Spurway said shortly and switched to weaknesses on the foreign news side. We were relying too much on agency material, he said. We needed three more good men. In Bonn, Rome and Moscow. 'We're at least well fixed in Paris and Washington, thank God,' he said. 'Peterson is no Sam White, but he's got good contacts around the edges of the de Gaulle circus and Thomas can float between Washington and New York until I get a first rate woman into New York. . . .'

He was musing aloud. I was, no doubt, a responsive sounding-board for him and he went on at length, until, suddenly, at about a quarter-to-three, he said: 'Let's go back and meet Morgan.'

'I've met him.'

'When?'

'Earlier this week, when I brought my copy in. You'd mentioned him, so I made my number with him.'

'Good for you.'

'I don't see how I would have got my copy into shape if I hadn't.'

'That's true. D'you like him?'

'A lot—at first sight.'

'He gets better as you go on—unlike most of Fleet Street. Let's go back, anyway.'

'No, you go back,' I said. 'There's nothing more there for me today. I've seen my proof. I've met Morgan. I've lunched with you. My day's done.'

'Have it your own way.'

21

I formally joined the *New Sunday* three days later, the fifth of August, a sunny Tuesday morning. The venture seemed so bizarre that curiosity ousted apprehension.

Spurway's office, as I've said, was rather like a compact chart-room in a small warship. He worked at a large desk with a high table set at right angles. Page and galley proofs occasionally spilled over this high table. The desk was always clear. Two armchairs in black leather and his own swivel chair, also in black leather, completed the furnishings of this aseptic, land-locked cabin which opened into a large editorial conference-room.

That morning Spurway took me straight into the conference-room. At the far end of the room eight or nine men were lolling around in more black-leather armchairs and sofas. A large conference-table with attendant chairs in the middle of the room was deserted. The conferees plainly preferred the relaxed comfort of armchairs.

Spurway took an armchair facing the crowd, waved me to an empty chair, and the session began. It was all very presidential but nobody seemed to think it funny. He began by introducing me. I only got a blurred impression of each man. I would begin to sort them out soon enough, I thought. Yet here, I suppose, is as logical a place as any to put down memories of my so-called colleagues.

Tom Morgan, managing editor, I had already met. He was the oldest man in the room: a trim, smiling, deceptively deferential Welshman of middle height and middle age. He greeted me with a ready smile and casual wave of the hand. I already liked and admired him. He had the quiet authoritative touch of a first-rate technician for a job and title which English journalism had appropriated and adapted from American usage.

Then Frederick Clifford Lee-Ellerton, political editor. He half-stood up, an enormously tall, gangling man in his mid-thirties, splendiferously turned out in a dark grey light-weight suiting of impeccable cut, palest grey shirt, stiff white collar, O.E. tie. He looked *en route* to a Foreign Office briefing or an embassy lunch. He stared at me from behind his pebble lenses, said quickly, 'Welcome to Cranks Corner,' grinned amiably and sat down suddenly, taking care to re-arrange the steel-edge crease of his fashionably narrow trousers.

Alan Pettiford, City editor, was next: short, plump, with a fiercely inflammable face and prideful military moustache. Seated there in brown tweeds and suède chukka boots he looked more like an adjutant in mufti on a day off from a mechanized unit than a City pundit with some academic standing as an economist of advanced Keynesian theories.

Then Edward Hales, news editor. A tall, handsome man with thinning fair hair, finely cut features. In his late forties, I judged. He was nervously tense, and, as I soon discovered, a chain-smoker.

Then Humphrey York, literary editor. Late-thirties, steel-rimmed specs, jowly, dark, curly, greying hair, looking more than an overblown sixth-former than a poet and essayist. Then John Hilton, art editor: middle height, black-bearded, blue-eyed, blue-shirted, blue-tweeded. Altogether a boy in blue. There were one or two others. They're not important to this record. They may come into the story later, but I doubt it.

For the next couple of hours I sat listening to them knocking spots off each other.

For me this news conference was a new experience. Mason's meetings had been short, sharp and to the point. By the time one reached his office, features, policy and assignments had already been decided. Discussion centred upon the approach, likely length, possible public and/or political reactions. Although the editor of a so-called liberal newspaper, Mason had been an autocrat on all such occasions, brooking no opposing views. The policy of the paper was clear-cut, he would say: FOR the under-privileged, AGAINST the overprivileged. 'Keep that notice on your typewriters and you won't go far wrong.' That the legend was perennially abused by his own treatment of his own writers never crossed his mind. Fortunate, indeed, the self-unquestioning editor.

That first editorial meeting at West House was an eye-opener for me. Here I saw Spurway's radio and television experience and techniques at work. He set the meeting going by throwing in ideas, challenging assumptions, up-ending conventional judgments, destroying ancient shibboleths, mocking anything and anyone. At times the meeting was almost out of hand with apparently mature men abusing each other like a gang of Greek patriots.

I was amused and amazed and stayed silent. This kind of meeting needed a new kind of technique. One, I realized, I would have to learn from scratch.

Twice Spurway said: 'What d'you think, Paul?'

I came back with reasonable replies, for I had been watchful of my colleagues and following their arguments fairly closely. Spurway laughed at the immediate fall in the vocal temperature of the room when I spoke. 'A little judgment come to judgment,' he scoffed genially. They all laughed. He disagreed with what I had said. Pettiford heartily backed up the first of my observations, Lee-Ellerton the second. But each time they were off again, hammer and tongs. The second time Spurway also agreed with the views I had put forward, and that was that.

The meeting broke up with a couple of decisions made

concerning future features and thirty mooted ideas destroyed and discarded. This was more ruthless treatment than I had seen in any newspaper office I had known, but it was certainly a method guaranteed to weed out the weak and threadbare notions which were too frequently shaped-up for features.

I left the room exhilarated and exhausted. Spurway seemed ready to start all over again.

Morgan walked with me along to my room. 'What a shambles!' he said. 'I think the editor eats three journalists for breakfast every morning, even before he gets in. Then he starts on us. But it seems to work. I've never known meetings like 'em. Have you?'

'Never,' I said fervently. 'But I rather enjoyed it.'

'It has its points,' he said. 'Clears the air and all that. But I hope when we start in a month's time we concentrate just a little more on constructive ideas rather than these morning massacres. But I think he'll stage 'em as we're going to press. That's my secret nightmare.'

I could see that, as managing editor, he already had troubles and would have more.

22

Curious that newspaper editors, especially of what are generally known as quality newspapers, always contend—even vehemently on occasion—that they are keen to produce papers that women will wish to read.

Our paper is far too masculine, they say. Our image is too man-made. So they continue to hold editorial meetings to which no woman writer on the staff is ever invited. Not even the woman's page editor. On the basis, no doubt, that, as she's given complete freedom on her own pages, she ought to be satisfied, and that her views on the other pages might be an irritant.

Even Spurway had slipped into the same routine. This was one revolution he might start, I thought, and raised the subject over our next lunch, but he was blatantly unconcerned. 'They're interested in two things: clothes and money.'

'What about men?'

'Way down the list.'

'What about politics?'

'One woman in ten thousand. Not worth bothering about. A lot seem to turn up at right- and left-wing conferences. Vocal minority groups. Women in name only. A few don't shave and most lack men's members. That's the only difference. Forget 'em.'

He grinned. 'Now let's get on with serious discussions. Women are made for one thing only. The rot began to set in when the first Western man began to talk to them as equals. The Arabs had the right idea in this division of life as in so many others. Forget 'em.'

'I'll put 'em aside: I can't forget 'em.'

'The philosophy of a realist,' he said, and went on to talk of the industrial coverage of the paper. No newspaper dealt fully enough with popular explanations of new processes, new inventions, he contended.

I let him rant on.

23

He showed no sign of diminishing his destructive approach to the journalistic life as we got nearer D-Day. He threw out ideas with a demoniacal flair. He was after kernels, he said. The cores, hearts, guts, yolks of ideas. Not skins, shells, peels, rinds, husks.

He called me in for discussions about twice a week, asking what I had in mind for the opening spread of *Faces & Places*. I had been living with the same problem for a month.

My first thoughts had been to ask for even more space and do a major piece on the Trade Unions of Great Britain with pen portraits of the leaders, an enormous diagram in colour, showing the interlocking arrangements of the T.U.C., finishing with a group of interviews with the old-stagers and the young and militant shop stewards. To this I hoped to add a financial analysis, to be worked out with the City editor, showing, in diagrammatic form, the total finances of each Union and its strength or vulnerability in staging long-term strikes. Another table would show the strike records of the respective Unions.

'Worth doing,' Spurway said, 'but later. Six weeks later. I think we ought to start with a fun feature. Sophisticated and serious, but basically entertainment. Something to make the Great British Public spit, in a mixture of spleen and laughter, all over its breakfast tables. Go away and think again.'

I then came up with the notion of a long piece on modern poets or modern composers. Serious poets and composers. How they work, how they live, what they earn, who they marry, what they feel about their public. With selections from their poetry and music.

Spurway went for the poets. The subject plainly appealed to the television man never far below his journalistic veneer. After I had outlined its scope, he got worked up over the notion, stood up from the desk in his small room and marched into the conference-room, striding back and forth like a demented Captain Nemo, talking, building-up, improvising, haranguing. 'I think you're right. How they live. Where do they live? Garrets, basements, cottages, council houses? What do they earn? In a good year, in a bad year. What kind of wives do they marry, God help us? Do they have children? Are they kept men? Are they lazy bloody layabouts, expecting us to pay 'em for their self-indulgent ways and sonnets? Or are they steady-working bastards like bank clerks and the rest of us? What do they eat? Do they eat or are they always drunk like Dylan Thomas? Are they dirty? Do they ever go near a hot bath? Or ever want one? Do they do any other work? Are they sincere? You could follow up with the modern beat painters. Not the fashionable goons the glossies go for, but the others. The breakdown gang of junk-merchants who call themselves artists. Look into them. Try and get into their minds. It's their mental processes that fox and fascinate me and the rest of the great lay public. Dig in, buster. Angle it into their minds. With television you have to be too bloody careful. You can ask the questions and they can lie like hell if they're good actors—as most painters and poets are. But you can nail 'em in print. Dig, man, dig.'

And so on and so on. He talked about his secular projects like a defrocked evangelist, now turned diabolo, advancing the cause of Lucifer, the words rushing out in an unstoppable but well-controlled spate.

So poets it would be. Then painters. Then a week of short paragraphs on a miscellany of *Faces & Places*. Then the major piece on the Trade Unions. Then over to some aspect of shamateurism.

'All I want,' said Spurway, 'is a few well-timed, modest libel actions on my hands. Nothing astronomical, but something noticeable, all the same. I want to see that Malcolm bloody Prior, our chief legal adviser, works like hell for his pay packet. And a few letters to the Press Council will also help to show T.J. he's in business.'

I had met Prior, a rather angular, pale-faced, equestrian-looking young man, somewhat older than he looked, I suspected. He talked in slow, well-measured barristerial tones as if he had taken in torts with his mother's milk, and had been taught at his prep school never to be ruffled by other men's more coarse-grained tones. He seemed made for Spurway's barbs and arrows.

24

For the two further Saturdays preceding publication we again rehearsed, producing papers based on existing features and current news.

One hundred thousand copies of each paper were printed and then pulped.

Spurway fiercely resisted West's policy of pulping, contending that to let, say, ten thousand copies of the paper loose on the market could provoke a tremendous and gratuitous publicity build-up of interest and curiosity amongst newsagents, wholesalers, advertising agents and the public, but Douglas Castell, the circulation manager, said that T.J. had decreed that only five hundred copies of each issue were to be retained for the records, internal discussions and post-mortems.

'What the hell does he mean by it?' Spurway demanded at the final editorial meeting before publication. He had invited Castell to the meeting.

'Orders, Mr Spurway. I didn't ask why.'

'I'll see him later. How did it look to you, Doug?'

'Pretty good.'

'Something worth selling?'

'I'll have no trouble there.'

'And what's the first print order?'

'Half a million.'

'Too few. It's mad. We'd sell two million.'

'It's a very highbrow paper, Mr Spurway. No offence, but it is. One of the top brass at W. H. Smith's who saw one of the copies from the dummy run said it was like a cross between the Third Programme and the Connoisseur—in colour. Neither of those is what I'd call a mass-market. Personally, sir, I think Mr West is wise in keeping the figure at a rational figure for the first two or three issues.'

'What would you call a rational figure?'

'I'd be more optimistic than Mr West. I'd go for a first print order of a million.'

'That's better, but not much.'

'It's twice as many, sir.'

'Supposing it's a runaway success?'

'I get the firm impression that Mr West doesn't intend it to be. You'll remember he said at the last meeting that a sell-out of a quarter of a million is no guarantee that one could have sold half a million.'

'We could try.'

'You're in a far stronger position than I am, Mr Spurway, to persuade Mr West to change his ideas. And all the advertising rates are based on half a million launching sale. But if you can get authority for more copies I will, of course, do my level best to sell 'em.'

'We'll see,' Spurway growled.

25

I lunched again with Spurway later that week, on the Thursday.

He had seen West on the previous day but had been defeated on his request for a larger print order.

'Of course, he's on firm ground,' Spurway grumbled, 'but I don't like it. He's taking too much care and no chances.'

'Surely his present investment is gamble enough.'

'No man with these colour machines under one roof in the middle of London is taking any kind of gamble,' Spurway said decisively. 'There are too many newspaper outfits shopping around for colour. West has beaten them to it and he's sitting on a gold-mine. He can't lose. If we folded he'd have another, bigger contract sewn up within a couple of weeks at eight times the run that we're promised.'

'Perhaps that's what he's after. Perhaps he's proposing to use New Sunday as bait.'

'That's crossed my mind, too, after you dropped the first acidic seed a few weeks back.'

'And he won't budge?'

'Not an inch. Not even by another fifty thousand. Says he's working on trade demands and likely advertising revenue, and I'm working on egotistical wishful-thinking. Would I like to see the guaranteed figures? he asked. I said yes. He showed 'em to me. Didn't mean a thing. No wonder these bloody Marxists always want to control the means of production. I do myself after I've had ten minutes with West.'

'A far cry from being his white-haired boy.'

'I may have started off with that spectacular piece of self-delusion. The relationship's rapidly going downhill now. We're mutually disenchanted, to put it mildly.'

'Sad, especially at this crucial moment.'

'Perhaps I'm imagining things. He's pleasant enough when we discuss editorial matters. He's particularly sympathetic to all my editorial whims and whines. But as soon as I step over the line into what he calls spheres of management he cracks down like a bar of cold steel.'

'Seems reasonable enough. Few editors would ask for more than you apparently get. Why not leave him alone with his managerial headaches?'

'I'm something more than a new editor taking over a rundown newspaper. All this is something brand new, creative, worth while.'

'But it's still his money.'

'You ought to be an arbitrator on a wages council!' Spurway scoffed.

'It's been suggested before.'

At that same moment I began to wonder whether the coolness might not be part of some far-sighted West scheme. But I took care to sow no more acidic seeds, stayed silent and let Spurway talk.

26

I recalled all that Mason had said on the first Saturday of *New Sunday*, a hot sticky afternoon at the very end of August, the air of West House heavy, in equal parts, with humidity and foreboding.

Tension throughout the building was explosive. No matter how frequently and realistically rehearsals are staged, the real thing is unpredictably, anti-climatically different.

We started early. Forty-eight of the sixty-four tabloid pages had been O.K.'d and sent to press the night before. That left sixteen news and sports pages to be dealt with on Saturday.

Faces & Places was chock-full of modern poets and their ways of wayward life. Reading the final proof, I was more than ever willing to eat my earlier words about colour. The pages were as different from the black-and-white pages I had always known as poetry—even modern poetry—is different from prose. I had spent a lot of time with John Hilton, the art editor, going over the transparencies, watching the evolving make-up. I soon realized that I was editing a feature unlike any I had ever worked on before. I was, in fact, in my own small section of the press, involved in a major newspaper revolution. And after it was done I knew I was a complete convert to colour.

Tim Morgan had begged me to O.K. my proofs by six o'clock on Friday. He wanted a clear deck for the news pages on Saturday, he said. Only a libellous statement inadvertently written into my pages, and queried by the lawyer, would give me the chance to remake. Malcolm Prior and his winger, Dick Warren, the resident lawyers, had cleared them. So the pages were sent away on Friday for plate-making.

I need not have gone in that Saturday morning, but I knew that nothing would have kept me away. In any case, Spurway rang to say he might need me on any profile piece that might blow up. He wanted, he said—as he had said before—to get the *Faces & Places* touch into other personality pieces in the paper.

So I stood around, behind the long news desk, watching Ted Hales, the news editor, Ken Wheeler, the chief sub, Hilton and Bill Montgomery, the picture editor, make up their pages from the galleys of text and the transparencies that came across from the picture desk.

I found it an exciting and absorbing experience to watch news pages being laid out six times faster than Hilton had taken over *Faces & Places*. He made his swift pencil patterns on the white tabloid layout sheets, preprinted in pale blue vertical rules to indicate the column measure, making allowance for headings, text and pictures. To someone like myself, reared in traditional newspaper usages, it was difficult to comprehend that within half an hour of this page-scheming, colour plates of the pictures Hilton and Montgomery judged and masked would be made and ready for the machines. All text had been computer-set. All pictures were metal plates within the hour. I was living through a typographical and production revolution made by West's money and Spurway's drive. I was duly respectful and doubly grateful that so much technical expertize still needed a basic starting-point, in most cases, of old-fashioned words written with old-fashioned pens, typed on old-fashioned portable typewriters.

The pace was terrific: so was the strain, but Hales and Hilton, Wheeler and Montgomery seemed to thrive on it. Spurway, hunched in a swivel chair in a corner of the newsroom well away from his group of skilled technicians, read the *New Statesman* as if he were in a Pall Mall club. Nobody would have thought he was at a crisis point in his upward climb, a make-or-break moment. With his out-thrust chin, black-grey hair, heavy horn-rimmed specs and large cigar he looked more like a man whose way ahead was already assured rather than a man on the edge of a newly discovered, highly activated volcano. I admired the attitude: it seemed without affectation of any kind.

'Nice to see you here, Paul,' he said, putting down his paper, getting up as I went across. 'How d'you like the general panic?'

'How could anyone keep away?'

'I may want you to rewrite one or two of the political profiles for the second edition. I may not. I like the look of Faces and Places. Perfect subject for a kick-off. Shows where we stand. No concessions to the great masonic and moronic masses. How many other first issues of any paper would start with such a subject? I ask myself and the answer is a bloody great negative. Just what I wanted. How d'you like the look of the rest of the paper?'

'Pretty good, I think.'

'Good enough for you to take back some of those dyspeptic mealy-mouthed words you uttered at lunch that day all those months ago?'

'Good enough for that.'

'I think so, too. Now all we've got to do is sell the bloody thing. Thank God that's Castell's job and not mine.'

'Is he good?'

'His reputation is. The two don't always interlock. I think he is. But he's always been on trad papers and he's a trad type. He seemed keen on the pages he's seen. That's something. But I doubt whether he understands a tenth of what we're saying and what I'm after.'

By then all the news pages were away and the sports pages were beginning to go away. The sports subs, at the other end of the large news-room, were working swiftly and quietly at their reports and statistics. Not a very sporting-looking crowd, I thought, watching their bent bald pates and paunchy-looking pullovers, but they seemed proficient technicians. We can't do better, Tim Morgan had said with his habitual glint: each a third-rate authority on his particular sport. Spurway, a knowledgeable games-player in his university years, also believed he had got a couple of first-rate sports feature writers, and was backing them: a thirty-year-old ex-grammar-school professional footballer with a broken knee-cap and aggressive prose style, and a five-blues Cambridge hearty with a chip on his shoulder about all scholars and sports administrators.

'Who the hell wants to read descriptions of matches he's either seen or not seen?' Spurway had said two weeks before at an editorial conference. 'It doesn't make sense. People want to read every single word they can about the sport that interests 'em: the technique of the game, the masters of the sport, their weaknesses, their strengths, their pay cheques, their homes, their wives, their ambitions. That's the kind of stuff to give 'em, not a day-old list of results they get from the BBC anyway. Our results and reports are going to be the sparest and sparsest in the business, but our sports gossip is going to be the best in the land.'

The afternoon wore on for another hour and then the paper was on the machines. Somebody—I think it was Castell—came to ask Spurway whether he wished to go down to the machine-room to take delivery of the first copy of *New Sunday*.

'Not bloody likely,' Spurway said firmly. 'The colour will look like mud, the headings will be all wrong, and the pictures will be upside-down. Send me up a dozen copies when the colour's running well and you think you've got a paper you can sell.'

Castell grinned and went.

I asked Spurway why West wasn't around.

'Because it's just another piece of property to him,' Spurway said. 'Another pile of pound notes, although he's likely to lose a lot of those tonight if I'm any judge. He's not the type to be caught into what he would doubtless consider a display of hysterical emotion. The kind of nonsense that's got us all by the short hairs this afternoon.'

He looked around at subs scribbling at their desks, reporters glued to telephones, operators in the wire-room, telephone reporters in their cages taking down copy from outside men and agencies.

'It doesn't seem to have got you unduly steamed up,' I said.

'My phiz is a well-trained mask of deed and thought. I'm steamed up all right.'

27

So we wrote, printed, published and distributed the first number of the first volume of that historic newspaper, *New Sunday*, the first national newspaper in Great Britain to be printed in full colour by the web-fed offset process.

There, on the thirtieth day of August, a sticky, late-summer Saturday afternoon, at ten-to-six a messenger brought up two dozen copies from the machine-room and distributed them along the news-room desks.

We reached for the papers tentatively.

'Good god, what's happened?—it's all in colour!' cried a wag.

'Merciful god, the colour's in register!' said another.

'It looks like a bleeding glossy!' said a third.

'Nobody's going to believe all this news happened if we've got time to make and print in colour,' said a fourth.

'That sounds like the beginning of a smear campaign,' said Spurway.

He was elated, but his elation was well under control. He began to ask what changes Morgan and Hales proposed to make for the second edition, how many pages it would be possible to remake.

He was once more a technician on the job.

28

Now, looking back, it is clear enough to me, and will, I dare say, be even clearer to those journalistic historians who will one day write their theses on the subject, that that first number of *New Sunday* was a revelation of what a newspaper could be and of Spurway's three-league step forward in his campaign to be the nation's first complete communications man.

In that first number, *New Sunday* scotched the old notion that an editor of any worthwhile newspaper has to come up through the grinding, gruelling apprenticeship of early years in Bolton or Bristol, Pontypool or Polperro, scribbling away about local murders, mayors and matches, followed by further years, sitting on his broadening hunkers, doing a stint of desk-work or trailing, on flattening feet, through the depressing corridors of the Mother of All Parliaments, before he can take complete command of a metropolitan news sheet.

To that kind of worn-out, wearing-out training Spurway had cocked a decisive snook, and, in a curious and even bigger way, so had West. For both men, the project had taken courage of a high order. But no two men were ever more disparate in character, more divided in outlook.

The truth was that *New Sunday* looked the kind of high-grade popular art a newspaper can be, ought to be. Each page was a visual pleasure.

For his news headings and display types, Hilton had used two weights of narrow sanserif throughout the paper. He had kept to a quiet but effective form of picture presentation. And when he had dramatic pictures he had, by working closely with Montgomery and Hales, given them every possible square inch the page could afford. Consequently the paper had a rare unity: it looked the same kind of paper throughout, spoke with the same tone of authoritative voice throughout. Thus the women's pages, which were given over to fashion in that first issue, had photographs in colour—taken in Paris—and headings in the same light sanserif type enlarged to enormous size. I had never seen typographical consistency carried to so logical and flexible a limit.

But what's the use of trying to explain a graphic concept in good old-fashioned words? I ought to include a miniature copy of *New Sunday* with every copy of this narrative. The hell with the cost.

Most of us were shaken and almost over-awed by the colour.

Pettiford, looking at his City pages, said: 'It looks like a dummy for the ideal paper you produce for a lecture on journalism as it could be and ought to be and you know never will be. With this colourful rag before me I almost believe in my own pontifications. By rights we should be toasting our millionaire proprietor as well as our revered editor.'

Tim Morgan was so relieved that the paper had met all the machine-room deadlines that he was delighted to have any paper, whatever its merits or demerits. Yet, examining the paper that he had supervised, page by page, he was bowled over. 'It's too good,' he groaned. 'It'll only sell fifty thousand copies. People will think it's a half-crown glossy and put it back on the bookstalls.'

Lee-Ellerton, re-reading his leader, was as pleased as a Prime Minister learning of a dicey by-election victory. He said: 'Hilton's presentation has given my words an authority I never intended. My name's Lee-Ellerton, not Macaulay. I shall be accused of false pretences.'

And so it went. Trained journalists, astonished by the revolution that colour and orderly design had wrought in their ancient craft, were fascinated by the distinction with which these novelties had invested their very own words. The photographers were jubilant.

Looking at *Faces & Places* I could scarcely believe that the elements I had discussed and arranged with Hilton had been translated and transmuted into the resplendent double-page spread before me. I had half-expected something along the lines of the Sunday colour magazines. Instead I was holding a brilliantly coloured newspaper. These weren't just feature articles produced in colour a month previously. Transparencies I had seen three days before here glowed in more or less natural colours.

Yet despite the heady excitement of the day, I had reservations. But these I kept silent to myself.

I knew I was in at the passing of an age. I had liked old-fashioned black-and-white, which seemed to me—and still seems to me—to give truth and urgency to a factual story. The use of colour somehow seemed to suggest that we were trying to point up some of our stories, to project them. I was suspicious of their authenticity. But I knew that I was a writer, my journalistic roots in Addison, Steele, Defoe, Wilkes and that great unknown, unkempt army of reporters and coranto-makers—hacks and trimmers on occasion—but with a few among them seeking to tell the truth as they saw it—in black-and-white.

Yet to turn one's back on colour was to turn one's back on progress and all that. All newspapers will be in colour within twenty years, I told myself, and groaned at the prospect, for, on an actuarial basis I should still probably be alive, still sadly and secretly yearning for the black-and-white yesteryears of my craft.

I was a sentimentalist, I told myself, a backward-looker, now involved against my inner will with a bang-up-to-the-minute newspaper, the most modern of its time. And, ironically enough, I had been brought there not by the lure of colour, but by the promise of more space in which to write more words of my own making, a carrot that has been dangled before the vanity of journalists since the days, no doubt, of Grub Street itself.

So I viewed my spread with a certain distrust, despite its portraits in colour, despite the drawing—also in colour—of the stone cottage near Corfe Castle where Alec Lamden's *Study for a Canto against Freedom* had been written, despite the clear-cut beautifully balanced sanserif type of the headings. I felt the way some of the others felt: that my words had been treated merely as a kind of columnar infilling for the pictures, as a springboard for Hilton's talent for typographical display.

Yes, despite these reservations, it was a moving and

exciting experience. And of course, for some, it was disappointing. Hilton and Montgomery had seen more clearly than the rest of us the potentialities of colour. They were quick to see all the mistakes they and the printers had made. But there was no going back. Already they were examining the pages under their magnifying lenses, plotting improvements for the second edition.

I also wanted to start rewriting my own feature, but Morgan barred that, saying he was taking no chances. The only pages to be remade would be news pages one and four and the sports pages. We had fresh transparencies in of some White City milers and, for the front page, a tragi-comic picture of a collapsed Coldstream guardsman on—or rather off—parade, flat on his belly, his rifle three yards away, and nobody giving him a passing glance.

'Corny!' opined Montgomery at the desk, dismissing the picture. 'It's all been done a thousand times before.'

'Don't be daft!' Hilton shouted. 'Of course it's been done before, a thousand times, but never in a newspaper in colour.'

Spurway, standing by the desk, backed Hilton. 'It's just what we want. It'll point up the difference between old-fashioned deadbeat black-and-white and brilliant brand new colour. It'll do it in a way nothing else would. Let's go.'

So in went the guardsman for the second edition.

29

And of course the paper was talked about and was sold out by midday Sunday.

'All four hundred and ninety-eight thousand copies,' Castell reported to Spurway's query at the Tuesday morning conference.

'And how many do we print next week?' Ellerton asked.

'I've been told to raise the print order by twenty-five thousand for the next four weeks,' Castell said, almost apologetically. He was a short, square, brown-faced, open-air type with lively blue eyes and the features of a very aggressive Red Indian warrior. He seemed authoritative on his several managerial subjects—from circulation to machines, from unions to paper surfaces—with a quiet, no-nonsense West-of-England burr that softened some of his tougher statements.

'Why, for God's sake?' Spurway barked irritably. 'That's chicken-feed.'

'You know as much as I do, sir. We all had that memo from T.J. I think, in some ways, it's a somewhat faint-hearted policy, but I must take my instructions from the management.'

'This is madness unparalleled. How many do your people think they could get rid of with the sky the limit?'

'We'd have a bash at another hundred thousand, at least. Curiosity's strong throughout the country.'

'Another hundred thousand!' Spurway barked. 'Why not another half-million?'

'It's a very expensive operation, sir.'

'We knew we weren't in the home-made ice-cream business. What the hell is T.J. waiting for? Does he want people to come in here and beg for copies?'

'Ask me another. I sent him a memo on Saturday night. He's replied, saying he'll be satisfied with a solid under-pinning of half a million at the end of the first three months. He will then be prepared to go up to six hundred thousand. Says he doesn't want to go by fits and starts.'

'But he won't get advertising backing on half a million with all the colour supplements selling way above that.'

'Well, those are his standing instructions until September.'

'And what are the advance advertising bookings like?'

'Not bad for the first month. Those that came in got good series discounts. Six insertions for the price of four. I don't know what the re-bookings will be like.'

'I'll ask Minton,' Spurway said, referring to the advertisement manager. 'T.J. must be mad. Anyway, he presumably knows what he's after. He's made too many fortunes for me to set up as his adviser on money-spinning. Let's get down to the problem as it concerns us. What have we got for this Sunday? No need for you to hang on, Doug.'

'I'd like to hang on for a while yet if I may, sir,' Castell said. 'It's useful to know how colleagues work and I'd like to know as early as possible what kind of product I've got to sell.'

'Product!' Spurway snorted. 'So that's what a twentieth-century newspaper has come to, is it? A product. A tin of corned beef? A soap tablet?'

'Now, please, sir, don't get me wrong. To me it *is* a product. I've got to sell it. And it's a hard Sell, believe me.'

'Cheer up, Doug!' Pettiford interjected gaily and calmly. 'Other ages were more romantic about the press, that's all. The way some journalists always are in any age.'

Spurway laughed. 'It's a label most wouldn't recognize.'

'I've got to sell the paper or product or whatever you call it,' Castell said defensively, with a grateful glance at Pettiford, but Pettiford had moved on to other thoughts, for, turning to Spurway, he said: 'Could I ask Doug one or two questions?'

'Why not? That's why he's here,' Spurway countered.

'How many machines have we got here?' Pettiford asked.

'Twenty, sir.'

'I imagine that's a lot more than we need for this operation?'

'A lot more.'

'Tell us in simple language what we've got.'

'I doubt if it'll mean much to you, Mr Pettiford, or to anybody else in the room,' Castell said, 'but in simple technical language we've got five Goss sixteen-unit lines, each line arranged as four octuples, with four double folders. Each machine has two three-colour satellite units. There's also a late news and seal unit to each octuple.'

'It's a miracle we can print on such jargon,' Lee-Ellerton said, recovering.

'And it takes all that hardware to give us a measly half-million forty-eight-page paper?' Spurway scoffed.

'Not all the hardware, as you call it, is employed, sir. Barely a quarter of the capacity is used.'

'And all for forty-eight pages.'

'Sixty-four pages with sixteen pages in full-colour, another

78

sixteen in two colours and the rest in black and white,'
Castell amended patiently.

'But how many copies could be printed on these machines?' Pettiford went on.

'Daily or weekly, Mr Pettiford?'

'Does it matter?'

'Not really, I suppose, once the organization got going. If the whole place was geared and manned for the exercise, I'd say we could print well over three millions. Each machine could probably push out forty thousand copies an hour. Yes, in four hours running we could do something over three millions. Probably four at a pinch.'

'Quite a gap between achievement and potential, it seems,' Spurway said.

Castell nodded.

'Rather what I had in mind,' Pettiford said. 'There's a lot of slack to be taken up somewhere and I don't see West as a slack provider.'

'Nor me,' Spurway said. He sat staring sombrely at the wall above our heads.

'Wouldn't you say, Mr Castell, that all this machinery suggests one of two lines of thought,' Pettiford said coolly: 'Either that Mr West has enormous confidence in the future of New Sunday or even greater confidence in somebody else wanting his machines?'

'Put like that, I can see that it might seem either way,' Castell agreed. 'Or both.'

We were all silent, brooding on the implications of Pettiford's words.

'Let's get back to next Sunday's New Sunday, shall we?' Spurway grunted.

He turned to the projected contents for the following issue, voicing his ideas in swift, compelling sentences. He said at one point, 'I want everyone to think of the feature he most wants to write—and write it. I want you to think of the feature you most want to see written and commission it—in your own field, of course, and through Tom so we don't get our lines crossed. . . .' And so on. We were back to the world he understood.

30

The weekly commentators on the press were vastly impressed by *New Sunday*, and I could see why: the paper was a newspaperman's newspaper, putting into page form all those dreams that all journalists have in their daydreams and nightmares.

'After *New Sunday*,' wrote one ex-editorial mandarin, 'British newspapers will never be the same again, for *New Sunday* combines, in one newspaper, techniques which have been hammered out in other media and were there for the taking. It has an on-the-spot authority which one is apt to get only from a BBC television reporter speaking into a mike from a battlefield or a crisis-area; it has the courage to take a worthwhile feature over four or five pages if deemed editorially necessary; its typographical layout is as bright and lively as that of *Elle*; its writing is first-rate; above all, its pictorial coverage of both news and features is as rich and rare as that of *Life* or *Paris-Match*. Altogether, *New Sunday* is a paper to make the editors of other so-called quality newspapers sit up and look very carefully at what they are offering their publics.'

Others, less magisterial, were, nevertheless, as fulsome.

And Spurway almost purred.

31

Two recollections from that time:

Dining Helen at the Étoile one evening a couple of weeks later I said, 'I've changed a lot of my ideas about Spurway.'

'How come?'

I began to explain my attitudes.

'You always prided yourself on keeping an open mind. You're proving it once again, that's all.'

'Did the pride show?'

'Don't be touchy. If anything showed, it was my pride in your capacity for keeping an open mind. Is that better? You were going to talk about Spurway.'

Even as I took up the subject of Spurway again I thought:

this is the kind of exchange that gnaws at marriage. What starts the thing going? Whose pride, anyway? The hell with it all. Instead I said: 'He's a hell-raiser all right, and he's in everything for Spurway Number One, but there's more to him than that.'

'Why not Spurway Number One, anyway? It's a sound philosophy. I rather admire it. Why not Mortimer Number One for a change?' She knew she need not have said it, didn't want to say it, but still she'd said it.

'Why not?' I said, biting my lip although I could have hit her, but I went on: 'But he's got an odd kind of leadership thing. Nothing inborn or inspired or stuff like that. Not even natural leadership naturally assumed. It's merely that he's such a congenital bulldozer others are apt to follow his sheer brute force and don't-give-a-damn attitude. He would have made a fine infantry officer.'

'In the Marlborough campaigns, no doubt.'

'Particularly then,' I said, noting again Helen's talent for following up cracks that infuriated with those that flattered, both within the space of three minutes. But why not one without the other? Or was that too much to ask?

After that things went better as I tried to sort out, for my own benefit, the particular and peculiar twists of Spurway's qualities of leadership. 'I'm sure he has no yearning for leadership,' I went on. 'He's a loner, a self-willed wolf. He just becomes boss willy-nilly. I begin to see that wanting to be boss-man doesn't necessarily mean a man wants to lead. Spurway cares so little for anyone, any authority, any Establishment that he's apt to cause other men to want to jump on his wagon out of sheer exhilaration. Spurway becomes a leader despite himself. I suppose it's happened often enough in history. He seems so much tougher and more arrogant than other men they're likely to force him into becoming their leader. Particularly somebody as articulate as he is.'

'But I can't agree with your idea that a man who wants to be boss doesn't necessarily want to lead.'

'He may just want to order other people about, to bully, to subdue. Dictators are never leaders in the way that Churchill, Marlborough, Wellington or Monty were leaders.

The true leaders are prepared, even if not exactly willing, to step down at the end of their tasks. No dictator ever voluntarily steps down. Ataturk, Franco, Salazar, Stalin . . . none of them ever thought or thinks about handing over, once the immediate job is over.'

'Perhaps they consider their job is never done.'

'That's always the great alibi.'

'And you see Spurway merely as the boss type.'

'So far, he's been a cog in a democratic wheel. But I think he's the stuff of which bosses and dictators are made. Fortunately, the English seem to have evolved a sufficiency of counter-checks for would-be-rogue-bosses.'

'But you approve of him more than you did?'

'It's not so much approval—who am I to approve or disapprove?—but there's a lot more to him than just plain Spurway. With luck, his bullying could be transmuted into leading.'

'Good old Paul!' Helen said. 'Always on the side of the angels.' Why was it, I asked myself, that the same words from another woman might well seem flattering, yet from Helen were virtually a sneer. Give up trying for an answer, I told myself, and went on with the meal.

32

I also doubt the truth of Helen's appraisal when I recall another vignette of those days. (*Vignette: a shape somewhat hazy at the edges*, according to my dog-eared dictionary.)

I was talking to Molly one midweek morning around ten o'clock. We had concluded, apparently to our mutual pleasure, our morning rendezvous. Harryboy always fell asleep after getting his oats, she said, whereas she often felt like a natter. So I let her natter: I could always continue with my own silent reflections.

'Why 'ave you put me money up without me asking?' she was saying.

'Because I'm getting more in my new job.'

'But I ain't doing a new job.'

'You get even better at the old one.'

'Which is the old one: this or dustin' and washin'?'

'Both.'

'If I 'ad any feelings about it you'd make me feel like a tart.'

'Perish the thought.'

'Well, I suppose I am a bit o' one, so why worry? D'you ever get a touch of conscience, Paul, having it off another man's missus like this?'

'Why, for god's sake? I don't know him. It's not as if he's my best friend or something. He doesn't drop in for meals.'

She laughed long and boisterously. 'You and 'im wouldn't 'ave much in common, I can tell you—except me, o' course.'

'D'you have a conscience?'

'I done too much of it in me time to start growing a conscience now. Anyway, he gets all he wants. I've never denied him when 'e felt like it. But it's a funny thing, I was thinking last night. Harryboy feeds better because of all this. Looking at 'im getting outside 'is steak and onions, I thought to meself, you're a bit of a kept boy, y'know, Harryboy. Made me laugh. On the quiet like.'

'Would it have made him laugh?'

Again she laughed. 'I dunno. He's not the jealous sort. Never asked me if I'd 'ad much of it before we married. Took it for granted, I suppose. The war and all that, and all them Yanks about. But it's funny, don't y'think?'

'What is?'

'My Harryboy being a kept man.'

'Only for luxurious tit-bits.'

She laughed. 'You can say that again.'

'Would you mind if you discovered he was being unfaithful to you?'

'I'd be down on 'im like a ton o' bricks. It's different for a woman. She's gotta fight for her security an' all. And there's another thing. No woman wants to make an honest man of the other feller, 'er bit on the side. Not many women want to break up another 'ome. Well, not often. But men always get so bloody involved—just like young boys with their first bit o' skirt. Besides,' she added with Cockney canniness: 'it

83

always costs men more. And the extra usually comes out of the housekeepin', in my experience.'

I laughed aloud.

'Well, it's true. All this 'ere costs me nothing. Anyway, what would you say if you found your missus was 'aving it off with somebody else?'

'She's a free woman.'

'You wouldn't mind even though you're keeping her and paying the rent?'

'Why should I? Her body's her own. I undertook to pay the rent when I married. At the moment we're marking time, so to speak. If she finds somebody else she wants to spend the rest of her life with, he can take the house and mortgage over, if he wants to.'

'Fair enough. Funny. All of it. The whole bleedin' thing's a mystery. But I'll remember that bit about not ownin' me body in case Harryboy ever does find out. Well, back to the old brush an' pan, I suppose. Like some more coffee?'

I said I would. She stood up. With reviving lust I watched the splendid body, now running to seed, gradually enclosed within its mundane garb. Fascinated, as always, I watched her load her great breasts into her bra, tug on her girdle, roll on her stockings. She did these things with a casual carefree grace of which she was as unaware as she was of the fact that everything about her stark, slack, sensual limbs spelled, for me, complete escape from S.W.3.

Little wonder I had raised her wages.

33

Spurway opened each Tuesday editorial meeting with the same question to Castell: how had sales gone?

Castell would bring out a small, black, loose-leaf notebook and reel off the figures for various areas of Britain.

The paper was plainly a South of England paper. That was certain after the second week.

It will work outwards, Spurway said. Most radio and television programmes of any intellectual worth were tested and launched in London, got off to a slow start in the Midlands, slower still in the North.

This is still a nation with too great a metropolitan concentration of talent, he said. Despite Manchester's everlasting persecution-mania about culture and the Hallé. Edinburgh was an exception—for a month a year—but only then because Londoners went up there. Apart from that, it remained a pretty threadbare Athens of the North.

Only Tom Morgan protested. 'There speaks a good old southern English gentleman,' he said, a Welshman surprisingly speaking up for Scotland.

'But it's true. Ask any television producer.'

'Only if he's a Scot or a Welshman,' Morgan said. 'Just to keep a sense of balance.'

We went on with the meeting.

34

On the fifth Tuesday after the first issue, Castell said sales were soft west of Henley and Oxford and north of Hull. Sales, like currencies, are always 'hard' or 'soft' in the specialist's jargon.

That was the first time I saw Spurway's self-confidence even slightly impaired. I had seen him momentarily set back by other men's opinions, embarrassed by contrary views, even knocked off his perch by a quick-fire *riposte* to one of his more contentious assertions, but this was the first time I had seen the sudden disbelieving, frowning stare at a speaker who could back his views with irrefutable facts and figures. In such a way must monarchs of old have stared at couriers bringing unwelcome news from far-off corners of their kingdoms. Little wonder the couriers had occasionally lost their heads, I thought, noting the narrow-eyed hostility with which Spurway regarded Castell.

'Why are we soft?' Spurway barked. 'We're a good paper. How many men have you got? If we pushed more copies out we'd have more to sell.'

'I've got four area managers and twenty-three men on the road.'

'Is that enough?'

'It's slightly over my budget and it ought to be enough if the paper were moving.'

'But how can it move if sales are pegged?'

'There's something in that, Mr Spurway, but T.J. won't budge.'

'Why not?'

'I was hoping you'd know that, sir.'

'Well, I don't. Are we selling all we print?'

'There are very few returns, sir. Very few.'

'What do your men report? Give us a quick round-up.'

'The main reaction, of course, is that the public is a bit punch-drunk with the avalanche of Sunday newspapers, and that after the first month, when the initial novelty of the new paper had worn off, only the upper-crust intellectual core of the country has put down regular orders for it. They're mad keen. You could put that down as a solid three hundred thousand, well above the daily sales of The Times.'

'That figures.'

'And the trade remains very keen. But, as they point out, a sixty-four page tabloid colour page at sixpence still looks a good deal less in bulk to the general public than, say, forty-eight pages—or more—in the larger sized Sunday Times with all its colour magazine at ninepence.'

'What about the colour? Doesn't that count?'

'It's impressive. Everybody agrees on that. But the Sunday Times and Observer have come back strongly in plugging their colour. And they're both spending a lot of extra money in the press and on the hoardings.'

Spurway went back to his basic contention: 'Could we sell more if we had more papers to sell?'

'I think we could. We could start getting to grips with the North, Edinburgh, South Wales, where these more intellectual exercises are appreciated, despite what you were saying just now. But until T.J. says go, I'm stuck.'

Looking round, I could see that everybody, or almost everybody, was tensed up. Only Castell, diagnosing and explaining, and Pettiford, listening and nodding, had the experts' tranquillity.

Castell continued, like a quiet and expert lecturer: 'The wholesalers think we ought to be very pleased with what has happened so far. They point out that we're selling almost twice as many as The Times, that we're holding back expansion by the other Sundays, especially the Sunday Telegraph, that we're essentially a Third Programme kind of newspaper, intellectually the most advanced of the day, and that sales approaching five hundred thousand add up to a remarkable achievement.'

'Words, words, words,' Spurway said. 'Bread and milk for infants. I call it a wash-out.'

'But what had you expected, Mr Spurway?'

'Something better than this.'

'How many?'

'Something well over a million after the first month and then a gradual rise towards the Sunday Times by the end of next year. As it is, we don't know what we could sell.'

'Your figures would have been very pleasant but well beyond my estimate.'

'It should have been possible.'

'Frankly, Mr Spurway, I don't think the market is there.'

'How can you tell until we try. You're certainly T.J.'s man. Have you seen him?'

'I saw him yesterday. He didn't seem unduly bothered. Has he spoken to you, sir?'

'I haven't seen him for a week. I saw him last week. I agree with you: he didn't seem unduly bothered. In fact, quite unconcerned. What did he say to you, exactly?'

'That the figure was rather above what he'd expected and that it would do very well for the moment.'

'He didn't seem at all disconcerted?'

'Not at all. On the contrary, sir.'

'Why, for god's sake?'

'I must emphasize again that what you've already done is a considerable achievement, Mr Spurway, considering the kind of paper it is, the state of the market, the holiday season and so forth. It's really a time for congratulation, not lamentation.'

'I'm not in a congratulatory mood!' Spurway snapped. He turned to Pettiford. 'How much d'you think we'd be losing on these figures, Alan?'

Pettiford uncrossed his legs and said as if he'd been working on the equation the previous night: 'About seventeen thousand quid a week or anything up to twenty thousand. Say, a million a year, give or take a hundred thousand.'

'D'you think West is the man to stand that?'

'It's not the proven West philosophy of business.'

Pettiford's grin partly dissipated the tension, but only partly.

'Then why is West smiling?' Spurway said plaintively, rather like a spoilt child querying a parent's irrational behaviour.

'Perhaps it's a new philosophy,' Pettiford said. 'He may consider it a reasonable price to join the Newspaper Proprietors' Association as a fully paid-up member.'

'What a hope!' Spurway snorted.

Pettiford went on: 'It may be a hobby for his old age. It may be something he had to do. But it's certainly not sound newspaper finance. Unless . . .'

'Unless what?' Spurway barked.

'Unless he's got other objectives in mind.'

'Such as?'

'God knows. Who am I to look into that labyrinthine mind?'

'So there it is,' Spurway said. He turned to Pettiford again. 'What sales-figure would provide an economic break-even?'

'I couldn't say. My guess was based on current printing costs and charges out. I'd have to see what the forward advertising bookings were. I'd have to see what overheads he was loading the paper with. What he was offloading on the printing side, which is a separate company, as you probably know.'

'I didn't know,' Spurway said.

'Our New Sunday is a very interesting and complicated piece of company structure,' Pettiford said, settling back in his chair. 'I'll explain it to you sometime if you've got five or six hours to spare.'

Spurway grinned. 'I'll let you know. Let's meet for a teach-in after we've lost the first million, shall we? Meantime, let's get on with planning what Mr Castell or the trade so spicily call our intellectually advanced Sunday newspaper, shall we? I won't take up more of your time, Doug. Mr Morgan will let you have a likely list of contents for your bills later in the week.'

Poor Castell. Crossing the room, letting himself out, he looked, I thought, more than ever like a courier withdrawing from the Doge's presence after reporting further Dalmation depredations by the Turks or the Genoese.

'Well, gentlemen,' Spurway said, 'you've heard the report. Some say good old New Sunday, some the hell with New Sunday. I think the best thing we can do is to go ahead and produce the best paper we can for our few, yet faithful, readers and have fun while we can. Meanwhile, lock up your contracts or hand 'em over to your banks or your solicitors.'

We all grinned, somewhat sheepishly. There was a noticeable chill in the room. Spurway tried to whip up some kind of enthusiasm for the coming Sunday's contents, but we were all dampened.

But that kind of atmosphere was a challenge to Spurway. He began to needle each of us in turn, calling for a brief outline of the ideas we were working on for the current week, ideas we hoped to be working on in a month's time.

Spurway called on me.

With Pettiford's helpful co-operation, I had begun working on a group of profiles of the computer men. I had long wanted to try to discover whether the mathematicians, constructional and electronic engineers and financial backers involved in the building of these machines, had any kind of communal world. How often did they meet? Did they talk a common language? Did one man's expertise slot into another's or were there several fringe areas of ignorance? Was commercial competition keeping apart scientists and technicians who should be swopping ideas with each other rather than concealing facts from each other?

I had started making enquiries, digging out data in a vast computer-building outfit in Lancashire and a smaller unit in Kent. I had discussed the problems of mathematical computation and communication with university dons and lecturers at Cambridge and Manchester. I had had some fairly spectacular but incomprehensible diagrams presented to me by one of the younger research men in Manchester. Hilton was trying to see whether they could be reproduced in a way that any layman could begin to understand. I had managed to get one of our younger cameramen, Norman Sheeler, into the laboratories, and he had come up with a series of superb portraits of these unknown boffins who were edging us into the age of automation.

I explained all this as coherently as I could. Others began to ask questions. Pettiford helped me out. The meeting began to come alive.

Spurway fired his questions. So did Lee-Ellerton. So did everybody else. Pettiford, Hilton and myself stood up, pretty gamely and successfully, I thought, to their concerted barrage. Within twenty minutes Spurway's technique was, as usual, paying off. This was the world he loved: a world of words and word-banging. But it was the spoken word he loved so dearly. That I saw and recognized more clearly at each meeting. In much the same way that the mathematicians I had interviewed grudged the time-interval, however fractional a split-second, between evolving the problems they fed into their machines and waiting for the answer, so Spurway grudged the time required for translating spoken words into written and/or printed words. He hated the inevitable loss of spontaneity, the dilution of impact, the eradication of timbre. And he would I could see clearly enough, always consider the written word a poor, if more respectable, relation of the spoken word.

At that meeting I saw quite clearly for the first time that *New Sunday* was no more than an interim interest for him.

35

The next day, half-way through the afternoon, Spurway rang through to my office: could I come in? He was in the conference-room in his usual chair, facing Pettiford, sprawled along one of the black sofas.

'Following his rather detached comments at yesterday's meeting, I've been firing a few questions at Alan,' Spurway began. 'I thought you might be interested. And I'd like to have another mind, apart from my own, to which financial details are more or less a blank. Does that describe your attitude fairly well, Paul?'

I nodded.

'Well, let's go back to yesterday, Alan. I've been thinking about all you said. Do you really think it's as gloomy as you hinted?'

'I didn't say it was gloomy. Far from it. I said it was a very interesting but a new departure for West.'

'You also said that, according to your rough estimates, he might be losing up to a million a year.'

Pettiford sat up in his chair. 'Now take it easy, Mike. It might easily be not all that gloomy. I'm not writing this paper off by any means. I think it's got a hell of a future. And its finances may well fit into West's extremely complex interlocking arrangements. The Chancellor may well be paying for a lot of what West is doing. And there's another angle: to coin a phrase, New Sunday may well be a sprat to catch a mackerel.'

'I can see we're a sprat so far, but where's the mackerel?'

'Hasn't it struck you that New Sunday might well be showing the paces of web-fed offset on a national scale for the other newspaper proprietors to take note? You don't think they're unwatchful of what's happening, do you?' Pettiford was plainly enjoying his expository session. 'You don't think West is going to leave those machines downstairs lying idle for six days a week, do you?'

'That had crossed my mind, as I've said before,' Spurway said, almost tetchily.

'Very soon, one or more of the big dailies is going to talk

turkey about using that colour capacity. Not one of 'em can afford to let another national daily get a head start like that. These machines can rattle off three or four million thirty-two-pagers as easily as they can do three hundred thousand sixty-fours.'

'Don't rub it in, but what about the tabloid size I was so insistent about?' Spurway said.

'My information is that the machines are versatile and adaptable enough to take on at least four other likely page sizes. I asked the machine-room overseer last Saturday what other variants of size were possible. He chuckled and said they'd already tried three.'

'Have they, by God? On whose orders?'

' "Management", as usual.'

'I suppose they were tested for that long before we got 'em?'

'Probably. The fact is the New Sunday size is a mathematical variant of the newsreel size of the three nationals that matter,' Pettiford went on. 'Hicks, the overseer, told me. All that presents no difficulty at all.'

'Continue with your sordid tale,' Spurway commanded.

Pettiford continued: 'You don't think West is the kind of man to invest three millions in new machinery just to print a Third Programme Sunday newspaper, do you? He —or one of his trend-spotters—saw this colour thing coming and the West machine-room is now three years ahead of anybody else's in this country, that's all. In a way he's carrying out a vast blackmail operation. He can play one popular rag off against another. That's one of the ways he's made some of his other millions. He'll now make several more. You watch. It's pretty shrewd stuff.'

'Very shrewd. For whom?'

'Not for us, that's for sure. Not only that,' Pettiford went on, warming up, 'but if one of the national dailies takes up the rest of the machine-capacity New Sunday could obviously be more easily kept going. Underpinned by that national's weekly print bill, as it were.'

'Supposing New Sunday is no more than a sprat to catch a mackerel, d'you think West would keep his money-losing sprat going once he'd caught his profitable mackerel?'

'Depends whether he's printer, publisher or just an old moneybags at heart.'

'At heart he's a cash register,' Spurway said vehemently.

'I've only met him twice, but I think you're right.'

'Well, then?'

'I think he'd flog New Sunday,' Pettiford said calmly.

'I suppose part of the price could be the absorption of New Sunday into an existing Sunday newspaper in an existing group.'

'That, too, had crossed my mind,' Pettiford said with academic tranquillity. 'It would make a lot of sense. It has all the ingredients of a perfect Sunday supplement of larger size and scope than the others. It would be the perfect ready-made answer to a pop Sunday's expansion programme. All this culture-bashing in colour added to the usual Sunday rag. It's a natural.'

'So you think New Sunday may be a decoy-duck?'

'Could be, probably is.'

'And we're all involved in a kind of sham Sunday?'

'Not exactly a sham. After all, it's doing a job. While it lasts—or is allowed to last. You can't call that a sham.'

'What would you call it, then?'

Pettiford reflected for a moment. 'I think my word would be "hollow",' he said evenly. 'Rather like an empty money-box, waiting for some Midas or other to pour in the pennies.'

'Heard of any Midas?'

'Not so far.'

'Well, let me know if you do. You've given me a lot to think about. I'm grateful for the exercise.'

'Sorry it had to be so macabre,' Pettiford said, getting up.

'Let's talk about your next month's programme, shall we?' Spurway said after Pettiford had gone. 'I was wondering, by the way, if you and your wife would care to dine with me next week—say Tuesday—if it doesn't upset your curious marital arrangements, of course.'

'Are your own so Darby and Joan?'

He laughed. I said I'd check with Helen.

36

Under the relentless, gentle, demoniacal drive of Tom
Morgan, I'd quickly got into the habit of OK-ing my proof
of *Faces & Places* by five o'clock on Fridays. By then the
pace was beginning to hot up and the production people
were glad to have me out of the way.

I usually passed the paste-up of the spread with Hilton
soon after midday and then took galley proofs back to Swan
Court. Sometimes I even arranged to take back page proofs.
If I found a literal or a mistake I could ring through. There
was time for corrections up till ten o'clock on Saturday
morning. But, ideally, Morgan liked to have my pages away
by six o'clock on Friday evening.

The general assumption, therefore, was that if I felt like
making a dash for freedom for the rest of the weekend, I
could, but Spurway had given the word freedom a twisted
touch from the word go. He liked his staff around on
Saturdays. Not only that, but he liked to keep one corner
of an early news page for what he called late personality
news. The world didn't stop living on Saturday mornings,
he told Tom, and he might want the *Faces & Places* touch
on other pages. From the first day of the first number, these
provisos had inevitably begun to chisel away at my supposedly free Saturdays. Fortunately, I had never banked
on them.

Basically, I shared Spurway's views. A political poltroon,
given to off-the-cuff malapropisms, or a pulchritudinous
authoress, gabby on the decay of occidental marriage, is as
likely to fly in or out on Saturday as on any other day. Or
the lawyers occasionally had their last-minute doubts about
a double-edged reference to an international trollop or a
national tycoon in *Faces & Places*. Or Spurway had one of
his Friday-night brainwaves and wanted something new or
something different or something wonderful as a Saturday
morning postscript to *Faces & Places*.

So I went in. Things were easier that way.

Saturday was also the easiest of all mornings to go in
because Molly didn't come in. Her Gary was home from

school and often enough Harryboy, too, was home from his long hauls. So I set the alarm for eight o'clock, got up, made my own coffee, buttered my own toast and read *The Times* in comparative comfort, undisturbed by the exigencies of illicit lust or demi-semi-family life. Occasionally I walked round to Milner Street if Helen rang and invited me. And sometimes, of course, I stayed over Friday night at Milner Street. It was a variable way of life.

37

The dates get easier to recall or check as the record proceeds.

On the morning of Saturday, October the eighteenth, as the cops declaim at Bow Street, I awoke alone and breakfasted alone. As soon, however, as I read in *The Times*, over my would-have-been leisurely breakfast, that Frensham Baker was to head the new bombshell Ministry of Social Welfare I knew I would be wanted on deck.

I got in about ten-thirty and went along to Tom Morgan's office.

'I've been ringing your place for the past half-hour,' he said.

'I left forty minutes ago.'

'Well, I told Annie to ring you. Then I told her to get me some coffee. First things first. I take it you've seen this Frensham Baker announcement?'

'That's why I'm here.'

'I thought so. The editor's already been on. Thinks you ought to do a profile piece for page three. Or even the leader page, if you feel like it. Or it might even rate a kicker on page one. Or at a pinch you can scrub Faces and Places and start again.'

'Of these infinite variations, which would the Managing Editor prefer?'

'At the moment, as kicker on page one. I'll probably have to turn it, but God knows where. We're crowded out with stuff as it is. We need a ninety-six-page paper. But I'd rather keep Faces and Places the way it is.'

'So would I. It's quite good this week.'

'You're strangely modest for once.'

'The quiet confidence of a man who knows he's done more than mere duty calls for.'

He smiled. 'I'll want your copy by two-thirty, Paul. Ideally, two.'

'Noted. Is there an official press conference?'

'Apparently not. At least, so the P.M.'s press office said half an hour ago.'

'They won't let a job like this go without blowing it up skyhigh,' I said. 'Give it another five minutes. They're probably trying to track down Frensham Baker. He could be anywhere between Oxford and Budapest.'

'You and the editor both knew him, I gather.'

'We both sat at his academic knees, so to speak.'

'Poor old Baker.'

Morgan's secretary, Miss Annie Bolton, tall, disdainful, pretty and competent, came into the office with two cups of coffee, gave one to Morgan and then, with a big look of renunciation, the other to me.

'Will you make your own arrangements about getting hold of Baker?' Morgan said. 'Or could you do a piece of off-the-cuff if he's gone to earth?'

'He'll talk. I'd wager on it. He's one of nature's biggest natural talkers.'

The telephone rang. Annie took it, listened, cupped the mouthpiece: 'Mr. Bell,' she hissed.

Morgan took up the telephone on his desk. 'Hello, Freddie. Early for you. What is it?'

He listened, sipping his coffee. Then he said decisively: 'No, I'm sending Paul. He's here now. In my room. The editor wants it that way and wants you where you are, wherever that may be. Your proof's just come up. You're seven inches over. Shall I cut?'

I heard a falsetto screech as Frederick Ewart Bell, Lobby Correspondent, rang off. Any suggestion that another might cut his copy had his sixteen stones moving fast from his home in Highgate or his home-from-home in Westminster towards his galley proofs.

Morgan said: 'Frensham Baker, as you so accurately fore-

96

cast, *will* be giving a press conference. In his rooms at Oxford
at one o'clock. Cheese and beer for all. All very undergraduate and so forth but very considerate, all the same.
You'd better take an office car and go. Annie, get on the
blower and have an editorial car round to the Ludgate
Circus entrance for Mr Mortimer straightaway.'

'What a way to spend a Saturday!' I groaned.

'You'll be back by five and finished by five-past-five. I
shall be here till one. No quality of mercy is straining here
for you, chum?'

'I'll be on my way. What about a photographer?'

He talked as he scribbled. 'I'll get Monty to lay one on
in Oxford. He's sure to have a contact there. I'll have a
despatch rider waiting there to bring the film back. Ring
your stuff through. By two-thirty at the very latest, so help
me God.'

'How long?'

'If it's really good, I can take eight hundred. If it's a
masterpiece a thousand. I'd prefer run of the mill and call
it seven hundred. I don't want to turn overmuch. We're
packed out as it is.'

'Good. I'll send it as it comes. You can cut. I'm off.'

'And don't let the fact that he was once your mentor
intimidate you today. The editor says he wants a tight,
tough piece with some needle in it. Says that's why he's
sending you. Any special reason? Weren't you a dutiful
scholar?'

'Too dutiful,' I said, and went.

38

I had Myers for my chauffeur, one of those steady, resolute
drivers who keeps high average speeds without living on his
passenger's nerves.

I closed my eyes and began to work on the opening sentences. Memories and images of Frensham Baker came
pushing in from limbo.

In a way, I thought, this new job was all part of an
inevitable progress. He'd wanted the job, the first of its

kind, and, in a way, he'd made it for himself, preparing himself for the task like a novitiate for the priesthood. Even his early days, over which he'd scarcely had control, had somehow helped. Well-to-do parents, boyhood in Manchester, Oxford, Civil Service, Oxford again. And now Whitehall.

I wondered how I should find him. I hadn't seen him for two years. Then he'd been showing signs of running to seed, the great rock crumbling at the cliff-edge, so to speak. But the inside strata had still seemed durable and intact. And men sometimes pulled themselves up at the threatening, seedy edge, took themselves in hand, trimmed down again, got set for the rest of their earthly span. Well, I would soon know.

I recalled how I had first met him and been put to work by him: my master and my mentor for three long fulsome years. I'd had unusual chances to study him as well as study for him, for I had devilled deeply for him for his first major survey. Indeed, I sometimes thought I'd spent more time studying him than my chosen subject, and probably knew him as well as anybody outside his own family circle.

His own family circle. The olde-worlde phrase made me smile. Frensham Baker, I'd always thought, had less need for family, family circle, family life than any man or woman I'd ever known. He was, to put it briefly and mildly, a one-man power-house of egomaniacal ambition. Like the rest of us, he had his appetites, but in him all normal appetites, desires, ambitions—although they had their place in his life—were subjugated by and to a passionless passion for power. Not the aimless quantitative power that Spurway seemed to be seeking, but a clinically specialized area of power. And now he'd got it. Or so it seemed. He'd always prophesied that he would be the first Minister of Social Welfare and he'd made it.

I recalled our last meeting. I was going down for keeps the next day with that rankling Second.

'A pity,' he said; 'what d'you put it down to? We all thought you were booked for a First.'

'Too much work on senility, probably. It got into the bloodstream.'

'D'you think it kept you from your books?'

'What would you think? Ten months' field-work?'

'I suppose so. You should have protested. You don't want to go on with the social survey business, I take it?'

'Life's too short and I need a job.'

'Your work here should help you get one.'

'I don't think I want that kind of job.'

After that he wasn't interested. So I'd gone.

No word of thanks for the exploitation of a score of undergraduates like myself, beguiled by his persuasive words and seeming idealism into whittling away their university lives recording case-histories in alms-houses in Liverpool, infirmaries in Essex, old people's homes in Croydon; interviewing doctors, almoners, National Assistance officers, health visitors, nurses and the rest; extracting statistics from legal reports, White Papers and Ministry data sheets.

Our efforts had helped to bring Professor Frensham Baker into the headlines of every newspaper in the land on the morning of the publication of *The Social Implications of Senility*. And there, indeed, are our names, duly recorded in very small type in the acknowledgements.

39

Myers made good time and we were passing through Henley-on-Thames an hour later and were in Oxford within two hours, despite the drizzle that was slowing down the weekend escapist traffic going West. We were bang on time.

At the College gates I told Myers to get himself a meal and return in forty minutes. Then I went in under the arch-way I knew so well, past the porter's lodge and across the quadrangle to the Master's Lodge.

A couple of undergraduates stood inside the bleak hall-way.

'Professor Baker?' a tall, bearded youngster queried. What was left of his face outside his beard blushed scarlet as he uttered his harmless question. I nodded. Why make his torture worse by saying I could climb the stairs blindfold?

'Will you go up to the rooms on the first floor?'

'You *are* Press?' demanded his shorter, tubbier companion, cooler and infinitely more aggressive.

Again I nodded and went up by the waxed oak stairway. The Master's Lodge had been built just before the Second War, a fair and daunting example of neo Georgian without, Cotswold crafts within. I rapped on the first floor door and went in.

About a dozen people were already there, Baker amongst them. He was deep in the brown-leather, deep-buttoned Chesterfield, his huge legs crossed, his leonine head well back, ready, it seemed, for a mass-tutorial. He was dressed in one of his hairy, fleck-tweeded suits; blue flannel shirt; heavy brown boots. It was his uniform; he changed the colour of the suits but not their style: he was still the muscular professor just about to leave his Snowdonian hotel for a quick burst up Moel Hebog and then back for an evening's fireside disputation.

Another undergraduate by the door showed me to a chair as the Prof boomed. 'Come in. Make yourself comfortable.'

He stared intently at me as I edged past his boots, kept on staring, then shouted: 'Is it? Yes, by God, it is. Paul Mortimer. How d'you do, Paul? Never realized I'd have the luck to have you coming here today. Come over here. Excuse me, gentlemen, one of my onetime students. Pray forgive the human weaknesses of nostalgia and nepotism. Sit here, Paul.' He patted a vacant seat by his side on the sofa. 'What's the time? Five-to-one. Let's eat and let's start. You can fire your questions, gentlemen—and ladies, I see, forgive me—with your mouths full, I daresay; I know I can. Late-comers can latch on as best they can. I don't propose to keep you very long. Or for you to keep me very long. You're busy. So am I. Let's start.'

He was hearty, authoritative, supremely self-confident. This was the way he had spent his days. Why change now? On the eve of publication of each of his surveys he had taken far bigger press conferences in his stride. He was used to holding inquisitors enthralled. This little affair could be taken off-the-cuff. He sat easily in his chair, despite the three photographers kneeling on the floor, hobbling around on one knee apiece, flashing twenty-to-the-minute, getting the best views they could of the noble head. I leaned across and checked that one of the cameramen was working for *New Sunday*. On that note of reassurance I sat back.

'Did the appointment come as any surprise to you, Professor Baker?' asked one of the men, moving towards the table and food and drink.

'Scarcely,' Baker said, grinning. 'If there was to be a Ministry of this kind—and it seemed inevitable—the likely runners were few enough and I would have backed my chances. Bring a plate of those ham sandwiches over here, will you, my dear chap?'

Everybody giggled. The plate came. 'Wade in, Paul,' Baker hissed.

'So you were expecting a Ministry of this kind to be set up?'

'Politics follow logic so rarely that it was almost a surprise —but not quite.'

Again a laugh.

'Did you have any forewarnings?'

'I'd been sounded, if that's what you mean.'

Others were arriving, pressing into the room, moving across to the table, but not upsetting the Professor. He took expansive bites at his sandwich. The questioners were in full bay by now.

'Will you leave the college?' asked a young woman, nibbling at her cheese and biscuits.

'Oxford has a notable tradition in granting generous leave of absence to its Fellows when deemed necessary.'

'Will you stand for a by-election or take a life peerage?' I asked.

'I shall take my chance to state my case on the hustings.'

We all laughed again. This was authentic Battler Baker stuff. Just like his telly appearances. Heavyweight Champion of Post-Graduate Oxford, as somebody had once called him.

'Has a safe seat been found for you?' asked the girl.

'I'm not interested in safe seats. I've asked the P.M. to find me an agreeably marginal one. I think my case is strong enough to see off any margin and any opponent. It's foolish to start a militant campaign with a pacific little squit of a by-election, don't you think?'

He gave the girl one of his boyish, electrifying smiles. The girl blushed. The smile switched off. He was ready for the next.

'Would you say, Professor,' drawled a willowy, handsome, droop-haired young man, who had entered the room more or less invisibly, 'that you had consciously prepared yourself for this great task?'

'I doubt whether anybody outside the prize-ring ever consciously prepares himself for a particular fight,' Baker said easily. 'Take a pew—several more chairs over here,' he added in an aside to newcomers. 'But in a world which is only at the beginning of welfare enquiry and practice, only the most benighted of economists would have neglected the studies on which I have been engaged for twenty-five years.'

'What was the start of your own social enquiries, Professor Baker?' asked the girl again.

'Early days in Manchester. Travels on foot to and from the Grammar School. The stirrings of economic conscience. The birth of social horror. Youthful idealism, in fact.'

'But you were comfortably brought up yourself, I've heard,' said a voice from the room. There were nearly thirty in the room by now.

'That's true. The contrast between my own comfortable human condition and that of others struck me very forcibly. I went to work on the subject.'

'Have you any ideas on the likely size of your Ministry?'

'Not at the moment. In a sense I see myself in the early stages of my new job as a kind of link-man between the P.M. and what I call the Socio-Economic Ministries: the Home Office, the Ministry of Health, the Ministry of Pensions, the Ministry of Housing and so on.'

'Is that going to endear you to the other Ministries and

Ministers?' the languid one asked, languidly cutting a sandwich into careful segments, despite the crush.

'In politics, as in the home, those we find most endearing are usually those we find most essential to our well-being,' Baker said blandly. 'I think I shall be endured at first and finally endeared, to coin a usage.'

We all laughed.

'Do you see your task as advisory, then, rather than what I might call operational?' asked a voice.

'I wouldn't care to see it in those rather cosy terms,' Baker answered. 'I have been told that the new Minister is usually considered to be something of an operational type.'

We all chuckled. I munched my own sandwich and drank more of the college cider: as good as it had ever been.

'Have you any burning priorities, Professor Baker?' asked another female voice.

'In my experience most so-called burning priorities are usually fit for burning,' Baker said. 'My priorities have been burning away for centuries. As I've said often enough before, we have, as a nation, certain continuing, inherited priorities, which, as I see them, are roughly in this order: the poor, the underprivileged, the imbecilic, the incapable, the old, the lonely, the ignorant, the vicious, the young.'

'Why "the young" last?'

'Because they are the young, of course. Because they have strength. Because they can fight. Because they are ambitious. Because their day will come.'

'Why the vicious?'

'Because as a nation we sponsored and fostered their vices.'

'And that goes for the imbecilic, too?'

'That and a touch of there-but-for-the-grace-of-God and so forth. I had a puritan upbringing which is apt to leave traces of religious superstition as well as social conscience in certain areas of my thinking.'

'Where does your welfare system—laudable as it is—put parental responsibility?'

'Where it belongs—in the home.'

'With no external responsibilities at all?'

'Of course, but to a lesser degree than is conventional these days. If we start in the home and concentrate on the home —and that means well-built, comfortable homes—we shall be on the way. Parents must be brought back to first principles again. I'm rather Victorian about these matters. But it's no good demanding the old-fashioned domestic virtues to be reborn in old-fashioned houses.'

'Do you propose to inaugurate any new national surveys or enquiries?'

'That will be a major part of the work of my Ministry. We have far too few real facts upon which we can base what I call rational, national, socio-economic policies. We have scarcely any knowledge, for example, of the number of empty yet furnished rooms which are currently unused in London and other great cities. Yet such rooms could bring some kind of shelter—even happiness—to young marrieds and others seeking a roof. They could help to bring down the appalling rent-levels that are charged for the most rudimentary accommodation.'

'Isn't that a job for the Minister of Housing?'

'I don't imagine he would bother about whose job it was if someone gave him the figures. Relevant, reliable figures make for action. I am, at heart, a data man. One can't act without figures and facts based upon figures. The Webbs showed that conclusively. It is one of the first great laws of politics. And certainly the most neglected. As I was saying, we all know these rooms exist—by the thousand— but we have no reliable statistics to act upon. Again, we do not know how many old people are starving to death at this moment in this over-fed Britain. We need to know these facts and similar facts in scores of other sectors of our national life, from gluttony to loneliness, from clothing to yearning.'

'Yearning!' three voices cried at once.

'Yes, yearning. What mankind hopes for is not always what mankind is persuaded to work for. It would be interesting to know the differences, to try to bring the two together.'

'Can you measure loneliness in statistics?'

'I shall try,' he said simply. 'As you imply, it is a difficult task. We need new instruments of measurement. Perhaps we need a Department of Metaphysical Measurement. I think we do. It might even be termed my own burning priority.'

Again we smiled.

'Where will your Ministry be housed?'

'Somewhere near Whitehall, I imagine. The Ministry of Works is digging around for accommodation now. Meanwhile, I've been offered temporary offices in the Department of Education and Science in Curzon Street.'

'Have you the nucleus of a Ministry?'

'Even nuclei. Myself. A secretary. Two statisticians co-opted from the Board of Trade. Four undergraduates who have opted to help. Not bad, I think, for three hours' empire-building last evening.'

So the session continued in an agreeable give-and-take. The Prof was in his most urbane, winning mood, a formidable master of the game. Twenty minutes later he began making noises of imminent conclusion.

Then we were finished.

We all stood up and began to edge towards the door, offering good wishes and thanks. Baker took me by the arm and asked me to wait. When we were alone he said: 'In a rush, Paul?'

'A fair rush. I have to write you up and dictate the piece to our telephone reporters in London. All in forty minutes.'

'I thought as much. Why not work here? It's much more comfortable. Where were you proposing to work?'

'In my car. Or raid one of the college rooms.'

'I have to rush off—temporarily—to a meeting over at the New Bodleian. Why not stay for tea?'

'No go, alas. I must get back to correct the proof. It'll probably be too late, but I shall try. Terrible things can get into one's text.'

'Printers were put here by Lucifer to drive writers mad. Another time, perhaps. I've been interested in your new feature in New Sunday. How strange that you and Spurway should both be involved in this new venture.'

'He sent his salutations,' I lied in good cause.

'Well-laced with a dash of potassium cyanide, no doubt,' Baker said drily. 'Is he well?'

'Depressingly so. He never lets up.'

'Is the paper doing well?'

'Well enough for the owner, apparently. Not well enough for Spurway.'

'The portrait is recognizable. Pray return my salutations to Mike. He was destined for a life amongst the headlines. Why did you call the feature Faces and Places, by the way?'

'Because it seems to cover most things.'

'Even ideas?'

'They squeeze their way in sometimes.'

'Love? Hate? Gratitude? Greed? Tenderness? Lust?' he queried, smiling benignly like an old Pharisee in disputation on the steps of the temple.

'Wouldn't you say most of those characteristics show in our faces sooner or later?'

'Touché.'

I laughed.

'But if they do—and some people are notable dissemblers —how do you arrange to have photographers around at the time?' he asked genially, smiling at his own witticism.

'We had a man here this afternoon, photographing triumph,' I said.

'Ah, well,' he said, resigned. 'Send me one of the less horrific prints, will you?'

I promised to do so.

'It must be an appalling, enthralling, neurotic occupation. You scarcely had what might be called the ideal training for it.'

'I had the perfect training. Listening to pensioners in South Shields and paralytics in Salisbury was the perfect preparation for listening to film-stars, politicians, admirals and the rest.'

'The rest includes professors, I dare say.'

I nodded. 'May I congratulate you on your appointment, by the way?' I added. 'In the crowd it was difficult.'

'I doubt whether it's a fit subject for congratulations.

Commiseration. Condolences. Bewilderment. Anything but congratulations.'

'But you wanted the job?'

He nodded. 'That's true; it's certainly a treadmill of my own making.'

'You could have stepped off the treadmill at any time.'

'No man can,' he said soberly. 'Alcoholic, smoker, drug taker, social climber, womanizer . . . few men escape their own treadmills.'

'Most of us enjoy 'em.'

Again he nodded. 'The Anglo-Saxons are notorious masochists,' he said slowly, almost reflectively. 'Congenital treadmill-seekers. Anyway, I'm glad you came, Paul, and gladder still to be of some slight service to you. Hand the door keys over to Miss Fowler as you leave. And I'm doubly glad to see you so agreeably—and, I imagine, profitably—employed. I once had the remotest suspicion that I had misused your talents.'

'Perish the thought!'

'I'm glad to have your comfort. Suspicion, memory or conscience, it persisted. Well, all's well and all that. Make yourself at home. The typewriter's there.'

'I'll come down and see my driver.'

'No, stay here. I'll ask Miss Fowler to tell him. No, I'll tell him as I go out. What shall I say?'

'Tell him to give me another forty minutes.'

'How do I recognize him?'

'A strong-chinned, black-haired, thick-set numero in a Humber Snipe.'

'Most expressive. Impossible to miss. The shorthand of Faces and Places.' He smiled, waved, and went.

40

I sat down at Baker's desk, unlocked his ancient Corona and set to upon my piece. I had been setting up the opening phrases whilst listening to Baker's answers and evasions. The words almost began to type themselves.

Half an hour later, I took up the telephone, asked for the

Fleet Street number, reversed the charges, and began to dictate to one of the telephone reporters at West House:

'Mortimer to Morgan. Heading quote caps THE WELFARE MAN unquote. Begins . . .'

And here is the piece. I copied it today from my copies of *New Sunday*. Not so old as stories go, but already the colours are fading, the paper yellowing:

Those who prefer admirals and judges, actors and actressses to look the part will not be disappointed in Professor Andrew Frensham Baker, their new Minister of Social Welfare. The Professor or the Prof as he is usually known in Oxford, looks the way such a New-Age Minister ought to look: a strong and handsome father-figure for the nation.

The head is leonine and craggy. The iron-grey hair, still boyishly thick, falls over a wide and noble but frequently furrowed brow. The grey-blue eyes are often steely but can be gay with laughter. The vast scimitar of a nose curves from bushy eyebrows to a well-shaped, mobile mouth. The pear-shaped chin is pointed, cleft and strong. In short, a consul's features set upon broad shoulders, a barrel chest and strong, well-braced legs.

He was born the son of a cotton import-export man in a sizeable way of business. After three years as a day-boy at Manchester Grammar School he spent three years as a boarder at Rossall, the Lancashire public school. From Rossall he gained an open History Scholarship at Oxford University. His career there was academically brilliant. He got Firsts in Economics and History, followed by a Fellowship of his College and of All Souls. He also found time to play for his College at rugger and lawn tennis, a game he still plays with what opponents term a technique of massive retaliation.

The new Minister's academic life was interrupted by the war. He started his martial career with a hectic stint at the Board of Trade, then, higher up, at the Ministry of Economic Warfare. For his backroom contribution to the war effort he was awarded the O.B.E.

After the war he returned to Oxford, first as Senior Tutor and then Master of his College. In 1948 he published his first book; the sober but sensational survey, *The Social Implications of Senility*. Like many other books of revolutionary impact, the Professor's enquiry has been widely praised and denounced, probably less widely read. Only specialists studied the book. For them the Professor's methods and findings were a revelation. He had borrowed the techniques of the polsters and marketing-men for his thesis and appraisals.

An Enquiry into Social Conscience, a wide-ranging denunciation of what Baker termed 'laissez-faire charity which begins and stays at home', was published three years later. In 1954 he published *Class and Mass,* which, according to some self-styled authorities on the Prof's life and works, is his favourite. Certainly, the book remains the least subjective study of privilege and money ever likely to be written before the promised classless society takes over Britain completely.

These studies could not have been written by one man alone, however energetic and brilliant, and it is a measure of the Prof's powers of persuasion that, through the years, he was able to coerce, charm or cajole battalions of undergraduate-volunteers into helping him dig out the facts on which his sociological enquiries so firmly rest. The Prof has a relentless passion for facts. 'Not those in the reference books or the Board of Trade returns,' he is fond of saying, 'but those in the faces as well as the lathes in the factories, those in the stomachs as well as the cash registers of shop-assistants, those in the hopes of mankind as well as our cemeteries.'

This curious combination of economic sleuth and outspoken humanitarianism has given to the Prof's books a vividness not to be found in comparable sociological enquiries. He contends, unequivocally, that there are no comparable studies. He says his own books are flesh-and-blood computers.

Despite his multifarious activities, the Prof has managed to retain an enviable private life. Thirty years ago he married Anthea Lowry, daughter of one of his Oxford professors. She was called to the Bar but never practised. They live in an old stone water-mill in a remote part of Herefordshire. There they grow cider apples, successfully and commercially. They have two sons, Joshua (20) and Timothy (25), both now at Cambridge, the former studying architecture, the other a post-graduate research physicist. They also have a 20-year-old daughter, Aminta, now studying medicine at University College Hospital.

One thing is quite certain: if this unusual man cannot change Britain's current views on certain major social problems within measurable time, he will quit politics, for Britain's politicians will be unable to change him. He has integrity, convictions, knowledge and considerable private means. They add up to an unusual combination to find in a twentieth-century radical professor. Such a combination of humanitarian principle and material independence was more frequently to be seen in Victorian parliaments. Certainly the House will be a livelier place with the arrival of the new Minister.

I checked and settled a couple of queries raised by the telephone-reporter, recapped the titles of the books, gave thanks, said farewell, and then sat back for what I considered to be a well-earned cigarette.

Relaxing, I rang through to West House again and asked for Morgan.

'How'd it go, boy? How d'you find Big Brother Bountiful' he asked.

'Bigger and bouncier than ever.'

'Done a good piece?'

'Just phoned it through. It may be a trifle long.'

'I like cutting columnists down to size. Come on back now and I'll stand you a noggin after the first edition.'

'Will you keep an eye on my copy?'

'Will do. Are you coming back? You don't have to, of course.'

'I'm on my way.'

'It's not a bad idea. Freddie would like a chat. And I know the editor would like to see you.'

'Anything in particular?'

'No. I just think they'd like to hear your views of Frensham Baker. He's a big man now and you know more than most about him.'

'I doubt that, but I'm willing to talk. I should be back soon after five.'

'Good.' He rang off.

I stood up and I took a last look round the room: the massed book-shelves, the gay chintz curtains, the bombé commode, the enormous leather Chesterfield and the trio of loose-covered armchairs. And books everywhere. Books on chairs, books on the chimney-piece, books on the window-seat, books on the writing-table. Plus a stack of those red-covered box files which, once upon a distant time, I had come to know so well: files full of statistics, graphs, diagrams, tables, trends and god knows what all, collected and collated to prove a point of poverty or privilege, senility or security.

I had always liked the room and it still held the air of purposeful research that it had held fifteen years before. This was no academic ivory tower but a workshop. Yet, like any other room dominated by books this one was also touched by a sense of serenity. In such a room a man could work. The way I could work in my own small book-filled room in Swan Court—and only there.

I locked the door and went downstairs to hand in the keys. Miss Fowler didn't look up as I put the keys on the pale oaken counter so I made no cooing noises from the years before. Instead I went out into the College courtyard.

The morning's rain had given way to high racing clouds and a blustering south-westerly. Smoke was rising above the grey roofs. I was caught once more into the Oxford nostalgia that is apt to grip a man for all his days, and stood in the Inner Quad. taking in the orderly façades of the College buildings. Then, decisively, I put weakness aside and went on. Ten minutes more and I would have succumbed and found myself trying to get a room for the night in College or, failing that, wandering round to the Mitre to try to get a room there. I might even have been tempted to take an agnostical pleasure in the modest pomp and circumstance of Chapel in the morning.

Instead, I made a slow way across the gravelled quad.

41

Caught in these reflections, I almost bowled over a man ahead of me. He turned to accept my apology. Then he looked again and I gave him back his stare of interest. We tentatively uttered mutual recognition.

'Hello, Paul.'

'David!'

I might not have been so successful in my swift recognition of the man in the rather woebegone grey tweed overcoat if the big, bald, bespectacled face hadn't been making a recent reputation for itself on various TV panel quizzes. Here was an image I could place: the professorial up-and-coming popularizer of the classics, the explainer of Euripides, the unraveller of Suetonius, the guide to Herodotus and so on. I had seen the face on the screen at odd times, had hoped against hope that the years weren't as ageing for me as they seemed to be for Gregory.

'Why are you here?' he asked.

'Interviewing the Prof. And you?'

'I live here.'

David Gregory had been up with me. I had known him fairly well, having had rooms on the same staircase. I had also crossed swords with him once or twice at the Union and in Hall, and we had occasionally discussed the hazy prospects of our future jobs. He had also worked for Baker, but never the far-flung field-work of myself and the other suckers. He had never been a friend but something more than an acquaintance. A Christian-name legacy remained. He had been a Scholar, a winner of prizes, a likely academic runner who had missed All Souls by inches. And that had rankled with him as it always rankles. And here he was: my own age, my own height, but a lot more bulk and a lot more cranium. The life of scholarship seemed to be taking its toll.

'Whereabouts?' I asked.

'Rooms above the Master's, and a house out at Headington.'

'What are you doing?'

'Senior Tutor. Classics if you remember.' His voice had a curiously defiant, even bitter note. I dodged it.

'I remember that, but I hadn't heard. Somebody told me you'd gone to Australia.'

'I did. To Sydney. I came back. The Antipodes and the Aeneid didn't agree. At least, not for me. The Prof fixed my return as he fixes most things.'

'Glad to be back?'

'I've been back a couple of years now. What about a cuppa?'

'No go, alas. I have to get back to London.'

'You're doing that gossip thing in the New Sunday, I notice. Faces and Places, is it?'

112

I nodded: it was description of a kind.

We had noticeably dragged our steps, walking slowly past the lodge, through the arch and out into the Broad. I wondered how I could painlessly break away. 'Pity you can't stay,' he said. 'Prof changed much, d'you think?'

'A few more kilos on the belly. An incipient dewlap. No more.'

A false move there, I thought, even as I said the words too aptly applicable to Gregory. He seemed to take the reference calmly and to apply it, of his own accord, also to himself. 'Occupational hazard. Too much chair and too much opining. And too much College port and afternoon tea, dammit.'

'But the old battering-ram still batters,' I said, recalling the give-and-take of the recent press conference.

'The old ram still rams, in fact,' Gregory said. Tartly, I thought.

'I'd forgotten that side of things,' I said, and then added, recalling a ribald undergraduate's quip from years before: 'The bull in the vagina shop still? I should've thought he'd have rammed himself out of action by now.'

'Why should he? He keeps in training.'

'Who's the lucky girl? Or should I say girls?'

'They're around.'

'Well, it's all part of the job, I daresay. Keeping up with the Welfare State and all that.'

'I daresay.'

Despite his bulk, Gregory seemed wholly lacking in any of that legendary plump man's jollity. Indeed, he seemed weighed down with angst of some kind or another. I found his manner fairly depressing and was glad to see Myers nearby, standing by the car.

'Can I give you a lift?' I asked.

Gregory declined. 'I've a Vespa parked down the road. Pity you can't come up to Headington.'

He looked so forlorn, standing there, in the fading, boisterous October afternoon that I was touched by unaccustomed compassion. Perhaps I was also touched by the thought that, by taking tea at Headington, I might be able to add to my out-of-date knowledge of Baker; a chance not to be missed.

'If we can fix your machine in the boot of my auto, I'd be delighted to come,' I said on the instant.

My change of plan seemed to hearten him.

'Forget the Vespa. It's as safe as houses. I park it in one of the College sheds. My wife can bring me down in the car to chapel tomorrow. I'll pick it up then.'

I opened the rear door of the car. 'O.K., Myers, let's go. Doctor Gregory will tell you where.'

I ushered Gregory into the car and climbed in after him.

The car began to move slowly along the Broad out into the High, crowded with undergraduates, shoppers and visitors from the surrounding countryside.

'I take it you like journalism or you wouldn't be doing it,' Gregory said, opening up.

'It's not a necessary corollary, but I do. And you, presumably, like the collegiate life.'

'Quite,' he said, but not very convincingly.

'I should have said it was the perfect life for a scholar,' I said dutifully.

'For a scholar with sufficient private means to cancel out ambition. I've one without the other.'

'The ambitions being . . . ?'

'Nothing spectacular. Master of a decent college. Or even headmaster of a decent school. Even something right outside this academic grind wouldn't come amiss.'

'Such as?'

'I don't rightly know. Dream life and all that, I dare say. Hangover from the hopes of early manhood. One is told at nineteen or twenty that one has a first-class brain. One is never told that life's material rewards rarely go to the so-called first-class brain.'

'But it has its compensations, surely?'

'The first-class brain gets addled,' Gregory said shortly. 'But one clings to the label for what it's worth. For reassurance, no doubt. One's always hoping someone or something will come along and test it out, stretch it.

114

Certainly nothing that goes on in this academic backwater will ever do that.'

'But you do the occasional television stint. I've seen you. You're very good. And you seem to be enjoying the experience.'

He giggled self-consciously. His answer was touched with a curiously self-deprecating pride. 'I quite enjoy being the poor man's guide to the classics from time to time. The Delphic Oracle of Television, as one of your rivals termed the performance the other day.'

I went on with a subject that plainly soothed him. 'Are you doing more of it?'

'When they ask. I enjoy the attendant dinners and the shekels, of course. And the brief escape to the London smoothie life.'

'I've seen you three or four times. Very authoritative stuff,' I said as convincingly as I could, remembering his heavy humour and ponderous punditry.

'Kind of you to say so.'

'Would a political plunge similar to Baker's have any appeal for you?'

'Not unduly. I envy him his vast new opportunities, of course. I'd be lying if I said otherwise. Straight on after the roundabout, driver. But it's not my line. I'm not cut out for the hustings. Curiously enough, Baker once suggested it.'

'Recently?'

'Fairly. But I'm not especially good with hecklers. I don't like people answering back. I'm the congenital lecturer. That's why I enjoy these telly jaunts.'

'But you were pretty good at the Union.'

'Not especially, although I was President. No, like many other men of my age I'm at a cross-roads of four culs-de-sac.'

Then, once again, that irritating cut-off, self-conscious giggle.

'A good expression. Forgive me if you see it used without acknowledgement.'

'I should be glad not to have it publicly attributed to my personal dilemma,' he said, noticeably more cheerful. 'But I'm afraid I can't guarantee its originality, although I do believe it's this afternoon's minting. And what about you?'

'Like most journalists I enjoy the grind, despite the occasional whine.'

'You're lucky,' he said briefly. 'Straight on, driver. I'll tell you when to turn.'

'Have you any family?' I asked, breaking the silence.

'Two girls. Two and four. And you?'

'One girl. Now ten. When did you marry?'

'In Australia. One of my pupils in the University of Sydney. '

'Romantic stuff.'

'Of a kind. And you?'

'Strictly unromantic. Separated. Once bitten twice shy and all that.'

He seemed to want to go on talking. Curiously enough, about marriage. 'Why did you separate, if it's not a rude question and/or answer?'

Myers, I suspected, had already, in his brief term probably overheard half the secrets of the private lives of the paper's staff. Or did editorial drivers automatically become occupationally deaf on their appointment? 'Difficult to say. Incompatibility of temperament still remains one of the world's best, yet least convincing, alibis. I'll settle for that. A lot of intangibles adding up to a tangible break.'

'You don't mind my asking?' he said, rather like a plump schoolboy asking for another cake.

'Not at all. It's a question I ask myself daily. No hope of an answer, of course.'

'Who has custody?'

'My wife, but I have access and see a good deal of her. And my wife for that matter. Once or twice a week, in fact.'

'Perhaps you've stumbled on the solution—given the necessary means, of course.'

'It's a solution of despair. Not to be recommended for universal practice.'

He went on with what I began to think was somewhat insensitive persistence: 'No divorce in prospect, then?'

'No point as things are. Re-marriage doesn't seem all that alluring at the moment.'

116

'Next turning to the right, driver, third house on the left. Just by the lamp-post.'

Myers stopped the car. We got out.

'I'll be about half an hour,' I told Myers.

'Quite all right, sir. Any time suits me.'

Little wonder that everybody on *New Sunday* wanted Myers for all their trips.

I followed Gregory up a flight of wide stone steps under a Victorian portico with fairly brutish Ionic columns. He let us into a lofty, uninviting hall. A smell of tired cooking hung on the air.

'I'll let my wife know we're here,' he said, opening a door into a room on the right. 'Make yourself comfortable.'

I went into the high square room with its large bay window. A couple of sofas, loose-covered in washed-out chintz, flanked either side of the gloomy fireplace. A heavy, circular, Victorian table in the middle of the room was piled with books and notebooks. A pair of oak bookshelves, set against the wall, near the sofas, was also packed. A tall, glazed, breakfront bureau-bookcase dominated the wall opposite the fireplace. Two nondescript red-and-green floral-design rugs covered part of the floor. The exposed floor-boards were stained dark brown. Dark green curtains, also dolefully floral in design, hung heavily at the windows.

The room had that ghastly cheerlessness which so frequently afflicts the homes of the academic middle-classes, with their vast pretensions to culture and none to domestic gaiety. Nothing in the room was colourful or personal. Nothing could possibly arouse any visitor's interest, let alone covetousness.

Curious in an Australian housewife, I thought. Weren't they all supposed to be passionately concerned about their homes, sunny colours and all that?

I crossed to the table and picked up one of the books, a recent copy of a book on Etruscan art, but it wasn't my line. I put it down and took up a copy of Malraux's *The Arts of Man*. That was better.

The door opened and a tall dark young woman came in ahead of Gregory, who was gamely carrying an overloaded

117

tray. She was as glowing and positive as he was grey and negative, especially in his baggy outmoded grey flannel suit. It's not possible! I thought instantly, for she walked like an amazon, prideful in youth and vitality.

How the hell did Gregory land a piece like this? I thought.

Black hair enclosed her face like a dark and gleaming helmet, dark eyes smiled gaily from the lively, tawny-skinned face. Her lips were full and red. Her nose was straight and small. Her chin was firm, well-shaped and dimpled. And she smiled like a girl who had just won a Championship of the World at something extremely open-air. She was, in fact, I swiftly decided, quite something. Gregory was a damned lucky chap.

He puffed out the introductions from behind the tray, then lowered the load on to the table. An enormous yellow tea-pot, yellow-and-white hooped teacups, jostled against sandwiches and fruit-cake.

'I was just about to have tea with the kids in the kitchen,' Nan Gregory said. 'I've left them with the au pair girl.' She looked out of the window. 'Your driver must come in and have tea with Heidi. I never miss a chance of improving her English. David, go out and inveigle him in.'

'It'll be good for her Cockney English, at least,' I said as Gregory went.

How did I like my tea? she asked. Strong? Weak? Milk? Lemon?

I liked the faint twang of her Antipodean vowels. As it came, I answered limply, still bewildered. I decided I was glad I'd come, particularly when I heard the captive Myers tramping through the hall *en route* to the kitchen.

Nan Gregory handed me cup and saucer and plate in that terrible ritual of the English tea-party. Then came the fruit cake. I took a huge slice, already cut. Nan Gregory then took her own cup and saucer to one sagging sofa. I took my load to the other. Her dress was fractionally too short for her comfort but fine for me. Her well-shaped amazonian legs well-matched her strapping body.

Gregory came back and lit the gas-fire in the fireplace,

bringing a sad warmth to the hearth but little to the room. He poured tea for himself.

He sat down next to his wife and began to talk about our distant past, but I was more interested in his recent past and firmly got the conversation back to the University of Sydney and Nan Gregory.

Like most housewives given a brief break for freedom, she was more than willing to talk, and took her chance. I was a more-than-willing listener. She talked about her life in Sydney, which she'd plainly loved; the climate, the sea, the sport, the lot.

'And how d'you like Oxford?' I asked at one point as she took breath.

'Love it!' she said decisively. 'Lots of entertaining characters—and some not-so-nice ones, too, of course. Lots of holidays, too. I'm all right so long as I can get back to Australia every year. Daddy pays, so why not?'

'Why not indeed? And your daughters?'

'I left them here last year for a month. I may take 'em next year.'

'Poor forsaken David.'

'He makes out. There's always enough hostesses around Oxford to take care of grass widowers.'

'Dried-up dregs of hostesses,' Gregory said lugubriously.

I was amused by her vivacity and lack of reverence for Oxford and its institutional pomposities and conventions which might easily have intimidated any young wife from Sydney. I also enjoyed listening to her unselfconscious Australian voice. Half an hour had hurtled away before I recalled my half-promise to Morgan to return by five. That was a forlorn hope. I waited for my chance, stood up and said I must be moving off. Mrs. Gregory went off to summon Myers.

'Your wife seems to enjoy Oxford life,' I said.

'No reason why she shouldn't. There's everything here she wants,' Gregory said, almost peevishly.

'There's everything for any other pretty young woman, but a lot seem to get bored rather easily. Or say they are.'

'My wife's always looked on the bright side of things,' he

said flatly. Then, leaning forward from the sofa, blushing like an awkward schoolboy, he said in a rush of words: 'She's so bloody bright you'd never believe I'm divorcing her, would you?'

I was winded both by his words and his ungainly ferocity. Like many another big, bald, fat man he was grotesquely pathetic in fury. I said limply: 'She's putting on a good act—if she knows. Does she '

'I told her three days ago.'

'It's rather an extreme course. Tough on the children. Isn't it something that can be patched up?'

'Not this time,' he said, still breathing heavily.

'Think about it carefully,' I said like a Dutch uncle, adding the man-sized lie that I'd often regretted my own hastiness.

'D'you think I haven't thought about it?' he barked. 'But why should I carry all Baker's bloody cans. Why should he have my wife as one of his little social welfare sidelines. Had the Fleet Street grapevine told you that?'

'Frankly, no,' I said quickly, hearing steps in the hall.

Gregory stood up as Nan Gregory came into the room. The silence shouted, and she looked quickly from her husband to myself. 'Your driver's gone out, Mr Mortimer. He seems to have left Heidi in a very lively mood. Thanks for the loan.'

We stood there awkwardly for a split-second. Then I moved to the door, making my farewells. Gregory shuffled after me, followed me down the steps and across to the car.

'I'm rather at a loss for appropriate words,' I said.

'Well, it's not quite what one expects to blurt out after one's invited a onetime acquaintance in for tea,' he said. 'I suppose that rather boorish set of questions I fired at you in the car touched it all off.' He looked rather shamefaced. 'Probably had to tell someone. The dam bursts and all that. And I suddenly remembered how you, too, had worked your hide off for that bastard ten years ago. Fellow-feeling at work, I suppose.'

'It got me a Second. You still managed a First.'

'My pay-off from the bloody man was delayed, that's all.

In any case, working for him killed my All Souls chances stone dead,' he added bitterly. 'And now this.'

'How long ago? This.' I moved my hand vaguely.

'A year, at least, but I've only known about it these last two months.'

'Does it still go on?'

'It still goes on.'

'Does Baker know you're going ahead yet?'

As if realizing he'd said too much, he didn't answer my question, but said abruptly: 'Forget it. You'll read all the details in due course, I suppose. See you again sometime.' He turned and went up the stairs, not looking back.

I got into the car and said, 'Let's go.' Myers said, 'Aye, aye, sir,' as if I were boarding an M.T.B.

Sitting there, relaxing, I decided that if I were as pre-occupied with ideas of journalistic integrity as I sometimes told myself I ought to be, the piece I'd finished an hour before now needed some serious amendments, but I doubted whether the lawyer would let them stay, even if I did have the nerve to write them in on the galley.

42

I was an hour later than I'd promised Morgan, and the first edition was well on its way by the time I got back.

I went down to the composing-room where I knew I would find him, smoking a nine-inch cigar, despite the NO SMOKING announcements. He was brooding over the plates of the pages, watching the comps at their make-up, scanning proofs as they were pulled.

He looked up from a proof of a sports page with a fine colour picture of Greaves scoring a goal with an overhead scissors kick.

'I liked the piece,' he said. 'Makes a good kicker for page one. I've turned to page three. Difficult to cut, damn you. Fortunately, we got some good pictures, too. How d'you find your old teacher or whatever they call 'em in these dreaming-spire outfits?'

'Master, no less.'

'So you implied in your piece,' he said and winked. 'We're slipping page one and remaking pages three and five for the second. Don't flinch. We're not dropping your piece or even cutting it. Freddie says he'd like to see you if you have a minute to spare. And the editor's been asking after your health, too. I'll stand you a drink after the second edition if you're still intact after those two brain-washers and your ancient Master have been at work.'

I said I'd come and find him later. Meanwhile, had he got proofs of *Faces & Places*? He took a couple off the spike labelled with his own name and gave them to me. 'Not even a comma changed. See you later.'

I went out from the composing-room, out to the lifts.

Up on the tenth floor everything was quiet. I put my head round the door of Lee-Ellerton's room. The soles of his enormous but exquisite Chelsea boots faced me. He was lying along the day-bed he had personally imported, reading a proof of the leader page. His six-and-a-half feet took the whole length of the sofa, the ankles of his seemingly endless, boneless legs resting on one of the arms. He was wearing heavy horn-rimmed specs, but took them off to rest them on his Adam's apple as I looked round the door.

'Come in, Paul. I liked your piece. How was the old homestead of lost causes? Still losing, I daresay?'

'Bearing up, especially now it's got a real live Minister in its midst.'

'And how was that old mountebank?'

'Rather cock-a-hoop, I thought.'

'Don't like him. Never did. Never will. Probably acute jealousy on my part somewhere along the line. He's certainly pulled off several things I'd given an eye tooth to call my own.'

'You know you don't think that.'

'Indeed I do. Those ghastly unreadable books of his are seminal contributions to the English social conscience—I trust my metaphor's not mixed—and it's no good denying it. Take a chair and tell a man from another place the latest Oxford tittle-tattle.'

I walked across to the armchair and flopped. I looked up to see Spurway at the door.

'Nice work, Paul,' he said. 'Just what we needed on a dull day for home news.' He turned to Lee-Ellerton and added in explanation, 'We both grew up under the old bastard.'

'Which accounts for the note of pupillary respect, no doubt,' Lee-Ellerton said.

'Baker's doing fine,' I said.

'I've had Baker already,' Lee-Ellerton said. 'I know in my aged bones that he's going to hog the news from now on. He loves it. Scholar and exhibitionist. A less rare and more horrible combination than one might think,' he added genially.

'He's also a fornicator of some standing, if that's the right word,' Spurway said. 'Did you know that? His sexual proclivities are less well-known than his social enquiries.'

'Curiously and infuriatingly enough, I've never heard that side of things,' Lee-Ellerton said. 'Does it make him more or less interesting?'

'Depends on the women, I daresay,' I said.

Spurway said: 'Women are much the same in Oxford University as in Oxford Street. How he finds time is the most interesting aspect of the circuitous story.'

'I met Gregory. Remember him?' I said, adding, 'Excuse the gossip,' in an aside to Lee-Ellerton.

'Pray proceed with your juvenalia,' Lee-Ellerton said grandly.

'Vaguely,' Spurway said vaguely.

'A rather portly Classics scholar. President of the Union.'

'Of course. I remember him. I've also seen him on telly. Big bald Doctor Gregory, the well-known Classical scholar and all that.'

'He's divorcing his wife and citing Baker.'

Spurway sat down in an armchair. Lee-Ellerton sat up on his sofa.

'Why isn't it in your piece?' Spurway asked instantly.

'I didn't get it in writing.'

'Why not?'

'Because it's not the kind of oddment a man scribbles out on the back of an envelope and hands across the table, that's why. Because it's not even with the solicitors yet. Because Gregory only told his wife three days ago.'

'Who told you?'

'Gregory.'

'Can't you quote him?'

I shook my head.

'But this is the story!' Spurway said, standing up, crossing to the window. 'What a way to start a new Ministry. Why the hell didn't you bring Gregory's story back with you, signed, sealed, delivered—and handsomely paid for, if necessary?'

'Because I couldn't. Because I'm not even sure Baker knows yet. Because it was told to me in confidence—as I'm telling it to you.'

'Why tell me, then?' Spurway barked. 'That Baker doesn't know yet is beside the point. Why wreck my evening, my weekend, my career?'

'Come off it, Mike,' Lee-Ellerton said. 'I thought we were just tittle-tattling. And it's scarcely a story we'd run in the paper.'

'Why bloody not?' said Spurway. 'We're still a *news*paper, aren't we? Even if we are so bloody high-brow, so full of Third Programme intellectual parlour games.'

'It's your paper. That's the way you've made it. We deal in written confirmation, not second-hand word of mouth. Isn't that the drill?' Lee-Ellerton said.

'Not so second-hand,' I said, stung.

'You'd swear it was true comment, Paul?' Spurway pleaded.

'It seemed like it.'

'Nobody engaging in a beautiful, majestic hoax out of malice to Baker?' Lee-Ellerton put in. 'I admit it doesn't sound like it.'

'Could have been, but not the way it was said. And the part fits Baker. It's a game he's always played, as Mike said just now.'

'But was never caught at,' Spurway said viciously. 'Poor old Gregory.'

'He's two years older than you!' I pointed out.

'That makes him very old this afternoon.'

'He certainly looks pretty antique,' Lee-Ellerton said. 'I've also seen him on the little box. A very unlovely personage, I would have said. Large bald nut with tufts of hair sticking out round his collar like a turkey fringe. Cod-fish eyes. Large double—or is it treble?—chin. That the chap?'

'A real identikit job,' Spurway growled.

'Uncharitable but recognizable,' I admitted.

'Never forget a face,' Lee-Ellerton said complacently. 'What's his wife like? All bow legs and twin-set, I suppose.'

'Not a bit of it. Quite a dish, in fact. Australian. Big handsome, tennis-champ type.'

'How old?' Spurway said, too interested for my peace of mind.

'Late twenties, I'd say. Looks younger.'

'Any brats?'

'Two girls. Very young, I gather.'

'One has to hand it to a brand new Minister,' Lee-Ellerton said. 'It's quite a way to start. How old is he? Sixty-one. It's not bad stoating, is it? How d'you rate your chances with the subs' wives at sixty-one, Mike?'

'I've made other arrangements,' Spurway said with no hint of levity.

He wasn't to be side-tracked by banter. 'I'm disappointed, Paul. Supposing this story breaks mid-week and we know we had it here all the time. Exclusive. Scoop. How will you feel about things then?'

'I'd say it was the luck of the draw, an accident of time.'

'You're not on that terrible Men is History lark now, Mike,' Lee-Ellerton chided gently. 'You're on a quality newspaper. Remember?'

'Can I forget it, surrounded as I am by a pair of top-quality newspaper nits, sitting on their ageing backsides letting the best story of the year slip past 'em. How can I forget?'

'Well, it's jest gotta be that way, pal,' Lee-Ellerton said in quite a good Western saloon bar drawl. 'The lawyers wouldn't let it go without confirmation. Ask 'em. It's dynamite. In any case, is it so extraordinary, a Minister being cited by a colleague? I seem to remember that the great and good Lord Melbourne was cited as co-respondent by a colleague.'

'I read Geography, not History, but I'll still bet it wasn't the day he got the big job,' Spurway said.

Lee-Ellerton grinned and then began to chuckle. But still Spurway showed no wish to join in the mirth. He went on: 'And how d'you think the P.M. will welcome a Minister of Social Welfare who's known as the Minister of Sexual Welfare or Warfare from the moment he's got the job?'

'But you know damn well the Prof's the kind of man who could live it down,' I said.

'Maybe,' Spurway admitted unwillingly. 'God knows he's by way of being a primeval force, but don't forget this so-called modern world is often a damn sight more censorious than the old and hypocritical Victorian one.'

'One of the results of the great levelling-down process,' Lee-Ellerton added. 'Moral laxity is one of civilization's more subtle achievements.'

'Maybe, but it's the way it happens to be. So it's a good story and you're letting it go. Why don't you get him on the telephone, Paul? We could tape his reply.'

'Perhaps the editor has a point there, Paul,' Lee-Ellerton said gently. 'Even if no judge would admit it.'

'No, he hasn't got a point,' I said. 'Supposing Gregory told me in a fit of black depression—as he did. Supposing it's not yet in the hands of the solicitors—as it probably isn't. Supposing he just had to tell someone—as he admitted. Supposing he's already had a bedtime reconciliation with this Australian Brunhilde wife of his. . . . Where do we stand then?'

'In a pretty shaky spot,' Lee-Ellerton readily admitted. He turned to Spurway. 'Would Baker have accepted this appointment if he'd known this was hanging over his head? It doesn't seem very likely.' He turned to me. 'Did Baker seem a worried man today, Paul?'

'Far from it.'

I turned to Spurway again. 'I'll ring Gregory if you like.' I didn't make the offer very forcefully.

'Why not?' Spurway said, very forcefully.

I crossed to the telephone and dialled the West House operator. 'Paul Mortimer here. Will you find the number of one Gregory, David Gregory, possibly Doctor D. Gregory, number eleven Reading Road, Headington, Oxford? Make it a personal call to him. I'm in Mr Lee-Ellerton's office?'

'Wouldn't you rather take it?' I asked Lee-Ellerton, too innocently. 'You're the political editor.'

'That's why I'm being politic and staying on this sofa.'

'Or you?' I said to Spurway. 'You could say how well you remembered him. He remembered you, too. The query would have infinitely more authority coming from the editor.'

'You started it. You're the man I put on the job. You finish it,' Spurway said curtly.

'I gave you a piece of confidential information which you —not me—want to turn into a headline. By rights the rest is yours.'

'Or one of the reporter's—if you're ratting.'

'I'll take it. What do we do if he says he is divorcing but we're not to publish the story?'

'We'll publish,' Spurway said.

'Not with me around you won't, Mike,' Lee-Ellerton said in a lazy but very steely voice. 'You'll have my resignation before you've even read the galley.'

'If this paper is going to stay alive we've got to let our readers know we're in the news business,' Spurway snapped.

'Even at the price of being out of business?' Lee-Ellerton said rather than queried.

'Even at that. I'm here to make this a newspaper as well as a culture-sheet.'

'This isn't a popular daily.'

'All news is the same. It's how you treat it. This is real news and the pair of you are running for cover.'

'How d'you treat divorce? As if it's a Foreign Office hand-out?' Lee-Ellerton demanded.

The telephone rang. Gloomily I crossed the room, waving

Spurway to the linked receiver. He sat on the edge of Lee-Ellerton's desk.

'Mr Mortimer? Doctor David Gregory on the line, sir,' the operator said.

I greeted Gregory, and immediately sensed his hesitancy. 'About what you said to me this afternoon . . .' I said quickly.

'What did I say?'

'Well . . . about your impending divorce . . .'

'Did I?' he said, and then after a pause, 'I don't remember. Doesn't sound like me. I think you've got it wrong somewhere.'

'In your sitting-room. And then again when we were talking by the car. As I was leaving. Don't you remember? About Baker . . .'

'I'm tired,' he said. 'Very tired. Forget it. Goodnight, Paul. Kind of you to ring but I've nothing to say.'

He rang off.

We replaced the telephones.

'His little phrase "forget it" proved your point all right,' Spurway said slowly.

I breathed my scant relief for that, at least.

'Where the hell does that leave us?' Spurway asked.

'He's had second thoughts, got cold feet, been bought off or thinks he blurted out too much.'

'He'll do it some time, that's certain,' Spurway said. 'You've got to keep in touch, Paul. It's a story in a thousand. It's just what this paper needs. It'll show that New Sunday is in the news as well as the views business. Give us the shot in the arm we need—but only if it's exclusive. We'd have to print more copies. Understand?'

He got up from his perch on the desk and stalked out of the room.

Lee-Ellerton, still on the sofa, rolled over on his back like an elongated porpoise. 'I had rather a good phrase in my leader, I thought,' he said. 'I speak of the Opposition's "invincible indisposition to oppose". Rather neat, I thought. What d'you think?'

'Quite pretty,' I said absently.

'The follow-up phrase isn't bad either,' he went on, approvingly. 'I quote: "Passive resistance in the face of an enemy may, on occasion, be heroic, enobling, even patriotic, as Mahatma Gandhi convincingly demonstrated, but passive resistance by an opposition in the face of a government is, almost invariably, pathetic, degrading, unpatriotic." Unquote. Would you agree?'

'Not bad at all. I think I'll wander down to the canteen and get some supper.'

I went out and down to the canteen on the fourth floor, ordered bacon and eggs, which always tasted rather well there, presumably because one was either very hungry or it's a difficult dish for even a works canteen to ruin.

I sat reading the *Evening Standard* front page follow-up to the morning's announcement of Baker's appointment. *The Londoner's Diary* had five or six pars on the press conference, amusing but cursory, adding its usual breakdown of Baker's probable income from all sources and a dutiful quote from his architect-trainee son. What else could a Saturday evening paper do with all those column-inches needed for Maureen Cleave, Ramsden, Grieg, football reports, cooking, Show Biz and the rest?

Morgan came in halfway through my meal. He waved from the counter and came across carrying two cups of coffee. He slid one across the Formica table-top.

'Our editor wants to see you on your way up.'

'I've only just left him. How're things going?'

'All right. Be nice to work on a newspaper where the machines run all night. We'll be through our run in two hours' time.'

'How's the paper, I mean.'

'Better. Gets better each week. Merely a matter of a race against time with the certainty of losing.'

'What makes you so certain—and so pessimistic?'

'A smell in the air. The pegged sales. Inside six months we'll be killed stone dead or absorbed in another paper.'

'You've been listening to Pettiford.'

'He makes a good case, but I also keep my ears open at the Press Club. I think West is after big game.'

Across the canteen I saw Prior, the senior of the two resident Saturday lawyers.

'Come with me,' I said to Morgan. We went across. 'What's the drill, Malcolm, when a divorce action gets set in motion. The legal drill?'

'Sorry it's come to that, Paul,' Prior said with a grin.

'Mine will never get on to such a logical basis. This is a story we're nibbling at.'

'Tonight?'

'No, but very urgent, the editor says.'

'Well, the solicitor fires in letters and then, when it's all lined up, the petition is served and notice of the pending action is entered in what is known as the Clerk's Book at the Law Courts.'

'Tweedledum versus Tweedledum and Tweedledee—that kind of thing?' asked Morgan.

'More or less.'

'Any chance of going through the entries over, say, the last couple of months?'

'It is not impossible. A barrister can go in, ostensibly to check an entry concerning his own client or clients. There's nothing to prevent him seeing another entry. Incidentally or accidentally, of course. Checking entry by entry would be rather frowned on, I suspect.'

'Usual old English humbuggery?' Morgan said, native Celtic aggression in every word.

'I know quite a number of Welsh barristers engaged in divorce,' Prior said firmly. 'Some of 'em are quite good at it, too. I have a Welsh grandmother myself.'

'Not enough to boast about,' Morgan said, grinning. 'A vitiated stream.'

'But it can be done?' I persisted, concentrating on Prior.

'There are ways. As usual.'

'If I scribbled a couple of names down now, could you arrange to stumble on 'em by accident—if they happen to be there, of course—and report to me by Tuesday or Wednesday?'

'I've no divorce actions on hand myself at the moment, but I've no doubt something could be done.'

I wrote *Gregory versus Gregory and Baker* on the back of an envelope and gave it to him.

'I could have wished the names made more of a visual impact,' Prior said, viewing the names. 'Montague versus Montague and Capulet, for instance. Something to leap out of the pages as one skims through.'

'You've got to work with what you've got, boy,' Morgan said. 'Come on, Paul, let's leave him to his Shakespearean imagery. I've work to do.'

Waiting by the lifts, I said: 'Are you happy in your work?'

'Not so much happy as enslaved,' he said, grinning.

'Same thing, I suppose.'

The lifts arrived together. 'You to the editorial sanctum, me to the editorial shambles!' he said and left me.

Spurway was sitting at his desk, studying early editions of our sabbatical rivals. 'Your piece reads well,' he said. 'We've done a better job than any of 'em. I've been brooding over this Gregory lark, Paul. I've cooled down, as you'll doubtless be relieved to hear, but I don't want you to let him get away. If this divorce is on and Baker's in it, I want the story for us alone. What'll you do?'

'I'll think about it.'

'That's not quite the dynamic reply I'd hoped for.'

'I've fixed with Prior to see whether there's any reference in the Divorce Court lists, pending actions and so forth.'

'That's better. When will you get the answer?'

'By Tuesday. I'll also dig up an Oxford story for Faces and Places and go up on Wednesday or Thursday and try to see Gregory again.'

'Better still. God, I'd give a lot to nail Baker.'

'Why the venom?'

'Don't know. Don't like him. Never liked him.'

'You never even worked your guts out for him the way I did.'

'That's true, and I still hate him.'

'But why? What happened?'

'He was always too bloody superior by half. Too busy parading that cold, brilliant, academic brain of his.'

'At your expense?'

'Probably. Everybody's.'

'He spoke civilly of you today.'

'I still hate him and all he stands for.'

'You probably had the knack of upsetting him.'

'I hope so.'

'I always found him rather a likeable bird, even though I thought he'd ruined my life at one stage.'

'How?'

I told the story as briefly as I could.

'How very odd,' Spurway said at the end. 'I often wondered why you went down under a kind of self-made cloud. I'd hate a guy who did a thing like that to me. Why don't you hate him?'

'In a curious kind of way that apparent undergraduate disaster gave me a life I've enjoyed—a lot more profitable way of life than a don's, judging by Gregory's remarks today.'

'That's not the point. It's the basic contempt he showed towards us all as human beings. Didn't you see it? I could see that side of him when I was up and it was there, clear as glass, when we had him as a guest one night on the Great Ideas show.'

I shook my head. 'I'm plainly less moved by these things than you are. You talk like some prideful hidalgo out of Cervantes.'

'I talk like Mrs Spurway's boy out of the Black Country.'

I laughed, but Spurway wasn't done. 'Contempt for his fellow beings runs through his whole bloody life,' he growled, sounding more like a Sicilian bandit with a family feud on his hands than an editor. 'My experience of him says so. Your story says so. This Gregory tit-bit says so.'

'His books don't.'

'Like Marx and a few other maniacs down the long road of history, Baker's fond of people as long as they're statistics and hates their guts as soon as they become neighbours. He has the congenital commissar's built-in talent for signing death warrants for his friends and foes alike.'

'Take it easy,' I said. 'He's still only a Minister.'

Spurway grinned. 'Stick close to Gregory, buster. That's all I ask. I'd like to slip *him* a truth drug and hear *him* on the subject of Baker.'

'He used to be fairly fluent on the subject. Even though Baker's helped him a lot in his career. Even before he had a wife and Baker had her. I imagine he'd be even more fluent now, helping to prove your point, once we got him talking.'

'I bet he would an' all. So get him talking. Pity he's not here now.'

He stood up. 'I'm off. This paper looks fit enough to live without its editor for the rest of the night. Tell Tom I wished him a fond farewell, will you? See you at the conference on Tuesday.'

I walked with him through to the upper hall. We both stood silently by the lifts. He sported neither hat nor overcoat, despite the nip in the air. He was, I thought, a big, tall, impatient citizen, marking time before he was off in another direction. Newspapers weren't for him.

The lift came. We muttered our farewells.

I went back to my room, scribbled a note to Gregory, addressed to the College:

Dear David: Sorry about the telephone call. Hope it didn't add to your labours. Let's forget it, as you say. I have to be in Oxford on Thursday, on an architectural mission. If you can lunch, I'd be delighted. Mitre one o'clock. No need to reply if you can. Do hope you can.

Paul.

By the same post went a reservation for a table at the Mitre.

That was the sum total of my evening chores before going down to the news desk to make my own farewell to Morgan.

43

On Tuesday morning a postcard from Gregory awaited me:
Delighted. See you at the Mitre one o'clock. D.

There was also a note from Malcolm Prior:

Dear P: Scoured these lists in best M.I.5 manner. Not a vestige of the names you want. Malcolm P.

Half-way through Tuesday morning's editorial conference, Spurway outlined the Baker-Gregory situation. After the ribald comments had died down, Spurway called for suggestions.

We kicked the problem around for almost an hour, but finally agreed that we were checkmated at every point.

Spurway scoffed at our lack of journalistic imagination, but grudgingly admitted defeat on his own account. He turned to me: 'You'll just have to string along with Gregory, then, Paul. Stick with him like a Siamese twin.'

'A distasteful prospect in the extreme,' Lee-Ellerton said. 'I call that a task well beyond the dictates of duty.'

'That's damn near mutiny,' Spurway said. 'Let's get on with our unwritten agenda for next week's world-beating New Sunday, shall we?'

44

The following afternoon, therefore, I travelled up to Oxford with Myers, sent him on his way, booked in at the Mitre, spent a pleasant evening on my own and prepared for the morrow's enquiries with an early night.

My intention was not only to lunch with Gregory but also to see and report on how undergraduates liked and/or disliked living in modern rooms in an ancient college.

I spent the following forenoon inspecting, by the grace and favour of Master and Bursar of that ancient college, undergraduates' rooms designed by a group of younger modern architects. I listened to the praise of undergraduates for their rooms, their commiseration for those exposed to damp walls and dicey plumbing, took coffee in the S.C.R., made my notes, and then spent an hour in Blackwells before wandering round to the Mitre.

Gregory was ten minutes late. I scarcely recognized him as the man of frustrated fury and despair I had seen the previous Saturday. He was flushed, smiling and, in a curious way, tense with suppressed excitement. Even his baggy grey trousers had been given a semblance of a crease. I was delighted and relieved. I had half-expected some woebegone, self-pitying rebuke for my telephone call. Instead, he ordered a large vodka, took it in a Cossack's gulp and said shouldn't we go in, he was so damned hungry? I agreed. I was also hungry. I was also mystified.

'You're a changed man,' I said, half-studying the menu, half-studying the man.

'In every sense of the phrase,' he agreed and giggled. I was so surprised I almost dropped the menu.

'Have you by any chance won the Pools or got the Mastership you were yearning for? If it's either, pray keep the story until Saturday and then let me have it exclusively.'

He giggled again and said: 'All out of my hands, old boy, but one or two things are moving my way and I'm letting myself play the unusual part of optimist for once. A rare experience for me, I don't mind admitting.'

'You should cultivate it. It suits you. Pity you can't share the good news here and now. Let me be the first to congratulate you.'

'I only wish I could, but I can't.'

He changed the subject, almost brusquely but still quite genially. 'Smoked salmon for me, I think. And then I'll settle for a well-done tournedos and lettuce salad.'

I chose smoked salmon followed by braised ham. To add to the festivities I chose a bottle of Johannisberger. We were away.

As he hadn't rebuked me so far, I said: 'You were disconcertingly cagey when I rang you the other night.'

'Afraid I was. I was tired. Right at the edge of things. I was glad to have seen you, but by the time you rang me I was down in the depths. I was fed up with everything and everyone. You came in for some of the general malaise, I'm afraid.'

'You've done nothing decisive since?' I queried, as casually as I could.

'What I said was said in a moment of depression. I want to forget the ghastly business. It's finished with.'

'I take it, then, you're making a fresh start?'

'Yes. I am.' After a long pause, and almost as a perfunctory afterthought, he added quietly, 'We are.'

He seemed tense again.

In the flurry of plates being set, brown bread being offered and red or black pepper queried, I studied Gregory He was biting his underlip hard. Globules of sweat shone on brow and cranium. His face was feverishly pink.

He was plainly undergoing a pretty fierce strain, whatever it was. I wondered whether it derived from his decision to remake his marriage or from some other cause. Well, it was plain I wouldn't find the answer simply or swiftly. I relaxed and settled down to enjoy my lunch. We talked of the College and the current crop of undergraduates, plans for future expansion, the ever-present never-present prospect for the road across Christ Church Meadow.

In view of Gregory's decision I thought it reasonable, at last, to ask about Baker. Almost racing through the answer Gregory said: 'The Master's disappeared completely. I imagine he's safely entombed in Whitehall by now, although I heard he was briefly in College yesterday en route for high places.'

'Full of plans, no doubt?'

'So I gather. I didn't see him, but I gather he was positively bursting with ideas. I hope he finds scope for some of 'em.'

'I wonder if this kind of power will change him?'

'Inevitably. It's a different kind and he'll come out of it a different man.'

'Would you have been tempted by such an offer?'

'Gregory giggled again. 'Not exactly my line,' he said. 'As I explained on Saturday, I'm all right opining, even debating, but I'm no good at planning, organizing, catalysting and all the rest.' He giggled again, even more nervously this time. 'My métier, let's face it, is researching and then explaining.'

The giggle was preposterous. Yet it certainly seemed part of Gregory's new persona. A reaction against the load he had been bearing for too long, perhaps? I set out to treat this new oddity of behaviour with patience and sympathy. I'd probably unwittingly acquired one or two myself from Molly's propinquity. New expressions? New gestures? New

136

grimaces? I must watch myself with care. On the other hand, I told myself, Molly was no strain. I imagined life between Baker and Nan Gregory could be.

'I wonder how Anthea takes it all?' I said.

'In her understanding stride, no doubt. She may not have heard of it yet, of course. Looking after all those orchards is a full-time job. She's scarcely been in Oxford twice these past five years.'

'Curious life they lead.'

'Very.'

'One of the strangest quests for power in our time,' I said, musing aloud. 'Statistics will prove anything, they say. Now they prove they can get a man a Ministry.'

'They got Webb a fair way on. And Beveridge. In a way Beveridge paved the way for Baker.'

'Baker could be one of the three or four most powerful men in Britain in two years.'

'He aims to do it in less.'

'Is he human, d'you think?'

'I don't think any man could answer that question,' Gregory said quietly and with what I thought unusual detachment in one who had suffered so recently from Baker's inhumanity. 'Like his kind of man in other spheres—great artists, writers, industrialists, even sailors, and soldiers—I think Baker's only partly human or fallible, if that's the word. With other men he's a remote and chilly character— despite the genial touches. He only comes alive with women. Even then, I suspect, he's only part warmed-up.'

'He's managed to keep his tepid side-lines pretty secret, all the same.'

In a quiet, almost clinical manner Gregory said: 'I think he chooses types who need secrecy on their own account. Other men's wives, not too desperately unhappy. Even other men's mistresses. He's never picked on some of the more adventurous unattached adventuresses around here, for instance. He's never selected any of the girls who occasionally show a yen for older men.' He added casually: 'Everybody does know, of course, but it's never blatant.'

'What does he offer them? Money? Furs? Books? Travel?'

A curious conversation, I thought; but Gregory showed no sign of annoyance. He seemed a totally different creature from the man I had listened to the previous Saturday. He said: 'I think he gives 'em an odd kind of strength, makes 'em believe in their own talents, intelligence, charm and all that. He listens to 'em. It's quite a rare gift. Merely being chosen by him is something up here, of course.'

'And when he drops 'em? Any trouble then?'

'Not so far as I know. He seems to have the knack of keeping 'em as admirers and friends, even after they realize their own reign is over and another's got the job. I don't think women mind that kind of treatment so long as they're not actually thrown out. Ultimately, I think most women would settle for conversation rather than fornication.'

Gregory was so detached he might have been discussing the sexual *mores* of the ancient Greeks. I said, smiling no doubt, 'He ought to hold seminars in the art.'

Gregory laughed. The waiter brought plates for the second course. I was momentarily annoyed. I had been a keen listener: As Gregory had shown such scant signs of sensitiveness, I said: 'You've apparently studied the subject. Do the ladies have any commonality of looks and so forth?'

Gregory blushed. For a moment I thought I'd overreached my hostmanship, but he said: 'Not at all. That's one of the astonishing things about it all. At first they were inclined to be small. In fact, at one time . . .' he broke off with a giggle before going on, '. . . there was a ribald quip about the mills of the Master grinding exceeding small. But some of his recent attachments have been quite big girls .I've come to the conclusion he has no particular physical type, so long as they're temperamentally complementary types for himself.'

'And how would you describe that?'

'Oh, somebody gay, light-hearted, respectful of his brain-power.'

'We all want that,' I said with feeling.

Gregory laughed. 'But rarely get,' he said.

Despite his heavy levity and analytical comments he

seemed abstracted, possessed by secret excitement. He giggled, fidgeted with his napkin and looked about as if searching for other faces. It was a restive, jerky meal and I was relieved when it ended.

Outside, in the High, he thanked me and said he hoped we'd meet again soon. A pity, he said, if, after these two meetings, we should fade out of each other's lives. And so on and on. I nodded dutifully and then, taking a long chance, I said: 'I have the feeling that you're sitting on the edge of what the fortune-tellers call a dramatic change in your destiny. Obviously it's something quite pleasant. What is it?'

He giggled and blushed again. 'In a way, your well-known intuitive streak hasn't let you down, Paul. Up to a point you're right. But it's something I can't talk about just now.'

'I'm picking up some books from Blackwells,' I said. We turned and walked along the Turl. 'Nothing I can publish?'

He shook his head.

'If you get a clearance, will you let me know first thing?'

'If I can, but quite frankly, I doubt whether I could.'

'You haven't fallen in love with another don's wife?'

He giggled and then, pathetically and almost apologetically, said hurriedly, 'I'm too much in love with my own.'

'I see your point.'

He looked round at me, suspiciously, and said: 'What d'you mean?'

'What I say. I thought she was a handsome, sweet-natured creature and that you were a lucky man.'

'Past tense, I notice,' he said with a touch of self-pity.

'Are a lucky man,' I amended.

His giggle had gone. He frowned. 'You're right,' he said firmly. 'I *am* a lucky man.' Then he added, almost in a whisper; 'Up to a point.'

'What does that mean?' I asked, but he shook his head and made no reply.

Outside Blackwells we renewed our farewells and parted. He turned and walked slowly towards Holywell. I watched him go. I was very puzzled indeed.

45

I spent the evening with Helen, dining in Milner Street. As it was to be an early meal, Marion was with us.

'How goes the job?' Helen asked as I stood by the kitchen door, sipping Dubonnet, watching her careful preparation of a highly personal *sauce bearnaise* with one hand and an expert tossing of French fried potatoes with the other.

'Let me do the potatoes,' I offered.

'Not on your life. "How goes the job?" I asked. Remember? Are you evading?'

I told her about Baker, Gregory, Nan Gregory and then mentioned Gregory's surprising volte-face during that day's lunch: the embittered Gregory on Saturday, the elated Gregory on Thursday.

'Perhaps she's promised to reform.'

'That may have come into it, but I think he would have told me about that. No, it was something more tangible than her faithfulness.'

'That's an intolerably cynical remark.'

'All right, then. It was something more material than her faithfulness.'

'That's better. D'you think he's been bought off? You say Baker's a rich man.'

'Like most rich men he's mean, especially to his girl friends. No, it's not that. Gregory may have been given a rise or a new job. Whatever it is, it's something extremely flattering to his ego. Mastership of a College maybe. Damn him if it is. That kind of academic titbit's just made for Faces and Places. I'll be furious if it turns into a general release.'

'Did you take to his wife?'

'She's a very handsome piece.'

'So you took to her. We're ready, let's go. Will you call Marion?'

I went upstairs, two at a time, to rescue my daughter from her prep. Head in hands she was rooted to her desk-cum-dressing table.

'Will you help me afterwards?' she begged.

'If I can. What is it?'

'Geometry.'

'Touch and go if I can. Always hated it.'

'Oh, how I wish all triangles were isosceles jobs!' she cried plaintively, rising, her brows creased with perplexity. My parental heart bled.

'I'll try,' I promised.

Our meal was gay with no intrusive thought of Spurway, Baker or triangles.

I stayed the night. I needed the rest after coping with Marion's triangles.

46

I spent most of Friday putting the week's finishing touches to *Faces & Places*. I worked late and slept late.

As usual, lured by the appalling toxic drug of the paper, I went in to West House, persuading myself that both journalistic and personal integrity demanded a final check of *Faces & Places*. Deadly errors lie hidden in the shortest paragraph, even after six readings by three pairs of eyes.

So I went in, finding no surprise in the quickening of my steps as I left the No. 11 bus on Ludgate Hill and turned back to the Circus. I suppose all men deeply absorbed in their quotidian tasks have this experience, taking their vast and rare good fortune for granted.

Final page proofs were lying on my desk. They had already gone to press, a pinned note from Tom Morgan informed me, but I began to go through them with loving hate. There was always the chance of a remake for later news, and none of the paragraphs had exactly the bull's eye rightness I always hoped to find, I knew I never would.

Self-pity was halted by Morgan's entry. He put down a ticker-tape slip on my desk. 'P.A. handout, just in,' he said.

I read: ANNOUNCED 10 DOWNING STREET THIS A.M. FOLLOW-ING APPOINTED LIFE PEERS: DAVID GREGORY, OXFORD DON; WILLIAM KIRBY, INDUSTRIALIST; T. H. R. NEWMAN, TRADE UNION LEADER. DETAILS FOLLOW.

'Know any?' Morgan asked. 'I don't want to remake Faces

141

and Places now, if we can avoid it. I can give 'em space elsewhere if you think they rate it.'

'I know Gregory very well,' I said dumbfounded. 'The others well enough to write about. Give me the best part of two columns, can you?'

'All right. I'm having pictures sent up to Hilton's room, and all the cuttings we've got sent up to you. Rudy will help you. John's busy downstairs. Meantime, I've sent both your pages away. Work on two columns.'

I went along to Hilton's room which opened into the studio. He was there with two of his wingers, Dent and Colyer, milling over a couple of early news pages and some of the culture pages. 'Put that literary self-indulgence away and bend your technological skills to this,' I pleaded.

'Rudy will help you out,' Hilton said. 'I'm off below.'

'Poor old you,' Dent commiserated, turning to me. 'Thought we'd sewn you up last night.'

'Life peers can mess up anything. Even the most beautiful faces and places. I hear you've got their pictures.'

'A pretty ropey trio,' Dent said judicially.

We looked through the photographs, 'Curious lot of phizzes,' Dent went on. He had come up the hard way, through scholarships from Lancashire to the Royal College of Art, but he had little time for the rest of the meritocratic world. 'Part of the great redistribution of patronage we're living through, I suppose. Personally, I prefer the crummy old aristocracy as it used to be. They know their place in the ancient order of things. These newcomers are such a bloody brash lot.'

'No more brash than Norman or Tudor upstarts,' I said, studying the portrait of Gregory. But Dent was still militant. 'I've seen that geezer on the telly, giving us all that ancient Greek crap. Makes me sick. Why the hell can't they devote a bit more time to the age we live in. Look at him. What kind of home truths can he offer us with a face like that? He looks like a bed-wetting old owl, intellectual and ineffectual!'

'You ought to be a caption-writer.'

He laughed. 'No thanks: It's a secret talent and I'm

keeping it that way. When dogs talk they'll work. Laying-out your high-falutin' pages is enough for me. Are you leading the paper on these bums?'

'Have your little joke. Two columns, run of paper. The appointments have just come through from the Press Association.' I looked cursorily at the portraits of Newman and Kirby. 'We'll need a heading,' I said. 'Any thoughts as you're obviously in one of your semi-literate moods?'

He laughed. 'What about "This week's Crap Game winners"?'

'You're better off—and safer—where you are.'

He agreed. 'I save this paper a libel case a week by never putting pen to paper.'

He took up a pencil, smoothed out one of the blank ruled make-up sheets and began the layout, drawing in the pattern of text and half-tone swiftly and authoritatively.

'How many words are you giving this trio of twerps?' he asked still drawing.

'Three hundred for Gregory. Two hundred apiece for the others. Say seven hundred and fifty in all.'

'Twenty-two inches,' he said as if in a trance and measured out the legs of type. 'I'll make these morons three inches single-column each. O.K.? You can have a forty-eight point heading across three cols.' He talked as he worked. 'How I hate their stupid, opinionated faces! I suppose a chap behind the counter in any shop begins to hate his customers the same way.'

'Relax. I'd better go and write the damned piece,' I said. 'I'll let the printer have it direct.'

I went back to my room, began to read through all the cuttings, each set in its subject-envelope from the library. The trio was lightly documented, for each man had lived out his life in a fairly anonymous setting of modest achievement. Only Gregory had begun to make any kind of public name for himself with his recent TV appearances. I checked their entries in Who's Who, lit a cigarette, sent Elspeth for coffee and began to write. Unlike most journalists I prefer, when given the chance, to write my text rather than tap it straight on to the machine, although like most journalists

I'm a master of a plodding two-fingered typing technique when up against time and on my own. That morning Elspeth took the sheets as I scribbled.

Half-way through writing the Gregory piece, I put through a call to Oxford. Nan Gregory answered. I congratulated her and asked whether David had yet decided on his title.

'He rather favours retaining his own name,' she said. 'There doesn't seem to be a current Lord Gregory, but we'll have to leave a lot of that side of things to the College of Arms, I gather. There was a famous and fairly recent Lady Gregory in the theatre, I gather.'

'Will it change your way of life much?'

'Not a scrap, I imagine. David will be in London rather more frequently, but he likes that. And I imagine he'll be doing more television work. He likes that, too.'

'Will he keep his College fellowship?'

'I think so. He wants to. He wouldn't want to lose touch with the University. And, after all, we need the money, too.'

'I suppose you've been inundated with congratulations?'

'We have rather.'

'Is David there? I'd like to add my tribute.'

'No, he's giving a lecture at Bristol University tonight and driving back late. Very late, I'm afraid. There's a dinner, too. Would you like him to ring you later tonight or tomorrow?'

I told her not to bother, I'd ring him during the week if need arose, I said, rang off and went back to my scribbling-block.

Afterwards I rang the other two: Kirby in Lincolnshire and Newman in Brockley, S.W.29. Kirby, according to his butler, was out shooting over his fenland acres. Newman, according to his wife, was attending a committee meeting or a study-group at Transport House. She didn't know when he'd be back. I pressed on with my scribbled lines, writing swiftly and deliberately, not stopping to lament the story of Gregory I couldn't write. That way lay frustration and delay.

I was finished within the hour, corrected the drafts of

typescript, and sent the copy down to the printers with a 'black' to Morgan.

Only then did I sit back to think.

But thinking took me nowhere. There were too few facts on which to base the thoughts. I had my own ideas, of course, but one missing fact can damn a story to oblivion. And from this story, I suspected, several facts were missing.

So far I had only Gregory's outburst and now his life-peerage to go on. I had no doubt that the two were connected, that the peerage had bought off an outraged husband's threats of action. What other explanation could there be?'

Morgan put his head round the door. 'The editor wants to see you.'

I went round to Spurway's room. He was standing by the window, staring out unseeingly towards St Paul's. Lee-Ellerton was in an armchair, reading a proof.

'Hullo Paul,' Spurway said. 'Looks as if you were right and Gregory had a price.'

'So it seems.'

'I imagine Gregory's divorce is now a very dead duck indeed. This was one move nobody ever thought of. What do you propose to do now?'

'What can anybody do? Baker got in too quickly, that's all.'

'A masterly piece of work,' Lee-Ellerton said.

'Bloody marvellous,' Spurway said in huge admiration. 'What I've been looking for all my life. To get the Monarch or the Mother of Parliament to pay the bills for one's peccadilloes. That seems to me a sizeable achievement by any standards.'

'It's certainly the neatest and one of the nastiest ways I've heard of for buying off a vengeful husband,' Lee-Ellerton said.

'It's a method that hasn't changed overmuch since Edward the Seventh, I imagine,' I said.

'I wouldn't agree,' Lee-Ellerton said. 'Newspapers are more inquisitive these days. And people more envious and malevolent.'

Spurway interrupted: 'Let's keep to this one, and leave the academic historical hair-splitting till later, shall we? You had your fun with your Lord Melbourne reminiscences last week and a fat lot of good they did us. As of this moment, as far as I can see into things we're thoroughly outwitted.'

'Thoroughly,' I said. 'Baker's wrapped it all up.'

'A pity. I'd've given anything to've got that bird on the end of a fork,' Lee-Ellerton said.

'Me too. Not so much him as the story,' Spurway added. 'As I've said before, it's just what this paper needs. A really good national-sexual-political-social scandal all our very own and all dealt with in the discreet, genteel, lethal way I know I can leave to the pair of you.'

'A pleasure denied, alas,' Lee-Ellerton lamented.

'Possibly only postponed,' I said without conviction.

47

So we published the potted biographies of the three new life peers. They were, said Lee-Ellerton, a lot longer and better scissor-and-paste jobs than anyone else had managed to dig out of their cutting envelopes and Tom Morgan was pleased to have them on time. Even Spurway was grudgingly appreciative.

I'd O.K.'d my proof by two o'clock and went round to Spurway's room. Lee-Ellerton was also there. In unspoken unanimity we wandered into the conference-room, and with the same unanimity took up the subject of Baker and Gregory again.

Spurway said: 'I can't believe there's no way into this story, Paul. I suppose you've racked your brains.'

'Never stopped,' I lied.

'You think there's no confirmatory word of what he told you in existence?'

'I doubt it. Unless he'd been to a solicitor. Malcolm says nothing was pending at the Law Courts.'

'I suppose a few people in Oxford must have known the state of the game between Baker and Mrs Gregory,' Lee-Ellerton said.

146

'They always do. But what can they do? Baker's not the first politician to buy off a risk of some kind with the offer of a title or office.'

'Few have acted so swiftly,' Lee-Ellerton said. 'Kings, yes, as we said this morning, but not embryonic ministers. After all he's not even in the House yet.'

'Presumably he said he wanted Gregory?'

'No doubt about that. Obviously he needed—or will need —a spokesman in the Upper House. Who better than one he's trained and one who'll echo his words? On the surface the appointment is a simple and logical part of the new Ministry set-up. Any P.M. would see that and act on a Minister's recommendation.'

'I didn't think there could ever be a perfectly balanced double-blackmail act, but this looks like it,' Spurway said.

Lee-Ellerton nodded. 'A well-nigh perfect equation. The only hope is that her new ladyship might upset things if she's eased out by Baker.'

'I gather all his cast-offs go on loving him,' I said.

'Anyway, it's damn long to wait,' Spurway said. 'I want a story I can run now, not in two or three years' time. And she's up to the hilt in it, too, if that's the right expression. I suppose there's no future in trying to get at her?'

'What could you hope to get?' Lee-Ellerton said. 'If Baker's still enjoying her favours they'll be laughing themselves silly over the neat way he's sewn up the *ménage à trois*. Most women would be impressed by the sheer artistry of the coup. She stays his mistress, she becomes a peeress and her housekeeping money is sizeably increased. What more could any woman want?'

'She might want a husband she respects,' Lee-Ellerton said, 'but I gather that's a pretty threadbare philosophy these days.'

'Wishful-thinking on the part of husbands rather than a philosophy,' Spurway said. He rang down to the canteen for tea to be sent up. Morgan looked in and was invited to sit down and join in the discussion. Lee-Ellerton was riveted by the whole story: for him it had a pleasantly eighteenth century smell about it.

147

'It wasn't unknown as late as Edwardian times,' Morgan said.

'Come! Come!' Lee-Ellerton said. 'Much nearer home than that. Far more recent creations than those can be placed to the debit of illicit sex, but this one does have something of the Charles James Fox era about it. I must write a piece on the subject one of these days.'

'Any time you like, as long as you drag Baker's name in,' Spurway said.

'I'm leaving that to Paul,' Lee-Ellerton said grandiloquently.

On that note we more or less left the galling subject. After tea I went back to my office, sent Elspeth off and once again sat in my swivel-chair racking my brains for a way into the triangle so neatly squared by Frensham Baker. But all I could think of was the triangle itself: Gregory at Bristol, beaming with pleasure as he received congratulations on his lecture and his honour; Baker at Oxford, Hereford or London, dreaming of his vast new future; Nan Gregory in Oxford, a lesser, more shadowy figure on that day of masculine achievement.

But wasn't Nan Gregory the one I ought to be doing something about? I thought.

I looked at my watch and it was some time after half-past three. Now was the moment to go to Oxford again, I decided. *Diminish the distance between yourself and your story* had been the continuous injunction of one of my earlier editors. I put a call through to the Mitre. I would let everything hang on an outsider's gamble: whether I could get a room there on a Saturday night in Term. After all, I didn't have to go. I'd done as much as any egghead columnist need do. The telephone rang. I spoke. Yes, the Mitre did have a room. Just one; yes, with bath.

So I stood by my silent, secret wager with myself and went.

First, I went along to Morgan and said I thought I'd go to Oxford: could I have a car and driver?

'Of course. Especially if you can let me have a brand new scoop before eight or nine o'clock tonight.'

148

'I doubt it, but it's all in aid of one, this week, next week, sometime, never.'

Why couldn't I have left well alone! I asked myself plaintively as I sat in the car alongside Myers *en route* to Swan Court.

Yet, in the flat, packing my bag with a couple of shirts and a dark suit and the rest of my gear I felt a pleasant sense of freedom. After all, it wasn't every man who could decide, on Saturday afternoon, to wake up in a University town on a Sunday morning, have breakfast in bed, please himself exactly what he did and all in the cause and course of business, and all at the ultimate expense of a multi-millionaire.

48

I was in Oxford by six and in my room with a drink and *The Evening Standard* by six-thirty. Then I made my second gamble and rang the Gregory number.

Mrs Gregory was out, but was expected back in twenty minutes, the Swiss girl—Heidi, was it?—confided. I left my message. Would she ring Mr Mortimer at the Mitre?

I went back to my drink, firmly reconciling myself to the probability that no message would be likely to get through or get answered. Well, I could ring again or relax and put in some needed reading and sleeping. Yet, half an hour later, half-way through running a bath, the telephone rang and Nan Gregory said: 'Mr Mortimer?'

I took a deep breath for a hard sell and started: 'I'm in Oxford, staying at the Mitre. I thought perhaps if you were on your own—or if David's back, both of you—you might care to dine with me. I'd like to toast your future happiness.'

'Excluding Heidi, the children, the dog and the cat I'm all alone,' she said, laughing.

'Would you care to come down? I'd like to offer *you* my congratulations over a meal and a bottle.'

'That's very kind of you. It would be rather a break from maternal responsibility and all that. In fact, it sounds far too good to miss. I love the Mitre, anyway, especially on Saturdays. Not that we go there a lot. You're not wearing a black tie, I hope?'

'Dark blue with white dots.'

She laughed. 'What time?'

'Say eight o'clock.'

'That would suit me fine. See you then.'

Soaking in the bath and reflecting on the cheerless house and the smell of tired cooking, my surprise at her ready acceptance of my invitation gradually diminished. I dozed off and came awake with a start in a tepid bath at nearly a quarter-to-eight. The rest was a rush, but I was downstairs at a minute before the hour, and was appropriately expectant as she came through the door into the crowded hall, a tall, handsome young woman, likely to get a second glance from men and women anywhere in the world.

She was wearing a black coat, buttoned only at the neck, over a flame-coloured silk jersey dress and high heeled shoes. She walked into the hotel like an eager young amazon, head high, black hair gleaming, splendidly sleek and serene. Only the shield and spear were missing.

I went towards her, took her coat and gave it into the cloakroom. Would she like a drink?

She said she'd rather have a drink at the table. So we went in.

'It was kind of you to think of me,' she said. 'It's exactly what I felt in need of. A bit of a celebration.'

'I count myself fortunate to find you free.'

'I had a rather heavy invitation this morning but shot it down. A College jamboree on the Iffley Road.'

I ordered two large Martinis.

'Too much college gossip, too little decent food. Your invitation sounded different. As I said, I like this place and I felt like escaping.'

The waiter came to the table. We ordered: smoked salmon followed by saddle of lamb. She said she'd like hock. I ordered a bottle of Marcobrunner.

'Have you been practising saying "Lady Gregory" aloud?'

She laughed. 'As a matter of fact, I have,' she admitted.

'David said you dealt in human vanity so I should have expected that.'

Her honesty amused me. The drinks were brought to the table. I toasted Lord and Lady Gregory. She smiled and drank.

'My first congratulations in liquid form,' she said. 'Quite strong, too.'

'Have you called your parents?'

'I sent Daddy a cable. I've only a step-mother. Two years younger than me.'

'When did David know?'

'Two days ago. Thursday morning. It's quite a strain, wandering around tight-lipped with that kind of weight on one's mind.'

'I suppose Professor Baker broke the news?'

She nodded, suddenly seeming to watch me intently as she did so.

I slowed down, changed gear. 'It will change David's life quite a bit, I imagine.'

'I hope not. I don't think it need.'

'As a television pundit he'll be double his fees with this new handle.'

'I hope so. Bringing up children on a don's income is no joke.'

'What will be your first act as Lady Gregory?'

'You're not going to print any of this?'

'Strictly off the record. Promise.'

'Frankly, I don't know. In some ways it'll obviously be a bit of a bore. As an Australian I ought to be sceptical of titles and all that, but secretly I'm not. Few Australians are. And I really get the best of both worlds. The fact that David's is only a life peerage squares my democratic conscience, and the fact that we've got daughters is also a help.'

'Is David delighted? Or did he suffer democratic qualms, too?'

'I think you're laughing at me, but I don't care this evening. Frankly I think he'll love it. And what's more important, I think he needs it, too.'

She finished her drink. I beckoned the waiter and ordered

151

two more Martinis, interested to discover whether drink might loosen her reminiscent tongue. 'Why *needs*?' I asked.

'Well, in a way, he's a desperately disappointed man. He should have had more out of life. He's been overtaken by one or two of his contemporaries and he's always worked in the shadow of the Prof. I know everybody's always saying that David's got a brilliant brain and all that, but it must be rather galling to him to see other men—with far less to their credit—getting ahead.'

'But does David put so much store by material success?'

'All men do. And David does more than you might suspect.'

'I'm surprised,' I lied.

'Some people are. But I understand. He was a poor boy, a Scholar, the son of a poverty-ridden vicar in Somerset, as you probably know, and he's never had any spare cash.'

'But he got you.'

'Now you're buttering me up, Mr Mortimer,' she said, but smiled.

The Martinis arrived.

'Let's drink these first,' I said. 'We'll broach the hock with the salmon. Tell me more about your life in Sydney.'

She liked talking. She talked well. She soon finished the second Martini. We began to eat. She was enjoying what I knew too well was a rare pleasure for any woman in Oxford: talking about herself in a city normally devoted to masculine monologue-rolling.

Her account of her early life was an unexpected and a highly unconventional narrative to English ears. From the age of fourteen, she had been taken by her father, a jute merchant, on all his selling trips throughout Australasia, China and Japan. By the time she was seventeen she was as widely travelled in the Southern Seas as any Conrad captain. She had, to a great extent, been educated by her father. 'He was a first-rate salesman and mathematician,' she said. 'Figures, words, and women were his playthings. I taught myself the rudiments of English Literature by reading and listening to him. So when I went to Sydney University with an Exhibition in Maths it was as a self-educated woman of the world on the one hand and a spoiled brat on the other.'

'How did your father and David hit it off?'

'Perfectly,' she said easily. 'By my third year at the University my father had really adopted another daughter. A Malaysian girl of nineteen. She was a kind of Pygmalion plaything for him. With certain advantages a daughter couldn't have. I think he was glad to have me off his hands.'

'Were you sad?'

'Not unduly. Daddy and myself were really both in the same boat. He'd been looking for—and found—another daughter figure and I'd found another father figure. David's only ten years older than me but he seemed a lot older, and I suppose he looks it.'

I was amused by her frankness. I doubted whether Gregory would have been equally amused.

I saw to it that she drank more than her share of the hock, keeping her glass well topped-up and quietly ordered another bottle. We switched to talk of her life in Oxford. She liked the place, she said, as she had said a week earlier. And most of the people. She was less fond of the climate. 'That's why I have to get away as often as possible. Daddy helps.'

'Where do you go when you don't go back to Australia?'

'Mainly the South of France or Italy.'

'Where in Italy?'

'Venice is my favourite spot—especially in July and August when it's boiling.'

'Where do you stay?'

'The Bellini.'

'Ah! Life amongst the fleshpots.'

'I . . . We've only been twice,' she said defensively.

'Does David like it, too?'

She faltered and blushed, looked down at her plate, put down her knife and fork, took up her glass, drank too much, gulped a little, coughed, put her glass down and said too hurriedly, 'David, no, . . . not David. I was on my way back from Australia. Broke my journey in Rome and went on to Venice. David prefers Rome. We usually stay at the Eliseo up by the Borghese Gardens. Delightful place with a

153

wonderful roof garden restaurant. Sometimes they try to switch one to their annexe, a place called the Park Hotel. Way out. I won't stand for it. Do you know the Eliseo?'

I shook my head. She was talking too much, trying to cover her tracks. She watched me furtively as she tried to talk herself back into some kind of composure. When her eyes met mine she looked away quickly, utterly disconcerted. She began to eat once more, hesitantly, ill-at-ease. She wanted to get away from Venice. That was certain. I needed to get back. I thought I'd try again.

'I take it David's not keen on Venice?' I said, in part-statement, part-query.

'I didn't say that.'

'I'm sorry. I gathered that.'

'There's no need to be sorry.'

'Right,' I said. 'So I won't be sorry. How d'you like Professor Baker?'

Again she put her knife and fork down. 'So that's it,' she said, suddenly resolute. 'I began to wonder whether it might be just now. I like Professor Baker very much indeed. You sound as if you dislike him a great deal.'

She was pale and bothered, but she had guts.

'I'm neither a great liker nor disliker. It's not really part of my job. If I'm anything I'm one of life's acceptors.'

'How big of you!'

'Relax. Nobody's biting you.'

'You're trying to.'

'Not excessively.'

'You're here after some dreary story, I suppose. David should have warned me. Instead he said you were one of the kindest people he'd known when you were up.' I began to wonder whether Gregory had told her he was proposing to divorce her. He certainly hadn't told her that he'd told me. Could I ask her? Instead I said:

'Well, I'm not an undergraduate now, and perhaps I'm not as kind as I used to be.'

'That's abundantly clear. What are you up to, anyway? What's your game? I know you're a journalist. Why don't you like the Prof?'

She was still switching, I decided, still trying desperately to turn the dialogue away from Venice. Even the bold defence of Baker was a red herring. For a moment I played her game.

'Perhaps because you like him too much. All men are envious if not jealous of another man's successes with the girls.'

'Nonsense.'

'Why else was David proposing to divorce you? You're a very good wife and mother.'

She became paler than anyone I'd ever seen outside a hospital.

'Who told you that?' she said in a faint whisper, her voice faltering over the words.

'I heard.'

'And what are you going to do about it?'

She was game to the last, but this time she was slower to recover. Yet when she did she was magnificent: 'David is not!' she said with a defiant flourish. 'And there's nothing you can do about it.'

'So I imagine. Now.'

'David says the Prof pipped your chances of a First. Is that why you hate him so much? Why you're being so ghastly now? God, to think I let myself in for this for the chance of a decent dinner!'

'I don't hate him. As a matter of fact I quite like him. With reservations, of course. But let's get back to *you* and the Prof. Why d'you like him so much?'

She was watching me carefully, but spoke up defiantly again.

'Because he's done a great deal for me.'

'Who wouldn't,' I said heartily.

'That's better,' she said, smiling faintly, picking up her glass again. 'I thought just now you were crowding me. I was a bit shaken.'

'So I noticed. Forget it,' I said. 'You told me all that was necessary.'

'There's nothing you can print,' she said defiantly. 'Or is there?' she pleaded.

'Nothing,' I admitted.

'Is that true?'

I nodded.

'Why don't we go on being friends?' she said suddenly, and with what I could only think of as extraordinary courage and magnanimity.

'Why not?'

'I've told you nothing,' she said, reassuring herself, not very successfully. She sounded like a scared schoolgirl in the hands of a prefect. She looked over her shoulder, around the room.

'Not much, anyway,' I said. 'Relax. Tell me more about your father.' I knew I'd get little more about Baker.

'Perhaps you are kind after all,' she said. 'I wonder what you really are. You certainly manage to put a chill in the air sometimes. Anybody ever told you?'

I lied again. 'Nobody. Across my flinty heart.'

She laughed, not very convinced, but began to tell me more about her father and her life in the University of Sydney. Gradually she relaxed.

The saddle of lamb helped: it was very good indeed. Later, over rhum baba and coffee, she relaxed still more, but there were no more unguarded moments.

I took her back in a taxi. We both agreed it had been quite an evening.

'Have I been indiscreet anywhere?' she asked as we settled down in the enclosing intimate darkness of the car. 'I mean, answering those ghastly things you said. Please tell me. Please.'

'Nothing lethal. Just the ghastly things I said. Nothing to spoil a pleasant evening.'

'Good,' she said, but she was still far from convinced. I could sense that, even in the darkness.

'But tell me this,' I said. 'Strictly off the record, what's the Prof got that's so especially appealing to women?'

'Oh, that's simple,' she said, almost in relief. 'He makes everything seem so easy—from ordering dinner to organizing a Summer School for Social Studies. You've no idea. One is swept along. All life's problems seem solved when he's around. Women like that. And he likes women. Us. Me. That's another rare characteristic in a man in this country —or in Australia for that matter.'

'He ought to write another social survey,' I said. 'How to be a heart-throb in three easy lessons.'

'You can sneer, but you won't get me mad again. I like him and he's been a wonderful friend.'

'And lover?' I queried.

'Oh, grow up!' she said. 'Stop talking like a caretaker in a monastery.'

I rode that. I even laughed.

'Rumour says he is,' I said.

'Rumour can go to hell.'

'And David, where does he come in?'

'David's doing all right.'

'That's apparent, but perhaps he'd rather just have a wife.'

'He might have done a week ago. Not now.'

She sounded very convincing. She tapped on the taxi window. 'By the lamp post, driver,' she commanded. I helped her out. She said a brief goodnight and went up the steps to her front door without looking back. I went back to the Mitre, puzzled, interested and with my own bad taste in my mouth.

49

After the conference on Tuesday morning, which usually ended around twelve-thirty, Elspeth said: 'A Mr Woodruffe phoned. Said he'd ring back about now.'

'What about?'

'Wouldn't say.'

'Well, I'm off to lunch. Tell him he can tell you anything.'

'I did, but no go. Probably couldn't believe any man trusted a woman that far.'

The telephone rang. 'The same,' Elspeth said.

I took my own extension and gave my name.

'I gather you're responsible for a feature called Faces and Places in your paper, Mr Mortimer,' the voice began. A pleasant voice, cheerful, relaxed, at ease with its owner. I agreed I was.

'You wrote a piece about Professor Frensham Baker last week and Doctor Gregory this week. . . .'

I agreed I had.

'I found them full of interest but somewhat short on facts.'

'Such as?'

'Difficult to outline over the phone. I wondered whether I might call and see you?'

'Why not?'

'What's a good time for you?'

'Any. What's best for you?'

'I work. Would six o'clock be too late?'

'It is rather, on a Tuesday, but I'll hang on if you think my piece needed any serious corrections. It's a dead duck now, but the subject might crop up again.'

'I think it might. I don't think your stuff needs correcting so much as amending, bringing up to date.'

'Significantly?'

'Completely, would be a better word. Whereabouts is your place?'

I told him. 'Come straight up to the tenth floor.'

'O.K.'

'Which is your college?' I asked, casually but suddenly.

'We seem unable to agree on words,' he said. 'Which *was* my college would be more accurate. I was sent down. But beta plus for a good try.'

I liked the voice and the chuckle and laughed in my turn. I pictured him as an undergraduate with one or two tit-bits of information to add to the story. I doubted whether they would be as crucial as he thought or I hoped. But every little helped.

I hung around until six when the reception-desk commissionaire rang through. I went out to the hall to meet my would-be informant at the lift.

He was a tall young man: dark-haired, dark-eyed, dark-skinned. He looked more like a Southern Frenchman or an Italian than an Englishman. He had no hat or coat. His suit, in a near-black cloth, was beautifully tailored. So was his very dark blue shirt. He was wearing an Old Harrovian tie I judged him to be about twenty-three, possibly twenty-four.

'Come and sit down,' I said, crossing from the lift hall into the large inner hall with its black leather armchairs set around low tables in casual invitation.

'I imagine you'd better start,' I said, sitting down.

'Why not?' he said easily. He crossed his long legs, set his knife-edge crease to rights as carefully as Lee-Ellerton set his, shot his cuffs, eyed me quizzically as if I were the younger man about to be inducted into some secret rite, and said with easy aplomb: 'Woodruffe isn't my name, by the way, but I've always rather liked it. I think we should be given the chance at eighteen or thereabouts to change the whole shooting-match. What do you think?'

'It's an idea, but I'm also a great believer in trying to work with what you've got.'

'Very praiseworthy,' he said, 'but supposing you'd been christened Marmaduke Mortimer or Montmorency Mortimer, what then?'

'By a curious coincidence I have both names,' I said. 'I find them very easy to live with. Now, would you care to stop being an undergraduate, forget your name is Higgins or Muggins and get weaving?'

He didn't rise to that. Instead he smiled and then apologized handsomely for keeping me late.

'You said you wished to bring my Baker story up to date. What's so antediluvian about it?'

'The omissions.'

'Such as?'

'The general air of Gregory's climb to fame and fortune by merit and all that. I found it all rather Victorian. Well, you've only been going a few weeks. I'm hoping you'll loosen up in good time.'

'Very funny, but the English libel laws are a great brake on loosening-up.'

'I'm a solicitor,' he said.

'Then you ought to be more knowledgeable and aware of the fact that we often leave out as much as we put in.'

He was unperturbed. 'There's an old-fashioned phrase about true in substance and in fact. You seem to have forgotten that.'

'There's also such a thing as written proof. Judges are very keen on it.'

'That's true,' he agreed amiably. 'Libel's not my special study, anyway. I imagine it can be a terrible bore. Perhaps I was over-hasty. My apologies. Do you pay for information, by the way?'

'Modest sums. Nothing extravagant. What d'you think yours is worth?'

'I don't really know. Either a great deal or damn all.' He smiled. 'It depends what the crux of the story is worth. To coin a phrase, I think your crux is non-existent. Sounds rather obscene, put like that, but I'm sure you see what I mean.'

I grinned. I rather enjoyed his refusal to be over-awed by West House and some of my big-brotherly rebuffs. 'Frankly, I don't,' I said.

'We'll come to that later, then.'

'When did you come down?' I asked suddenly.

'Just over a year ago.'

'Which college?'

'I was at Cambridge,' he said, too smoothly.

'I don't believe it, but have it your own way.'

'Why don't you believe it?'

'Because the Baker-Gregory story is an Oxford tale through and through.'

'In essence I'd agree with you, but there are one or two naïve touches which place it deeper in the provinces.'

I laughed and said: 'Only an Oxford man would have said that.'

He laughed in his turn and said: 'Did you know that Gregory is proposing to divorce his wife?'

' "Was" would surely be more accurate?'

For the first time the young man's assurance seemed shaken.

'You knew!' he said, surprised.

'Of course I knew.'

160

'How?'

'I heard.'

'Who told you?'

'Gregory.'

'Gregory! It's not possible!'

'How would I know, then? Baker is scarcely likely to have told me. Mrs Gregory is scarcely likely to have told me. The solicitor is scarcely likely to have told me—unless you're the solicitor.'

'I'm not,' he said hurriedly. 'When did Gregory tell you, by the way?'

'You're supposed to be telling me things. Not vice versa. Actually, he told me ten days ago. On Saturday the eighteenth of October, to be precise. Today's the twenty-eighth, isn't it?'

He nodded dully and then sighed. 'I begin to see what you mean by leaving out as much as you put in.'

'I'm glad to have got the point across.'

'Why d'you think it's all off now, then?'

'I think Gregory's been bought off.'

'By whom?'

'By Frensham Baker. By a life peerage.'

'I think so, too,' he said quietly. 'How many other people think so, too, would you say?'

'Not many. One or two of my colleagues here. A few more in Oxford probably. Not hundreds. But why don't you like Baker?'

'I haven't said that.'

'It comes out.'

'Long before that is why I don't like my father. I think it's his obtuseness,' he said, genially. 'Then comes why I don't like Baker. I think it's his hypocrisy. Then comes why I don't like Gregory. I think it's his face.'

'All very youthful, emotional responses.'

He laughed.

'So you've nothing new to tell me?' I went on.

'So it would seem,' he said, getting up.

'Don't go,' I said, still seated. 'You may have other oddments I could buy.'

'Don't rub it in. The selling angle wasn't very important. I just put it in to give what I thought was the authentic touch. To kid myself I wasn't coming here solely for revenge. Rather the way these spy chaps take token payments for selling the secrets. I just hate Professor bloody Baker's guts, that's all.'

'You're not married, by any chance?'

He laughed loudly. 'No, not that. He hasn't cuckolded me.' He laughed again. 'I rather like that. No. No. Other reasons.'

'Tell me how you came to know what you told me already.'

'Gregory came to see us about divorce proceedings twelve days ago. On Thursday, the sixteenth of October.'

'Us being your firm of solicitors, presumably?'

He nodded.

'Tight time-keeping all round,' I said.

'So it seems now.'

'And when did Gregory call it off?'

'The following Tuesday, the twenty-first.'

'Short-lived resolve. Tell me one thing: d'you know whether Mrs Gregory had been informed?'

'Gregory said she hadn't. That it was going to be a big shock to her. But I think she knew.'

'Why?'

'I think she must have known for the peerage thing to have been so quick.'

Not bad, I thought, but said: 'Perhaps he was merely proposing to shock her, bring her to her senses.'

'It's possible. We shall never know.'

'I think she knew,' I said. 'But it's not all that important now, is it? Could he have got a divorce, living under the same roof and all that?'

'If he could have proved he hadn't either condoned the liaison or cohabited with the respondent, he'd have been on fairly firm ground. It happens more frequently than you might think. He had plenty of proof, I gather.'

'Well, anybody's entitled to call off a divorce, I suppose.'

'Oh God, yes. Ought to be more callings-off. Half the cases we get could be patched up, I'm sure. Sexual bitterness is the usual reason they're not called off. It's impossible to overrate sexual vanity in either sex, especially chaps.'

'But few get smoothed out by the offer of life peerages, I imagine.'

He grinned. 'That's true.'

'Who runs your outfit?' I asked.

'My old man.'

'Family business?'

He nodded and then added: 'Mainly him.'

'How many people in the office know about the proceedings?'

'Only my father and his secretary.'

'How far did things go?'

'A letter to Baker, that's all.'

'But it did get moving?'

'That's the way I see it. Gregory must have heard on some private grapevine—possibly from his wife—that Baker was going to get this Ministry. That must have been the last straw. In revenge he came straight up to London, talked to my father, fired off this letter, hoping to shake up Baker. I doubt whether he had a price for buying-off at that time.'

'Possibly not. So Baker got the letter on Friday morning?'

'I imagine so.'

'And went ahead, accepting the Ministry, giving the press conference on Saturday, knowing all this was afoot. Pretty cool stuff. One's got to hand it to the old monster.'

'In a way, I suppose.'

'He must have seen the P.M. on Friday or Saturday, got the O.K. and dealt with Gregory on Sunday or early the following week. Gregory certainly knew by last Thursday, when I lunched with him.'

'So you know Gregory as well as that?'

'I was up with him.'

'So you know it all,' the young man said limply.

'Does anybody else know all this in your office?'

'Only my father's secretary.'

'She doesn't talk?'

'Only to me occasionally.'

'You cultivate her?'

163

He nodded. 'It's very easy. She's quite a dish. I like her a lot.'

'I see. About your age, I suppose.'

'Year or two older.'

'That's the only way you could have known?'

'I'm apt to go through my father's papers from time to time. Keeping in touch and all that,' he said blandly. 'I came across the carbon.'

'With the secretary's connivance.'

'More or less. After all, my father says he wants me to take over the business one day, but I don't think he keeps me in the picture the way he should.'

'How old is he?'

'Late sixties. I'm an old man's son.'

'So there's a little time to go yet.'

He grinned. 'Not all that. He always said he'd retire at seventy. He won't of course. Fathers never do. Meantime, one can't start too soon. But between these two armchairs I don't think I'll last the course. I hate the whole bloody business.'

'You certainly won't if he learns you've been here.'

'How could he?'

I let that go.

'So you hadn't served any kind of petition or even prepared one?'

'Good God, no. Only that first warning letter to Baker.'

'So there's been no general whisper in the office?'

'Not a word.'

'And Gregory could easily have been calling in about his life peerage. I suppose he'll need legal advice on that.'

'A good deal, one gathers. But that's mostly done with the College of Arms. My father's been looking after the Gregorys' affairs for some years. His father, a clergyman, had some odd bits of legacies. So had Gregory. And Mrs Gregory has some money and there's a children's trust involved. I suppose I shouldn't be coughing up these details. But in for a penny . . .'

'What about the carbon of the letter to Baker?'

'Destroyed by now, I imagine, but it couldn't be counted as evidence.'

'And the original?'

'Presumably destroyed, too. I can't see Baker hanging on to that little oddment, can you? I imagine its destruction was part of the bargain between Baker and Gregory.'

'The crux, so to speak. What you came in about.'

He grinned. I went on: 'So there's nothing physical to show for what you've been telling me?'

He shook his head. 'Afraid not. Not a damn thing.'

'I take it there's nothing illegal about destroying letters if both parties are agreeable to the notion?'

'Perfectly legal. Goes on all the time. Usually regarded as rather an admirable solution if there's been much acrimony in the air.'

'So there's absolutely nothing there to pin on Baker or Gregory?'

'Nothing.'

'And you've no other written evidence?'

'None.'

'So you had little enough that was crucial to add to my piece?'

'Don't rub it in,' he said with a rueful smile. 'You seem to know it all. Sorry I kept you late. I suppose newspapers usually have loads of this kind of unconfirmable fire and brimstone they can't publish.'

'Usually.'

'Tough luck.'

'Forget it. Why don't you like soliciting?'

'Mainly because I'm so bloody bad at it. I really wanted to act. I was quite good at the . . . Footlights. I wanted two years in a good rep.'

'And your father turned it down?'

'And my mother. And my grandfather. And the Old Establishment ether-pad.'

'You could have made a break for it.'

'Not really. I would have lost my allowance. They've really been jolly decent all round in their own diehard cast-iron way. Anyway, I'm too fond of my E-Type and the birds generally to be any good as a runner in the Old English Martyr Stakes.'

'You'll be a pillar of the Establishment by the end of the road.'

He stood up. 'Maybe yes, maybe no. I'm really looking for a convenient brick to chuck through one or two windows. I've always been thrown out so far. Two prep schools, Cambridge and one engagement. A series of death wishes I seem to have turned to my advantage in a gruesome kind of way.'

'What about your Cambridge exit? Did you turn that to your advantage?'

'Once I'd promised to enter the family business I got the Jag and things began to look up in a big way.'

'What's your real name?'

'I'll drop you a note sometime in case you ever want to sue your proprietor or divorce your wife.'

I stood up: he had nothing more for me. I took him out to the hall. Waiting for the lift, I said: 'Why don't we have lunch later his week or early next week? I'd like to brood over what you've told me and see if there's a way round it.'

'I'll brood too,' he said. 'Nothing I'd like better than to sink Frensham Baker without trace.'

'Why the venom?' I asked.

The lift came, opened its silent doors. He let them close again.

'Dunno. Atavistic stuff. I hate him.'

'He certainly arouses some fierce responses around the town.'

'Why should he get away with it?'

'Why should you get away with going through your father's letters?'

'Oh, that's like the more innocent by-ways of incest: strictly in the family circle. I wouldn't try going through the L.C.J.'s papers. Or would I? It's this public domain that matters. Or so I tell myself. What d'you tell yourself here?'

'Much the same kind of thing: the public domain, a fit territory for editorial enquiry.'

'One always hopes one's grown out of this kind of juvenile vindictiveness,' he said, 'but I haven't. I know Baker would rationalize the whole thing in a couple of minutes. The nation needs his healing touch. This fly suddenly gets in the ointment. He can't kill the fly. At least not at the moment. So he smoothes it into the ointment. The sophistry of the end justifying the means. I hate it and I hate him.'

'You weren't at Cambridge,' I said quietly. 'You were under Baker—as I was.'

He grinned. 'My venom gave me away, did it? Do you hate him too?'

'Not exactly. I've tried to analyse it: I think I'd sum mine up as respecting and detesting in equal portions.'

'Not bad. Did you work for him?'

'Did I not.'

'So did I. Did he bitch your degree?'

'I tell myself so. It's the kind of excuse all First-missers are looking for. But Gregory got a First so maybe I'm a self-deceiver. On the other hand, Gregory took damn good care to keep out of Baker's provincial excursions.'

He chuckled. 'None of that high-flown nonsense comes into my loathing of the old phoney. I wasn't that kind of scholar. I'd never have got more than a lousy Third. But I did a hell of a lot of foot-slogging for him all over the country, and then in my third year I got caught into a trap of my own springing. Woman in my rooms and all that. Usual thing. Could have been glossed over with a fine. I thought it would be anyway, especially after all I'd done for him. But not a bit of it. Decided to come the old Cromwellian puritan line with me. What was the College coming to? So the old stoat sent me down. No appeal. Just like that. It rankled. Let's face it, I wouldn't even have got a poor Second, but when I think how much I'd done for him and the way he had his bits of skirt around the place. I could've killed him.'

'And still could.'

'More than ever now he's got this job he's always wanted, and just used the political set-up to suit his purpose.'

'From his point of view it's unimportant. All these protests we're making he'd dismiss as envy, venom or conventional oddments of middle-class morality. And he could also make out a very good case for the motion that Gregory will be very useful to him in the Upper House.'

The young man shook his head and pressed the lift button again. 'To think I was so near the chance to destroy him and now I can't do a damned thing. It's galling, to say the least.'

'Have lunch next Wednesday,' I said. 'Scotts. One o'clock.'

'I'd like that,' he said quickly. The lift door opened.

I held my hand over the beam which closed the door. 'As it wasn't the Footlights were you any good with the O.U.D.S.?'

'Outstanding,' he said, grinning. 'A reg'lar Burton.'

'You should have chanced your arm.'

'Needs the kind of muscular development and stamina I haven't got,' he said. 'I'm basically a sprinter, not a weight-lifter.'

I took my hand away and waved farewell. The doors closed.

50

Discovering Woodruffe's true name was child's play. I sent one of the junior reporters, Wynter, to Oxford on Wednesday with a note from myself to the College secretary, saying that, as an old member of the College, I wanted to trace a young Harrovian who had unfortunately been sent down, was now a solicitor, and so on and so on.

Wynter came back in the late afternoon. 'Storey's the name. Timothy Morant Storey, now a junior partner in Storey, Storey and Morant, Solicitors, of Bedford Row,' he announced triumphantly. 'You didn't tell me he was only sacked last year. One of the girls in the secretary's office was still gooey-eyed at the memory of the heart-throb.'

The information wasn't of vital importance, but I was grateful, especially as Storey rang me on Wednesday morning.

'Woodruffe here, Mr Mortimer,' he said. 'You kindly suggested that I might lunch with you. Is it still on?'

'Of course.'

'You suggested I might brood over any possibilities.'

'I did.'

'Well, I did, but my brooding has got me nowhere, so I'd be lunching under false pretences Not only that but I've also got a somewhat presumptuous request.'

'Carry on.'

'I'd like to bring the so-called confidential secretary I spoke about to lunch?'

'Why not? You implied she's a good-looker.'

'She's that all right.'

'I think it's an excellent idea. Forget the false pretences line. I'll book a table for three. What's her name, by the way? We don't want a tableful of pseudonyms, do we? As far as I'm concerned you're T. M. Storey.'

He laughed. 'Not bad, but I imagine it was dead easy with the clues I left lying around. I'm usually known as Tim Storey, by the way. And the girl I'm bringing along is Clare Munro.'

'I can take that as pretty authentic?'

'The whole truth and nothing but.'

51

They made an unusually handsome pair, I thought, as the head-waiter showed them to my table by the window in the upstairs restaurant. Miss Munro was certainly a good-looker: tall, willowy, dark chestnut-to-bronze hair, high cheekbones, small, fine features and big brown eyes, heavily shadowed. She was wearing a black-and-brown jersey two-piece under what I judged to be a brown seal coat.

We ordered drinks, then our meal and wine. Storey didn't waste time. Waiting for the smoked salmon he said, 'I told Clare all about my interview with you the other evening. She's hopping mad about my father's behaviour in this affair.'

'What else could he do?' I asked. 'Gregory's his client. I suppose his first duty is to his client.'

'Not if he thinks his client is flagrantly involved in a national scandal,' Miss Munro said.

'Supposing Gregory had been bought off with money?'

'I think that would have been O.K. so long as it was Baker's own money,' she said.

'A life peerage is a kind of national pay-off, as I see it. At our expense,' Storey added.

'Or the P.M.'s gift, don't forget,' I said.

'Only via the Monarch and the People. We're all involved.' Storey said. 'Big words for me to be using, but it's that kind of situation. They don't often come my way.' He grinned.

'Are there any Law Society rules in these matters?' I said.

'If any solicitor has reason to believe that he's being inveigled into aiding or abetting anything smelling of official bribery, corruption and all that jazz he has a duty to the State overriding his concern with his client,' Storey said. He was almost breathless after the recital.

'Noted,' I said, and then: 'What does Miss Munro think?'

'I think the whole thing stinks,' she said coolly, and took up her sherry.

'Have you told Storey senior your views?'

'I mentioned my qualms. He told me not to worry my pretty head with such things, but I think his not-so-pretty head's a lot more worried.'

'What d'you think he ought to do?'

'Tell Gregory that he must reject the peerage. That if he's willing to be bought off it must be by some private deal with Baker, not by this kind of thing.'

'I doubt whether money would buy him off. He's always known Baker's a rich man. I knew. We all knew.' I turned to Storey: 'You probably knew.'

He nodded. I went on: 'He's known this thing's been going on for ages. If he'd been after money he could have tackled Baker ages ago. My own view is that he started this thing in a moment of particular anger or frustration or both. Probably, as we agreed, when he heard a far-off whisper of Baker's coming appointment. Then, to his vast surprise, Baker came back with this stupendous offer. How could Gregory resist? As a pay-off it's perfectly tailored to his personal measurements.'

'I think so, too,' Miss Munro said quietly.

'And you think it ought to be exposed?'

'I think so.'

I took a deep breath and said the crucial words: 'Would you be willing to expose it?'

The waiter brought the smoked salmon to the table. We were all silent as he set the plates before us. With maddening solicitude he checked the table for a sufficiency of brown bread and butter, for red pepper, for the black pepper mill. With a coolness and assurance well beyond her years Miss Munro waited. As the waiter left she said: 'That would be too easy for me. I've nothing to lose. Any good secretary can walk into a job these days. But it would put Tim into a bit of a spot with his parents and so forth. It would poison several lives forever.'

'Don't mind me!' Storey said, cutting into his salmon.

'But I have to mind you.' she said quietly. 'You're the only one who's booked to lose anything.'

'Except Baker and Gregory, don't forget,' Storey said, grinning.

'And Mrs Baker and Mrs Gregory, don't forget,' I said. 'And their children. It's a chain reaction once it starts.'

'I've thought of all that, heaven knows,' she said.

'But you still don't think they ought to be allowed to get away with it?'

'No, I don't, but I'm terribly bothered by the thought of people in glass houses and all that. It's inevitable.'

'You haven't cooked up a crooked O.B.E. for yourself along the line, I hope.'

She laughed: 'No, but we're all so vulnerable.'

'Everyone is privately vulnerable,' Storey said, seriously, almost magisterially. 'We're all consenting males in some racket or other. But it's usually private. It's when we're vulnerable publicly that we're there to be shot at. Our shared morality, as old Devlin has it.'

'Fair enough,' Miss Munro added.

I was already intrigued by the understanding and maturity she had shown, but I was still more surprised when, after Storey had said gaily: 'So what are we waiting for?' she said simply: 'Supposing it did come to a showdown,

Tim. You'd have to come into it. You'd break your father's heart. And your mother's. And you'd be terribly vulnerable if it all came out in newspaper headlines. Supposing Baker replied immediately by saying what is, after all, the truth: that he'd sacked you. And he would. Your tale would look like an old sour-grapes-revenge story. Supposing it came out that I'd been the girl in your rooms? How would it look then?'

'It still wouldn't explain the peerage.'

'True enough, but supposing your father then denied ever having sent the letter on Gregory's behalf.'

'Very tricky,' Storey admitted.

We were silent for a long minute.

Storey broke the silence: 'So we let him get away with it. Nobody will ever know. A few might suspect, but by that time Baker will have moved on from Nan Gregory to another willing piece, and Gregory will be a Lord-in-waiting or something special. Everything will have been forgotten. Is that the way you see it?'

'More or less,' I said. 'The way things are shaping.'

'But you hate it, all the same?' Clare Munro said.

'In a fascinated kind of way,' I said.

'Well, I do,' Storey said. 'And I'm not so fascinated. He's been getting away with everything all his life.'

'Is it honesty in public life you're after or private revenge?' I asked.

'You may have a point there,' Storey said reflectively and smiled. 'I'd say it's an equation somewhere between the two. Say twenty per cent purity in politics, eighty per cent the Storey personal vendetta.'

'It's not that way for me,' Miss Munro said coolly. 'It's one hundred per cent private vengeance.'

'Come, Clare, not just that,' Storey said, chuckling.

'And why not?' she asked. 'All these things are personal, finally. Why should he send you down and finish off your university career like that for doing exactly what he does all the time?'

'He covers his tracks more skilfully,' Storey said. 'As every schoolboy knows, it's being found out that matters in this antique land. But I admit he's a Public Humbug Number One.'

'I vote we go after him,' Miss Munro said.

Our plates were taken away.

'Think carefully what you're saying,' Storey admonished her before turning to me: 'Supposing we did go ahead, how would your paper set about it?'

'Very tricky. Our two resident lawyers would want rather more proof than we've got now.'

'More than our words?' Clare Munro asked.

'A good deal more.'

'But they'd help. Especially yours,' Storey said.

'It would have to be a matter for the editor,' I said. 'He might be prepared to take a chance. I think he would. Frankly, I wouldn't. I'd rather be on the side of the lawyers for once. I'd want some kind of written proof. The original of that letter, for example.'

'That's asking for the moon. And more,' Miss Munro said.

'The rest is your word against his.'

'*Our* word,' Storey emphasized. 'And one of them, take note, a solicitor's word.'

'You're not a solicitor yet, Tim,' she pointed out. 'And you jolly well know your reputation would be tarnished in any court of law. You're far too prejudiced a party.'

'As the girl in my rooms, so are you,' he said.

Minute steaks and salads were brought to the table. Again we were silent, watching the waiter's deft handling of the dishes.

'So we're cooked,' Storey said judicially, as the waiter left the table.

'More or less,' I agreed.

'Well, it's a delicious lunch. As I said, I feel we came here under somewhat false pretences.'

'Scarcely that. It's just a case of checkmate.'

'It's pretty infuriating, whatever it is.'

'Maddening,' Miss Munro said.

I wondered how serious their relationship was.

'If my editor decided to go ahead, to fly a dicey kite, so to speak, would you both string along?' I asked.

Miss Munro nodded. Storey said vigorously: 'Any chance?'

'It's possible. He's got rather a curious kind of animosity towards Baker. Rather like yours.'

'Haven't we all? Was he sent down too?'

I shook my head. 'He was up with me, but he avoided the Baker network. Far too shrewd. No, he just hates Baker. Partly, I think, because Baker gets away with the things he'd like to get away with himself, and partly because Baker's probably getting close to the kind of power he covets himself.'

'I'm sorry for him, then,' Storey said. 'But I'll back him in this venture if he goes ahead. Why don't you hate Baker?'

'I rather like him in a ghastly kind of way. He's got so much more energy and vision, drive and conviction than anybody else I've ever met. I always think he should be forgiven for any waste-product excesses.'

'That's far too tolerant a view,' Storey said. 'He's a paranoiacal humbug and I'd like to see him in the gutter.'

His voice held such bitterness that I was momentarily shaken. Miss Munro restored the balance. 'My, my, Tim. You *have* got it bad,' she said coolly.

He certainly had.

He shook his head as if surprised by his own outburst.

I began to question them—subtly, I hoped—about the complexities of their own friendship. There were difficulties, she implied. They had to move warily in order to avoid office gossip or Storey *père's* suspicions. But why? I wondered, but that was their affair. I thought they had an impossible task and told them so. She agreed. He pooh-poohed the notion.

I liked Clare Munro more and more. Her looks made liking very easy. I had also begun to respect her judgment. I also liked Storey. A lot. He had that British boyishness which I deprecated in a young man already in his twenties. It can, nevertheless, prove a disarmingly attractive characteristic.

174

52

I went back to West House and sat in my office brooding over the checkmate. I was paradoxically relieved and irritated. I shared Storey's sense of frustration and anger that Baker should get away with his double-dealing, but I was also aware of my profound relief that I shouldn't be playing the part of a crusader on the public's behalf.

I thought I should perhaps bring Spurway up to date on the affair, and, on the thought, got up and went round to his room. I poked my head round the door: he was deep in discussion with Morgan and Lee-Ellerton and I made to duck out, but he called me in. 'We need all the help we can get. I'm trying to persuade these people that we need a new kind of leader page.'

'The editor wants to put pictures in the leader itself. Even mentioned the possibility of a cartoon,' Lee-Ellerton groaned.

'Why not?' Spurway barked. 'If it makes our point more graphically or adds strength to your weak-kneed prose, why not, for God's sake?'

'I just don't like the idea, that's all,' Morgan said.

'The leader would stand a better chance of being read if it's brought to life. Why must cartoons always have a set place in the paper, miles away from the leader when it's dealing with the same subject? Normally I'm against cartoons, but we seem to have a winner in Larsen. Let's at least try to give him a chance.'

'He gets his chance along with the rest of us,' Lee-Ellerton protested.

'It would be too much of an innovation,' Morgan said.

'Papers change,' Spurway barked. 'They open out. Leader page features need projecting. Compare the leader pages of the Sunday Times or the Observer now with the leader pages they were doing ten years ago. You couldn't recognize them. And I aim to lead, not follow.'

'And I want to be treated seriously, not laughed out of Fleet Street,' Lee-Ellerton said faintly.

'What's your view, Paul?' Spurway said.

'I don't think it matters whether you use a cartoon, a photograph or any other graphic device so long as the words are worth reading in the first place.'

'That's what I say,' Lee-Ellerton said in a rush of relief.

'All right, I'll leave it for this week,' Spurway said, 'but I'll bash away again next week. Take warning. You're a gang of diehard defeatists. So get your shaky defences ready. What was it, Paul?'

'About Baker.'

'Anything new?'

I told them of my first meeting with Storey and that day's lunch. At the end they were all silent, each man, I knew, racking his brains for a way out. Or, more accurately, perhaps, a way in to the story.

'In its infuriating way it's a classic checkmate situation,' Lee-Ellerton said at last. 'Baker's got Gregory by the short hairs. Gregory's got Baker. Your Storey fellow's got 'em both, but Baker's got him. A real checkmate.'

'I've already used the phrase,' I said. 'Think of another.'

'It's too bloody classic for me,' Spurway said. 'I'd like a little baroque escapism.'

We all laughed.

'Supposing we took a chance by innuendo and Baker hit back,' Spurway said, musing aloud. 'D'you think young Storey and his bird would string along with us?'

'I think so. In fact I'm sure they would.'

'It's a somewhat dangerous game, isn't it?' Lee-Ellerton asked quietly.

'Very,' Spurway said.

'I'd say the limit,' Lee-Ellerton said. 'There's absolutely no black-and-white confirmation of any kind.'

'It's all very inflammable stuff, Mike,' Morgan said warningly. 'You could send the whole damned paper up in a sheet of flame.'

'Not a bad end. I'd rather that than wake up one Saturday morning to find West had signed our future off the map. You can't trust any multi-millionaire who's losing a few thousand quid a week.'

'The lawyers wouldn't let it go,' Lee-Ellerton said.

'You'd have their resignations on your desk in an hour.'

'Lawyers are easy to find.'

'New Sunday newspapers less so.'

Spurway grinned. 'You've got a point there. All right. Then the alternative as I see it is a confrontation, the great new word of our decade. You, Paul, will confront Baker with his villainy.'

'Proof of his villainy would be more convincing.'

'Too true,' Lee-Ellerton murmured.

'Why not implied proof of his villainy?' Spurway said. 'Then listen to what he's got to say. He might give himself away. He might even crack under the threat of the strain.'

'If you believe that, you'll believe anything. You know as well as I do that Baker's made of teak. He'll never give himself away and he'll never crack.'

'Teak has a splitting-point,' Spurway snapped. 'I forget what it is for the moment, but I dare say the timber boffins could tell us. I still think you ought to try. What alternative can you offer?'

'None so daft, at least.'

He laughed. 'Then let's try that one. Find out where he is and talk to him tomorrow.'

'You're not serious, Mike,' Morgan said, aghast.

'I bloody am.'

To my astonishment, Lee-Ellerton said quietly: 'I think it's not such a bad idea. It would show Baker we're on the scent. It might even shake him. It may lead on to something more positive. It's worth trying. I'd quite like to come along.'

'You can an' all,' I said with my first glimmer of enthusiasm.

'You'll stay here,' Spurway said, 'and get this damned fusty-musty-dusty leader page of yours under way. I think I'll come along with you, Paul. Nothing like keeping one's hand in. Too long since I went out on a television interview. Any so-called creative type neglects leg-work at his peril. Try and track Baker down. Tell him we'd like to come and see him.'

'If anybody's likely to crack, wouldn't it be Gregory?' Lee-Ellerton asked quietly.

'You're right,' Spurway said quickly. 'We're so bloody busy thinking of strong-arm Baker we forget the stool-pigeon. Of course. At least, I'd say so, judging by Gregory's pictures and the little I remember of him. He looks pretty mushy at the core. As far as I'm concerned it doesn't matter which of 'em cracks so long as it's one of 'em. Which shall we try, Paul?'

I knew I had to stake a claim. 'Let's start with Gregory,' I said. 'When?'

'Tomorrow, of course. We might even go on from one to the other if they're within walking distance.' He was already on his way. 'Well, I asked for leg-work. Let's see what you can lay on. If you can get Gregory let's leave it at that. We'll decide about Baker after that.'

'I don't think we'll have to. If I get Gregory, Baker will soon know about it, that's certain.'

'You've probably got a point there, buster.'

53

I went back to my room in a mood of deep depression. After all the talk, this is where the action begins, I told myself glumly. I didn't like the prospect one little bit.

I told Elspeth I needed to track down Gregory.

'Start with his College number,' I suggested. 'Then his home. It's still a bit soon for the House of Lords, I dare say.'

He was at home. He was very friendly. 'I was just scribbling a note to you, Paul, to thank you for giving Nan dinner last Saturday. A very kindly thought.' He gave no indication that she had confided overmuch in him. Probably kept it to herself so far, I thought. She knew well enough that to have told him would have scared him.

'A very selfish thought as I happened to be staying at the Mitre. Sorry you were away. I have to be in Oxford again tomorrow, by the way. Any chance of lunching?'

'I'm afraid I can't.'

'Pity. I particularly wanted to see you.'

'Anything I can answer now?'

'No. It's rather an off-the-record query. Rather personal, in fact.'

'Can't you fire it off now?'

'No, it's a bit, well, difficult.'

'Will it take long?'

'Not more than ten minutes.'

He was plainly perturbed. 'Is there anything I can brush up on before you arrive?'

'No. A few questions. Now you're in the news they're likely to be inevitable for a few days. A point I'd like to check with you before I print it.'

'About what?' I could sense his growing apprehension.

'I'd rather leave them until we meet.'

'Can you come to the Master's Lodge?'

'Of course.'

'After lunch then? Say three. Would that suit you?'

'Couldn't be better.'

'Ask for me at the office in the Lodge, will you?'

'Will do. Nan well?'

'Very. You're sure there's nothing I can do now?'

'Nothing at the moment, David. See you tomorrow.'

'Good.' He didn't want to hang up. He would be alone with his fears and forebodings. I said farewell and hung up.

I decided against trying to get Baker. We would stand a better chance with Gregory alone, although Gregory, I had little doubt, was already on the blower trying to contact Baker.

Let it rest, I told myself. If Gregory's alone we may stand a chance. If he goes scuttling off to Baker and Baker's also there, too bad. There was always the chance that Baker might advise Gregory not to see me: it was a possibility, but remote, I thought. Both of them would want to know for certain if we were on to something. Knowing something of Gregory's fears, I had little doubt that he would want to know the worst. He was scarcely the kind of man who could live with this kind of threat overhanging his day-to-day existence.

54

We left West House soon after midday on Thursday the sixth of November, a dull steel-grey day. Myers was driving. Spurway had organized a sizeable picnic luncheon-basket, which we opened *en route*. He was delighted at the prospect of the excursion and the confrontation. He was, I thought, rather like any tycoon trying his hand at a new electric typewriter or, more accurately, an ex-television boss trying a nostalgic hand at the old routine.

He dispensed his provender with democratic breeziness, passing Myers a wing of chicken, enwrapped in a delicate tissue of Kleenex for Men. The sporting gesture was well in character, for Spurway looked more than a little sportive himself, in a lovat tweed two-piece suit and dark-brown suede bootees.

Over coffee, taken in guarded sips from plastic cups, Spurway said: 'Ever seen one of these?' He put his cup on the deck and held out a small plastic box, the size of a match box. I shook my head.

'Little Japanese item I picked up in the States last year,' he said. 'The best bug-box I've ever seen.'

'What does it do?' I asked, guessing.

'Records!' he said simply. 'That's why I'm wearing my poacher's jacket.' He opened out his jacket and showed me an enormous patch pocket. He gently tugged at a flat plastic container within the pocket.

'I won't take it out now,' he said. 'It's too comfortably housed, but this gadget takes down any conversation on tape, thanks to this hearing device.'

'Have you ever used it?'

'Several times in fun. Never very seriously. I'm hoping today will prove its worth.'

'Is it admissible in a court of law?'

'Could be at a pinch. Has been known, I believe, but it's at it's most useful, I imagine, for its persuasive powers.'

'Very handy,' I said limply. This was a new kind of journalism to me and I hoped I was taking it with appropriate sophistication.

'Very. Well, let's hope it doesn't let us down. Have some more coffee.'

'No, thanks,' I said gloomily, conscious of the fact that my ideas of newspaper precept and practice were getting very limp indeed.

'What'll we do when we get there?' Spurway asked.

'We shan't have much free time, but I can always fill in time very agreeably at Blackwells. What about you?'

'Never spent much time there. I knew that if I did I'd become just another one of those undergraduates pinched for pinching books. Always found the place too tempting.'

'I had my temptations, too.'

'You probably weren't living on the kind of shoestring grant I was. I'm not basically an Oxford type. It never got under my skin. I'm no nostalgia man.'

'I hadn't been back myself for twelve years, until you sent me back on this Baker story.'

'Curious, the way all that dreaming spires stuff gets a grip on most of its alumni. Old men in love with their own youth, I suppose. Gets worse as they get older. Never had it, never will. What about you?'

'I left the place in too much bitterness.'

'Baker seems to have brought a lot of bitterness to those who worked and studied with him, don't you think?'

'Probably part of the price a few individuals need to pay for Baker's benefits to humanity at large.'

Spurway laughed. 'When I get back to TV, the first programme I'm doing is an enquiry into the private hells created by some of the world's best-known do-gooders. It really needs colour. Are you looking forward to this lark this afternoon?'

'Not much. Not at all, in fact. It's all yours and you ought to conduct the quiz.'

'I may at that. I'm looking forward to the whole venture. I realized last night I haven't done a real roasting, grilling interview for five years. I'm carrying around too much admin fat, mentally as well as physically.'

'A pity you had to choose today and me to help you keep your hand in.'

He laughed. 'I'd have liked to have seen you on the job solo, but I think I may have to bulldoze things a bit.'

I groaned. He grinned.

'Are you enjoying Faces and Places?' he asked suddenly.

'When I get a chance to get down to it. This Baker thing seems to be turning into a full-time job.'

'That sounds good, but it's as wrong as hell. This Baker is a very pleasant little sideline to keep your news values in working order.'

'Wish I thought so.'

'You'll admit that if we make the story stick it'll be a story in a thousand?'

I agreed. Not very enthusiastically.

'Well, buster, whether you like it or not that's why we're here.'

55

Myers put us down at the College gates.

We crossed the courtyard to the Master's Lodge. Miss Elizabeth Fowler was expecting me, if not us, and made a show of remembering me, but not very willingly. I asked for Gregory.

'Oh yes, Doctor Gregory left a message. He says he'll see you in Professor Baker's rooms. I'm sure you know your way up.'

'Same old smell,' Spurway said as we went up to Baker's rooms. I knocked. The unmistakable voice boomed, 'Come in!'

Inside the room, Baker was standing by the window, Gregory was sitting on the sofa. Baker seemed very much at ease: Gregory very nervous indeed.

'Hello, Mike,' Baker said. 'I wasn't expecting this additional pleasure.'

'Hello,' Spurway replied. 'Glad you see it that way.'

Gregory nodded nervously to each of us in turn. Baker started the proceedings: 'As I gathered from David that you were going on to see him, I thought I might well be present, as I imagine it's his new job you'd like to talk about. Save your time and ours.' He spoke with enormous equanimity.

'Why not?' I said.

'Good idea,' Spurway said.

'Well, I suppose you're both as busy as we are, so shoot,' Baker said in his best hearty-Master manner.

Spurway began: 'It's less about your new tasks. We've really come to clear up, if possible, certain rumours of divorce that are beginning to build up in Fleet Street.'

'What an extraordinary opening. Why come here, for heaven's sake? I'm as interested in Oxford tittle-tattle as the next man, but I'm scarcely a fountain-head.'

'These rumours concern you. The pair of you.'

'Do they now?' Baker queried like a ham actor in a seaside rep. He turned to Gregory: 'Hear that, David?' Then, quickly and aggressively, as if to let us know he was ready and in fighting form, he said, 'Well, if the interview's to proceed along those murky lines of innuendo and so on, perhaps we'd better keep the record straight.'

He turned from the window, crossed to the large bombé commode, pulled out the top drawer to display an impressive array of electronic equipment. 'We'd better let the old Grundig do its stuff. Might as well have an authentic record of the proceedings, don't you think?' He switched on the machine. 'Now where were we?'

Spurway grinned. I almost guffawed. Gregory looked desperately unhappy.

Slowly and carefully, as if he were dictating an opening paragraph for a feature, Spurway said: 'The rumour is that you, Professor Baker, and you, Doctor Gregory, were involved in the early stages of a divorce case and that this case has now been dropped. True or untrue?'

'A curious rumour, to say the least,' Baker said, ignoring the question. 'I imagine you gave no credence to it. You are here, I imagine, to warn us to be on the alert to quash any repetition of the rumour in these academic areas.'

'We're here on what might be called a modest fact-finding mission.'

'In what way?'

Now, in his turn, Spurway ignored the question. 'It might also be considered as a warning,' he said coolly. 'But not, perhaps, in quite the way you seem to think.'

'In what way, then, may I ask?'

'Rather than go on with this kind of cat-and-mouse game —which I never believe in anyway—I think I ought to tell you where my paper stands in this matter. Briefly, it's come to our knowledge—and from what we judge to be a pretty authoritative source—that Gregory sent you, via his solicitors, a letter warning you that he proposed to start divorce proceedings, citing you as co-respondent.'

'What an extraordinary story!' Baker boomed. He turned to Gregory. 'What's your view, David?'

'I don't like it,' Gregory almost quavered in what might have seemed a highly equivocal contribution.

'Neither do I!' Baker said quickly, plainly not liking his junior partner's plainly failing nerve. 'What next?'

'The implications in the story are obvious,' Spurway said. 'You received his letter, according to our sources, on the eighteenth of October. David's life peerage was announced on the twenty-fifth. That seems to me and my reporting staff a curiously coincidental pair of dates.'

'A devilishly well-contrived smear if ever I heard one, Baker said calmly. 'Reminds me of some of those wartime black radio smears. Justifiable in times of national crisis, no doubt, although I had my reservations even then. Quite intolerable in a so-called responsible newspaper. You get two facts right, add a dirty third, and lo and behold, you have a man's reputation in jeopardy.'

'Which would you say are the two correct facts?' Spurway asked quietly.

'My Ministry, and David's peerage of course.'

'And the rest you regard as innuendo.'

'Of course I do. Innuendo of the filthiest kind.'

'Our source is authoritative and not given to innuendo.'

'Your alleged source being?'

'For one, the solicitors.'

'Who are?'

'Storey, Storey and Morant of Bedford Row.'

'Never heard of them. Have you, David?'

'They happen to be my solicitors,' Gregory said in a thin voice.

'Well, that would be a logical name to introduce into this kind of beastly game when the smear's intended to stick,' Baker said easily, even grandiloquently. He turned to Gregory again. 'Have you known them long?'

'They've always looked after my business, such as it is. You may remember young Storey was up a couple of years back. In fact I was rather instrumental in getting him into the College. His father begged me to do what I could and I'm afraid I rather leaned over backwards to get him in.'

Baker was listening to Gregory with a heavily furrowed forehead: the picture of a man struggling to recall memories from the past. 'Storey, Storey,' he repeated portentously. 'Wasn't he the chap I sent down? Woman in his rooms and so forth?'

'Against my protestations at the time, Master, you may remember,' Gregory said, covering himself glibly, I thought. He was looking in slightly better trim. He had probably been well-primed by Baker against just such an eventuality as this. The words were coming a bit too slickly. Despite Gregory's early terror, much of the interview seemed to be going like a well-rehearsed dialogue, well-suited to Baker's purpose.

'You ought to have a clearer memory of him, Prof,' I said. 'He did a lot of work for you, I understand, one way and another.'

'Many undergraduates do,' Baker said easily. 'You did yourself. But I remember now. Of course I remember. He kicked up a fuss. Whined a good deal around the place. Tried to pull a few strings such as they were. That the chap?'

'Well, it was Storey you sent down. I wasn't aware of the whining, as you call it,' Gregory said, gamely but pitifully.

'I do call it whining. He should have been more manly. I suppose he's the originator of this smear.'

'Your letter didn't come from him,' Spurway said harshly. His face was flushed. The initiative had been plucked from him. He didn't like it: he wasn't used to it.

'Fortunately, I know nothing of any other Storey. As far as I'm concerned, the only Storey I know was sent down and that's that.' Baker paused and then suddenly snapped at Spurway: 'Have *you* ever met this young man by the way?' He sensed escape and a sudden position of power.

'I have not,' Spurway said.

'Or his father?' Baker said, too quickly.

'How did you know he had a father?' Spurway countered.

'I assumed he had.'

'Why?'

'Curiously enough, most of my undergraduates have fathers,' Baker said, beaming like a phoney old archbishop. 'I doubtless met Storey's father while he was up. Did I meet your own?'

'You met my mum. My father died too young. I doubt whether you'd remember the meeting, anyway, although it had its memorable moments.'

'Can't say I do,' Baker said coolly. 'A pity.' He turned to Gregory: 'Perhaps you'd check, David, to settle Mr Spurway's query. Perhaps you don't need to as you know the family.'

Gregory nodded. 'There is a father.'

'I hope you're now satisfied,' Baker said to Spurway. 'Have you any further curiosa to add to this preposterous story before I ask you to leave these rooms?'

'I have a copy of the letter sent to you,' Spurway said quietly. It was a desperate doomed throw of an unloaded dice. He knew he was defeated.

Baker was triumphant. 'I imagine that nobody would venture this kind of smear without having one or two pieces of worthless, so-called documentary evidence. I believe judges, like historians, are more pre-occupied with original source material. They are highly suspicious of alleged copies, as you should know. As I said when you arrived, Mr Spurway, I have very little time. Indeed, I have none left. Unless you have more substantial accusations to make against Doctor Gregory or myself I must ask you to leave, or I shall call the police and charge you with trespass and threatening behaviour. Have you anything more to say?'

'Only that I'll get you. And you, Gregory,' Spurway said, almost hissed. He was furious: hence, I thought, the Drury Lane line.

'Bombast and nonsense!' Baker scoffed, but Gregory looked less assured. Baker turned to me. 'As for you, Paul, I'm astonished to find you lending your talents to this gutter journalism.'

'It's not only journalism that has its gutters.' Spurway interjected.

'Anyway, I want no more of it or either of you,' Baker said as if we were both still undergraduates. He added: 'And now, a very good afternoon to both of you.'

He crossed towards the Grundig. As he put out a hand to switch off the machine I took a chance. 'Where do you stay when you are in Venice, Prof? D'you still cultivate the Bellini?'

He swung round. 'What d'you mean by that?' He swiftly mollified his venom. Too swiftly. 'What an extraordinary question? Are you thinking of going there, Paul? To Venice, I mean?'

'I've been. To the Bellini, I mean. I may be going again. When were you there last?'

Gregory had got up from the sofa and had crossed to the window. There he turned. Perhaps he thought himself safer from giveaway tension with his face in shadow. Baker switched off his machine.

'Heaven knows. A couple of years ago,' he said easily. 'I've been in the city a score of times. I usually stay at the Danieli. But what a curious question to ask.'

'Not so curious,' I said. 'You stayed at the Bellini with Mrs Gregory last August.'

'Don't be so insanely ridiculous!' Baker shouted. Gregory said nothing.

'My information is that you did,' I said. 'Why don't you put the Grundig on again?'

Baker was suddenly fidgety. His assurance had gone. But he was still game. 'You must be mad!' he almost shouted. He was suddenly under strain.

'Not so mad, I'd say,' Spurway said. 'Let's get going, Paul.

I think they'll want to talk over their Venetian trips. Have you any other questions for our old Master?'

'Not today.'

'Thank God for that crumb of comfort, at least,' Baker said. He took out a large silk handkerchief and blew his nose. He watched me carefully from behind the folds of foulard.

At the door Spurway said: 'Unless I hear within the next twenty-four hours that this preposterous life peerage has been declined I shall publish a piece on the whole sordid story in Sunday's issue of my paper that will get the whole thing moving and blow you both sky-high.'

'Don't be so asinine and juvenile, Mike,' Baker snarled. 'You haven't a shred of evidence to support your scurrilous story—and you know it. And what's more I'll fight you to the last ditch. And so will David. It's quite intolerable that people like yourselves can come down here and utter your footling threats. Well, here are two people unmoved by your second-rate bullying methods.'

'I don't think there's two,' Spurway said. 'Try counting 'em.'

'Do your damndest!' Baker shouted. 'And now leave my rooms!'

We left.

In the car Spurway said, 'That Venice touch was helpful. Why didn't I know about it?'

'I'd half-forgotten,' I lied, and told him of my dinner with Nan Gregory.

'Did you follow it up?' he asked. 'Our stringer in Rome —Marzotti I think the name is, yes Lucio Marzotti—could have gone up to Venice to check. We've probably got some kind of contact in Venice, anyway.'

I shook my head.

'You'd better put it in hand as soon as we get back. Very remiss of you. All the same, I was very relieved. I wasn't doing so good until that little item cropped up.'

'Let's check by all means,' I said, 'but what will the hotel register say? Merely that Professor and Mrs Baker stayed at the hotel.'

'What about the passport numbers? You don't get away with things as easily in Italy as you do here. I've had experience.'

'But it's damned difficult getting these facts out of a continental hotelier.'

'That's why I say send Marzotti with a fistful of lira.'

'They might help, of course—if it comes to a case, with affidavits and the rest of the works. But if it comes to a showdown Anthea Baker will back up her husband. I can guarantee that. She's known all about his philandering antics for years past. Even in my time.'

'No jealousy?'

'Might have had at first, but I doubt it. Her kind of cold-blooded English beauty doesn't get steamed up over physical unfaithfulness. She's probably rather relieved. Leaves her free to get on with her own life.'

'What's she like?'

'Big, bony, handsome blonde. But I haven't seen her for over ten years.'

'So you think it's no go?'

'Well, it's certainly worth having Marzotti's researches into the matter.'

'Why didn't you do it?'

'Touch of remorse perhaps. The way I got the data. By giving Mrs Gregory too much to drink.'

Spurway grinned. 'Remorse has no part to play in any Fleet Street day or diary. But it was a well-timed titbit to toss into the controversial whirlpool. The Prof was beginning to have the best of the battle. I didn't like the way things were going. The Bellini touch evened things up.'

'I suppose so.'

'Like hell it did. Enough for him to switch off his Grundig.'

'So I noticed. What about your own little bug-box?'

'I think his Grundig cancelled that out. We'll try it, all the same.'

'So what have we got now?' Spurway began to tick off the items on his finger tips. 'One, Gregory's confession to you. Two, the testimony of Storey and his girl-friend. Three, this Venetian excursion. Four, my bug-box. Any advance on this flimsy quartet?'

I shook my head.

Spurway spoke. 'Extraordinary, isn't it? Infuriating. We know for certain that one of the most squalid pieces of political jobbery in recent years has been carried out under our very noses and yet we're absolutely bloody helpless. Not a shred of acceptable let alone admissible evidence. But I'll nail that bastard Baker, especially after this afternoon, if it's the last thing I do in Fleet Street.'

'How long does that give you?'

He laughed. 'It gets nearer each time I see West. Now, buster, how do we nail the Prof?'

'We'd better concentrate on the weakest link.'

'Gregory, you mean?'

I nodded. He nodded agreement. After reflection he said, 'How long before he's Lord Gregory, d'you think?'

'About a week or so, I suppose. These things seem more flexible than knighthoods, but they seem to have speeded the due processes up.'

'Our only hope is still to try to break Gregory,' Spurway said. 'And fast.'

'But if he breaks he gets nothing. He loses his peerage, confesses himself to be the seediest kind of social-climbing crook as well as a cuckold. He daren't break now. And he'll be supported by two pretty tough cookies: his wife and Baker.'

'You mean the longer it goes on the stronger he'll become? It didn't look that way today.'

'He'll get his peerage and then nothing will break him,' I said. 'The first time somebody calls him Lord Gregory there'll be no turning back. He'll be invulnerable as far as we're concerned.'

'Don't rub it in, buster. We'd better do something pretty lively, then.'

'Or nothing at all.'

'If you think I'm going to let a story like this go by default, you're mad.'

'Some of the best stories have never been published, thanks to lack of scraps of paper.'

'Don't come that old-man-of-the-sea stuff with me. I've told you: I'm going to publish this Baker story if it's the last bloody story I ever publish.'

'As it may well be,' I said in fairly sepulchral tones.

'If I publish a story—however thin—he'll have to bring a case. True or not true?'

'True.'

'He, at least, couldn't let it go by default. True or not true?'

'True.'

'A case of this kind will take at least three months to get into the courts.'

'Agreed.'

'Meantime, questions will be asked in the House. Other people will start digging for dirt. It will either be considered as a breach of privilege and I'll be hauled to the bar of the House or I'll have to disclose my sources—unless I want to go to gaol—which I don't. In a curious kind of way, what we've got now would be more convincing in a House of Commons Committee Enquiry than in the Courts. Would you be prepared to come along and say your say.'

'Of course.'

'And Storey and his girl-friend?'

'I'm sure they would if it gets as far as that.'

'Well, that's not bad for a start.'

'It's not good. Anyway, it's the start that's tricky.'

'All right. So we want every tit-bit of confirmation we can lay our hands on. Marzotti had better go up to Venice tomorrow. Better still, tonight. Ring him when you get back. I'd better meet your young solicitor friend, too.'

'If it's coming to a head, you'll have to.'

Then I asked the question that I'd been coming to since the whole damn thing had started: 'How are you going to bring it to a head?'

He had plainly worked that one out, for he said: 'I think I'll get Freddie to write a general piece about life peerages, the kind of people who've had 'em in the past five years, what it means in dignity, cash, coats-of-arms and the rest. I'll get him to slip in a reference to qualifications with a glancing blow at Baker's well-known friendship with the Gregorys, particularly Mrs Gregory.'

'It could sink into limbo if Baker plays it cool.'

'I'll have to write it myself so that he can't.'

I was relieved. I had thought I might get snarled up in the references and innuendo. As if reading my thoughts, Spurway said: 'The best way to flush him out would be a more direct piece in Faces and Places.'

'Would you care to write it?'

'I'll probably have to. I can smell your distaste. I'll write it with the help of the lawyers. Making 'em write something to invite a charge of libel rather than rewriting the guts out of everything to avoid it will be a change.' He chuckled.

'They've got their job to do,' I said defensively.

'A newspaper lawyer can't lose. He's like a doctor. He advises you. You take his advice. You still get landed for libel, but you've no case against your own bloody lawyer who let you in for damages. They ought to be liable—like surveyors or builders. We ought to write clauses into their contracts.'

'I like our pair.'

'I like 'em, too, but I think they're pretty squeamish.'

'They're trained to be squeamish. We pay 'em to be squeamish. They have to weigh their words more carefully than most of us.'

'*Our* words,' Spurway amended.

'*Our* words, then. Which are too often apt to go to *our* heads.'

'True enough. Now I want some words that'll strike straight at Baker's flinty heart. Write a paragraph that you'd put in Faces and Places that you think would make him rise.'

'Is that an order?'

Spurway laughed. 'Call it a psycho-quiz. If it's really good we'll run it on Sunday and wait for results. This Sunday's the day. We can't wait a day longer. We'll both have a bash. I'm a non-writing editor, but I'm willing to have a go.'

Spurway's challenge. I realized, was well-directed, and I was only mildly surprised to discover that I had, sub-consciously, been playing around with the opening words for such a paragraph. Spurway switched on the light. I took out a small notebook from my pocket and began to scribble. Spurway took out an envelope and started on his version.

The life peerage, I wrote, *recently granted to Dr David Gregory, the Oxford Classics don, is of particular interest as showing how these honours have, in some instances, become almost family affairs. Professor Frensham Baker, the new Minister of Social Welfare, and Dr Gregory have been friends as well as colleagues for some years. Ever since, in fact, Dr Gregory did a considerable amount of research on the new Minister's earlier sociological studies. After he had taken a brilliant First in Classics, David Gregory was appointed to Sydney University as Professor of Greek Studies. He returned from Australia at the request of his former tutor and was offered the Professorship of Classical Studies and a Fellowship of his old College. He returned with a young Australian wife, an ex-student, and it is no secret in Oxford that Professor Baker, who is well known for his interest in women's higher education, has found Mrs Gregory a staunch ally.*

I read my effort to Spurway.

'Too tame!' he said. 'I want something more like this.' He began to read: 'With the elevation of Dr David Gregory, a doubtless admirable but virtually unknown Classics don, to a life peerage, more than one voice in Fleet Street and Whitehall is asking whether the granting of life peerages isn't becoming too much of a closed shop and family affair altogether. Professor Frensham Baker is likely to prove a useful and forceful Minister of Social Welfare, but does this mean that he also has the right to nominate for a life peerage, almost as a matter of course, the husband of the lady who has, on occasions, been both his holiday com-panion and hostess in Oxford? Mrs Baker lives in a remote farm in Herefordshire.'

'Prior will want a lot of that changed,' I said. 'I can just imagine his words. "The implication, sir, that the offer of a peerage was a plain, unvarnished piece of jobbery in return for the wife's favours is clearly implied and actionable in law." '

Spurway laughed. 'Well, it's what I want. Too hot for you, Paul?'

'Far too hot.'

'Would you take it in your column?'

'Only under protest. But you're the editor.'

'Well said.'

Among the notes waiting for me on my desk was one from T.J.: Would I dine with him on the following Thursday? 8 for 8.15. Black tie. R.S.V.P. Chairman's office.

I told Elspeth to say I'd be there, and then to get through to Marzotti in Rome.

Marzotti came through half an hour later. I outlined the editor's instructions. He said he'd go up to Venice first thing the following morning. From there he would ring me or cable. He sounded capable and said he knew his way around Venice. He sounded unperturbed by the nature of the assignment. Spurway, at least, would have been reassured.

I spent that Thursday evening in an armchair at Swan Court, catching up on some neglected reading and putting the finishing touches to *Faces & Places*. But finally I gave up and got closer to my own nagging thoughts about the Baker-Gregory affair.

I was still too responsive to the Biblical injunctions of my youth, I decided. Let him who is without sin and all that. A sure sign of fence-sitting in any journalist.

What were my own peculiar domestic arrangements to do with Baker's? I asked myself a dozen times. Mine were strictly private. They hurt nobody. They might be reprehensible, but I kept them at home. I didn't ask the State to pay for them. Baker did.

That was the crux. Yet, a still small bourgeois voice piped up: Perhaps Baker is a bigger man than you are, Gunga Din. Why should the world's threadbare moral code be applied to him, when he, at least, is making a man-sized effort to lessen the ills of the world? If you bring him down, is there another man equipped by training, conviction, drive and imagination to take his place?

The answer was a resounding No.

Left to my own responses, I knew, I would have let the thing disappear into the limbo of things too hot, too equivocal, too subtle, too personal to handle. I would have left Baker to get on with his self-invited tasks, let Gregory strut around with his life peerage, let Nan Gregory take what she wanted from both of them.

56

But it was all fond, illusory, wishful-evading as far as Spurway was concerned.

Half-way through the following afternoon, the internal telephone rang and Elspeth said, 'Yes, sir,' and then to me, 'The editor says could you wander around with your improvements on the paragraph he wrote yesterday.'

So I wandered round.

Spurway was standing by the window. 'Did you polish up those sentences we—or better, I—wrote?'

'I had a shot.'

'Good, let's have a look.'

He scanned the words. 'Not bad,' he said, 'but I still prefer my own. More rugged and pointed. We'll have both versions set and see what we think of 'em in type. We'd better get both the lawyers to vet 'em too. We've got to make this par the most casually explosive thing we're ever likely to publish. What would you call my version?'

'Nuclear.'

'Good. I don't mind what the description is so long as the noise makes Baker jump and act.'

'I suppose you've thought about it from every angle?'

'I like to think I have. One never does, of course. One always overlooks a gap in the fence. Always.'

'You've considered all the consequences, I mean?'

'Most. Mention a few.'

'Well, the simplest. That we haven't a single piece of supporting evidence in black-and-white.'

'We've been through all that. We have my tape-recording. That could be pretty damaging.'

'What's it like?'

'Pretty ropey,' he admitted, with a grin.

'Even if it's allowed.'

'Which I doubt.'

'Would West let it come to a case? Is it the kind of thing he wants?'

'It hasn't come to anything yet, God dammit!' Spurway burst out. 'What with Freddie and Tom losing their nerve and now you, I've little enough support. Is this a newspaper or a girl's finishing school?'

'I'm all for it on two conditions: one, that we find some kind of evidence in black-and-white. Two, that we try to give one sustained thought to what might happen.'

'Give some, then.'

'Well, as I see it, if you print this paragraph, Baker can do one of three things: he can ignore it . . .'

'He couldn't. Not in Oxford. The meanest-gutted parish pump in England.'

'Agreed,' I said. 'May I continue?'

'By all means, M'lud.'

'He can fire in a writ, or he might write direct to West and try to get round you that way. How keen is West on a peerage?'

'Show me the newspaper boss who isn't, but you don't think Baker's got any more in his gift, do you?' He grinned. 'T.J. wouldn't settle for a lifer. He wants the real thing.'

'I'm not suggesting that at all, but if this paper brings discredit to the Government, news of a peerage won't be dropped through his letter-box for a year or so yet.'

'Plenty of time. He's not even hitting seventy yet. That's youthful stuff these days.' Spurway was still enjoying himself.

'And if the writ comes?'

'We'll fight.'

'You say "we'll fight". Does that include West? Have you got his O.K.?'

'Not a chance.'

'And if West wants to settle out of court?'

'That's his affair.'

'And if he's forced to make a major apology in the paper?'

'That's his affair too. I probably wouldn't be around by then.'

'And if Baker decides to fight?'

'That's my affair. That's the part I'm looking forward to.'

'So you're determined to publish?'

'I think so. In fact, I'm sure so. I hate Baker's tiny guts too much to go back on it now. So, buster, you'd better dig, dig, dig. Frankly, I don't think there's much more to dig out. For better or for worse, I think we've got most of the relevant material here, for what it's worth. Sad but true. He's covered his tracks too damn well.'

'Why are you so venomous about him?'

'Because I'm a newspaperman.'

'Sure that's all?'

'Partly that and partly because I don't care to see another man getting away with what I couldn't get away with. And because I object to a man's private peccadilloes being subsidized by me—and you, if you like. Perhaps you don't mind.'

'I do, but I obviously don't take it so seriously or emotionally.'

'Then you ought to be ashamed of yourself. Newspapers—like TV, like the theatre, like the films—are emotional business. Any form of communication is. How can you communicate with other human beings by computers? It's not on. Flesh and blood come into it. Envy, greed, lust, love, tenderness. I ought to sack you on the spot for such a cold-blooded statement. Lucky for you I made you sign that contract.'

'I'm still not satisfied. You've shown no signs of being so choked up by other men's faults and failures at other times.'

'Subjectivity comes into it, of course. That's the essence of an emotional response, isn't it? I'm allergic to Baker and all his works.'

'Why?'

He walked towards the window and was silent. Then he swung round and said quietly: 'Because, deep down, I envy him, I suppose.'

'I think so, too.'

'But I also envy Nelson, Einstein, Epstein, Delius, Sibelius, Cocteau, Cousteau, the whole bloody lot of the larger-than-lifers. Who doesn't want to see his memorial made before he dies?'

'Millions.'

'Balls. They're the non-livers, the accepters, the dead-heads.'

'If you're so keen on the larger-than-lifers, why are you so set on bringing this one down?'

'I told you. Envy. And because I want to know what makes him tick. Because I want to see whether he's as big as he thinks he is. Because I'm a newspaperman and I want to press on.'

I laughed.

'Well, what's your view?' he countered.

'I'm not sure. My own ideas of truth about this affair are too clouded by the impossibility of getting at any kind of absolute truth about my own affairs. I don't even try any more. They're a bit too shady at the edges. And I have an idea that what Baker's after is bigger than anything we're after.'

'So you think that justifies his actions.'

'Not justifies. Excuses, perhaps.'

'You're too charitable.'

'Perhaps—like you—I'm too subjective.'

'What d'you mean by that?'

'Well, I couldn't get steamed up by all the newspaper ballyhoo over the Profumo lark. Given half a chance I'd have liked a crack at one or two of the girls in the case. Wouldn't you?'

'Maybe, but you're getting your sights jammed or whatever the damned expression is. It was Profumo's lie to the House that got him down, not his sexual deviations.'

'Nonsense. Churchill lied to the House. So did Cripps. And scores of others. Every Minister lies to the House.

Barefaced lies. Lies shown to be lies within a week. **Lies** forgotten within a month. But this was a lie about **sex.** Not sterling or war. And that the British public won't stand for. It was the sexual envy Profumo aroused that **set** all the moralizing hypocritical hounds baying. And so **it** will be in this case if we tell the story. All the sexual suppression, frustrations, inhibitions of the British **will** have full foul play. Look at the way six hundred **M.P.s** discussed prostitution in this country without one of 'em mentioning he'd ever had a tart. Look at the way **they** discussed Wolfenden without one of 'em admitting he was a bugger.'

Spurway laughed. 'So you think we ought to drop it?'

I laughed. 'I don't know. I'd probably let it drop. I'm just glad I'm not an editor, that's all. You once asked **me** if I had ambitions in that line, and this is one of **my** reasons I haven't. I'm happy to think the decision's **all** yours.'

'Thanks a lot. And thanks for polishing up my deathless prose. Probably makes you an accessary before or after the fact or something.'

'Confirms me in my job as a hireling, that's all. You'll use your own version.'

He nodded his agreement: but he hadn't finished needling. 'If you're so riddled with conscience, **why** shouldn't you throw it in my face? The job, too?'

'I found it an interesting technical exercise.'

'So is firing an intercontinental missile, I dare say.'

I laughed. 'What does the technician do with this?' I asked, handing him the typed invitation from West.

'You go, buster. As a technician for yourself and **as a** spy for me. I shan't get an invite this time, that's for sure, and I want all the data I can get on West at the moment. I don't like the way he's acting one little bit. I smell burning somewhere and I don't like the smell.'

'What are his bun-fights like?'

'All very chaste and *comme il faut* and so damned dull you could scream. Taking your wife?'

'Not asked.'

'It's better that way.'

As I was leaving the room he said, 'By the way, Paul, I'd rather you didn't come in tomorrow.'

'Why not?'

'I may or may not run this piece. If I do, it's pretty sure to be my version. I may even hot it up a bit. I need reaction from Baker. I think the best place for it will be Faces and Places, and I want it to be quite clear that it was my decision to put it in. I'll probably have the lawyers' resignations on my hands before midday, in any case. So stay away.'

'I don't mind being around.'

'No, it's better this way.'

'You once told me there was nothing altruistic in the Spurway make-up. What's this, then?'

'Merely clearing the decks for action.'

57

But I did go in that Saturday. Spurway's secretary rang me at Swan Court soon after nine and said the editor would like to see me for an hour.

I went in, looking in first on Tom Morgan. News was almost non-existent, he said, and even what there was was lousy. Faces & Places had gone away the way it had been written.

I went on round to Spurway's room. As I went in he buzzed a number on his inter-com machine: 'Care to come in, Alan?' He then buzzed Lee-Ellerton, asking him to come through, too.

'Let's go into the other room,' Spurway said as Lee-Ellerton joined us. We went through into the big conference-room and sat down.

'Tell the others what you told Tom and me this morning,' Spurway said.

Pettiford pursed his lips, brushed his moustache and began: 'Briefly, it's this: I gather from one or two of my chums in the merchant banking world that T.J. is well on the way to concluding a deal with one of the nationals whereby they'll switch entirely to colour for their existing daily and Sunday. If it comes off, it'll be one of the biggest printing deals—if not the biggest—ever pulled off in this country.'

'West, I take it, isn't proposing to sell, merely to rent out his machines?' Lee-Ellerton queried.

'So I understand. It's much the same thing that Thomson does for the Guardian in London and for the Mirror at Withy Grove in Manchester—but on a vastly bigger scale, of course.'

'What's the other group going to do with its existing machines?' I asked.

'Some of them need replacing. There's some talk of 'em being used for a projected new London evening paper and other weekly oddments—so I gather.'

'Which group is it?' asked Lee-Ellerton.

'That I can't nail. Obviously it's one of three at the most, but there have been several red herrings to confuse the issue.'

'Who are your informants?'

'I've a couple. A youngish boffin in a merchant bank and a broker I know who's fairly well in with White, Behrens and Monson.'

'Might have guessed,' Lee-Ellerton said. 'How far advanced is it?'

'Fairly well on, I gather.'

'Anybody else on to it?'

'One or two of the City people are sniffing hard, but, so far, it's been absolutely top-level stuff. No more than West and three others in it.'

'With not a crummy old journalist in sight, I dare say,' Spurway said.

'Goes without saying,' Pettiford said. 'This is big business. What would a scribbler know about that?'

'Speaking as a split-personality, Alan—half-scribbler, half-City-gent—d'you think an editor should be in on a lark like this?'

'Of course he should—if he's on reasonably close terms with his owners. And I don't see how you can run a decent paper if you're not.'

'Well said. Take it from me, it's possible, but not easy,' Spurway said, grinning.

'West hasn't mentioned anything to you?'

'Nothing.'

'I always thought you were pretty close to him.'

' "Were" is the word. Thanks, Alan. I wanted the others to know.'

'What is reputedly going to happen to this rag if your spies are reliable?' Lee-Ellerton asked.

'Absorption, I suppose. But I have heard one whisper that New Sunday will be stepped up to become a three or four million supplement to the present black-and-white Sunday, whichever it is. That would certainly give the other Colour Supplements a real jolt. It makes sense, of course. At least twice their sales and larger in size and scope. It would be a formidable proposition for advertisers. Clean up the market, I'd say.'

'So we'd be the New Sunday Supplement?' Spurway barked. 'A giveaway sheet?'

'It's an alternative I've heard bruited abroad, but I doubt whether we'd still be known as New Sunday any more.'

'Decline and fall on a Gibbonian scale,' Lee-Ellerton said.

'And when shall we know for certain?' I asked.

'Could be a week. Could be a month. Not much longer than that, I'd say.'

'One can't help admiring him,' I said. 'If Big Business is the jungle it's said to be—and I think it is—West certainly did his Combat Course pretty thoroughly.'

'I rather agree,' Pettiford said.

'You're both too damned detached,' Spurway said.

'I write about these things happening to other outfits, other people. Now it's happening—or may happen—to me, us, you, it. Very interesting,' Pettiford said coolly.

'Doesn't it infuriate you, then?'

'Personally, yes. But I came here with my eyes open.'

Spurway turned to me. 'Would you go on doing Faces and Places for another group?'

'If I got the same kind of freedom.'

'For another editor?'

'Isn't that the same question?' The others laughed. 'Wouldn't you be around, then?'

'Not a chance.'

'What would be your feelings about West, Mike?' Lee-Ellerton asked, scarcely able to hide the mild malevolence of his enquiry.

'Mainly a search for full-scale revenge,' Spurway said without a moment for reflection.

58

Normally, on Sunday mornings, I was tempted to look through the opposition papers to see how their offerings compared with those of *New Sunday*. But not that Sunday morning.

After our mid-morning Saturday discussion I wasn't surprised to find in *Faces & Places* the Spurway version of the paragraph each of us had written in the Humber on the way back from Oxford.

He had added some extra touches plus a final sentence which showed how seriously he meant business. No paragraph could more explicitly have initiated legal reaction.

There it was in full under the heading OXFORD CIRCUS.

With the unexpected elevation of Dr David Gregory, a doubtless worthy but virtually unknown classics don, to a life peerage, more than one voice in Parliament, Oxford, Fleet Street and Whitehall is asking whether the bestowal of these lordly distinctions isn't becoming too much of a closed shop and/or family affair altogether. We are all, by now, accustomed to the use of this levitational device for easing aged or difficult party politicians into Another Place, but this most recent honour seems inexplicable by any standard. Professor Frensham Baker, the new Minister of Social Welfare, seems likely to prove a useful and forceful politician, but does this mean that he also has the right to nominate, almost as a matter of course, the husband of the lady who has, on occasions, been both his Oxford hostess and holiday companion, to a life peerage? Mrs Baker, as

I reported two weeks ago, lives apart from her husband in a remote farm in Herefordshire.

I managed a long-drawn whistle just before my teeth began to chatter, and turned to the opposition for some kind of comfort.

The front page of the *Sunday Times* Business News Section carried a short piece under a double heading *Newspaper Link-Up?* The story 'from a usually reliable source' reported that T. J. West was negotiating with a large London newspaper group for the printing of a daily coloured section and suggested that if agreement were reached and experiments proved successful, the project might mean the transformation not only of one of the popular national newspapers into the first British colour daily newspaper, but of the whole British press. Discussions were also concerned, added the source, with the future of *New Sunday*.

Pettiford wasn't the only City Editor with reliable sources, it seemed.

I went to Milner Street for lunch and afterwards took Marion to the V. and A. to see an exhibition of posters. Later I took Helen to supper at Scotts. I was preoccupied all day.

59

During the three months I had been a Sunday newspaper-man, I had discovered the particular pleasures of not working on Mondays, that most doleful of days when the rest of the world's breadwinners are sitting in trains, coughing in buses, strap-hanging in the Underground.

These pleasures were particularly sybaritic that November.

Molly, too, enjoyed her more leisurely approach to cleaning the flat on Mondays. By the time she arrived to begin her weekly round, I was usually drinking my second cup of coffee. Molly would then make a fresh brew which we proceeded to drink whilst discussing our respective weekends.

I was always entertained and appalled by her racy descriptions of the unutterably boring experiences she was prepared to live through in order to preserve domestic peace, from visiting unloved in-laws to journeying with Harryboy to stockcar racing meetings on the outskirts of London during the summer, or to Chelsea's home matches at Stamford Bridge in the winter.

We then went back to bed.

But the morning of Monday, November the tenth, was different in one chilling detail. Five minutes before Molly arrived, I was scanning the *Daily Express* after spending too long over *The Times* and *The Guardian*. At the foot of the front page, in the usual briefs on the usual weekend crashes, were the names of Timothy Storey, 22, and Miss Clare Munro, 26, killed in a four-car pile-up on the M4 between Reading and Maidenhead. I sat at the table, limp and cold with shock. They had both been so young, so very much alive. And lodged between this sense of loss and pity was more subjective and self-pitying apprehension: where did our story stand now?

I was still caught in bemused bewilderment when the telephone rang. Spurway said: 'Have you seen about Storey?'

'Ten minutes ago.'

'It puts us in rather a spot. Perhaps I've been too hasty. I see now how much I was banking on Storey being around. Our story was weak enough as it was, but with the two of them it might have stood up. In fact I think it would have done—ultimately. Now I don't think we've got a chance. No counsel in Britain would take on the case, except to pick up the cheque.'

'We'll soon know.'

'That's true. Don't lose heart.'

'I'll wait till tomorrow. I suppose we'll have the solicitors' letters in by then. What d'you do with 'em? Send 'em on to West with a note?'

'This will be big enough to go up to West straightaway. Ministers of the Crown don't get libelled every week. Were you proposing to go into the office today?'

'Not a chance. Were you?'

'Haven't decided yet. See you tomorrow.'

I put the telephone down almost regretfully. Spurway's flat, assertive voice had, at least, a show of self-confidence about it. I doubted whether mine had even the faintest undertones.

Molly arrived, shut the door behind her, bumped her backside firmly against the timber and said: 'With that, I'm putting my weekend right be'ind me. By gawd, I've had a time of it. Ever since I left 'ere on Friday I've been somebody's bleeding slave. Would you like some more coffee? I need an expresso like Burton needs Liz.'

In Molly Cowell's willing and capacious arms I ousted thoughts of Frensham Baker's life, Timothy Storey's death, Mike Spurway's troubles. And my own.

An hour later, around ten-thirty, I put a personal call through to Marzotti at the Bellini in Venice. To my great surprise he answered.

'I thought you'd be back in Rome.'

'I have work to do here,' he said blandly.

'Any results?'

'Within the next twenty-four hours, I hope. It has been a severely complicated business.'

'Why so long?'

'To discover such details as you request is very difficult. I do not know how it is in England.'

'Not so easy, I imagine. I've never tried.'

'I am glad to hear that.'

'What have you found so far? Anything?'

'Only that Professor Baker had a double room and bath here. That the bill was made out to him. That he paid by travellers' cheque. I sent all this in a cable an hour ago.'

'What about his companion?'

'These matters are strictly between the hotelier and the police. In Rome it would be simpler. Here, I have to make new friends from old contacts. It is a slow business. But I will let you know by tomorrow something. It is very very difficult. People are not what you call forthcoming.'

'Ring me at West House whether you've been lucky or not.'

He promised to do that. We rang off.

I had some more coffee.

Mason rang me just before eleven. A bit of a nerve, he said, but was I free to have lunch with him that day? We fixed on Rules. He was very grateful.

Later, having chosen our frugal meal: avocado pear followed by grilled steak, Mason said: 'I'll do the sales-talk first, then we can relax. It's this: the grapevine says big things are happening in your part of the world. As you're a Sunday and we're a daily, I want to make sure I get the news as soon as—or sooner than—any other daily.'

'What does the grapevine say?'

'Roughly what the Sunday Times hinted at yesterday: that West is having high-level talks with two—some say three—major groups about printing a colour daily.'

I was surprised. I thought he might have got on to the Baker story. I had been looking forward to his views of likely repercussions.

'It's a logical step, I'm told.'

'I suppose it is for the big boys. I'm not so keen myself. I suppose it will affect us sooner or later. Can't avoid it. If it blows up and you're in a position to let me in early on the story, will you?'

'Willingly.'

'Good. That settles that. I like the stuff you're doing, by the way. I assume you enjoy doing it.'

'Correct.'

'I've learned a bit from watching it. In fact, I've learned a lot from watching the paper as a whole. It's a newspaper-man's paper.'

'Edited by a television man.'

'I take back a lot of what I said about Spurway. I still don't like him, but he's got real feeling for the projection of news. Especially foreign news. It's not a collection of snippets. He evaluates the news even as he presents it. It's a rare talent and one we're apt to neglect in the newspaper business.'

'It's one of Spurway's big things. He's got three young rewrite men who'd be section editors in a good news magazine. They're the rare combination of hatchet men *and* writers and the best-informed trio in the foreign news business.'

'And I like the way the paper's put together. I haven't enjoyed just looking at a paper so much since that ill-fated Marshall Field New York job, *P.M.* You probably never saw it.'

'Indeed I did. In my first cheap students' tour in the States after Oxford.'

We went on nattering until half-past two. As we parted at the corner of Henrietta Street, Mason said: 'If these rumours mean a new way of life for you, Paul, I hope you'd drop in and see what we've got to offer.'

'Civil words in a time of tension.'

'I mean 'em. I've learned a lot.'

'Did you see the piece on Frensham Baker, by the way, in Faces and Places?'

He nodded. 'Indeed I did. Sticking your neck out, aren't you? I hope you cleared it with the lawyers.'

'Not exactly.'

'How much truth is there in your snide remarks?'

'A lot.'

'Baker's a tough egg. He'll come back at you.'

'I think so.'

'You sound as if you want him to?'

'Spurway does.'

We said our farewells. Mason looked very thoughtful.

60

That Tuesday morning we had no editorial conference. At ten o'clock I was reading the cable from Marzotti when Spurway rang through to say that he and I were wanted in West's room at eleven.

'It looks as if the capsule's gone up in several directions at once. My blast-off was bang-on, I like to think.'

'You mean this Sunday Times report as well as Baker?'

'What more d'you want?' he demanded. He sounded cheerful. 'I'm cutting the editorial meeting, but I'm having a quick discussion with all senior staff about that Sunday Times piece. Now. You'd better come along.'

In the conference-room Spurway spoke quickly and to the point: 'I imagine you all saw the piece in the Sunday Times Business News. I'm glad to say that Alan Pettiford, as usual, was ahead of the City grapevine. He told me of this two weeks ago. I thought it so outlandish a notion that I hoped it couldn't be true. Anyway, we've got a good paper going and we'll have to wait and see. I rang Mr West on Sunday but he was away. I tried to see him yesterday and again this morning, half an hour ago, but he wasn't available. I'm seeing him at eleven o'clock on this and other matters. We'll have our usual editorial conference later today. I'll let the rest of you know what I learn—if anything —as soon as possible. Meanwhile, we'll carry on along the hoary old lines laid down, I'm sure, by some antique Chinese philosopher: as if we're living forever yet likely to die tomorrow.'

They wandered from the room, a disconsolate, bewildered crowd. Spurway kept me back.

'What's our line?' he asked when we were alone. 'With Storey out of the way, we're pretty well cooked, aren't we?'

I agreed.

'Have you had any other details or only what you saw in the Express?'

'No more. Headstrong young ass, but a charmer. He lived and died for that damned E-Type. Appalling waste. D'you think we assume Baker's fired in a solicitor's letter?'

'I don't see how he hasn't. My piece was an open invitation, let's face it.'

'By the way,' I interrupted, remembering, 'Marzotti's cabled a reply about the Venice hotel. Apparently, Professor Frensham Baker and a Mrs Baker did stay at the Bellini last August. Marzotti's staying on another couple of days to try to check the entries further. It's not much, but it may produce something.'

'Marzotti probably wanted a few out-of-season days in Venice at our expense.'

'Not a Roman in November.'

'That's true. Surely the entry for the woman would have her passport name and number?'

'I'm assuming that's what Marzotti's after. It's a tricky business, he says, getting hold of the actual entries.'

'I can see that. I wish him luck,' Spurway said, taking out one of his beloved cigars. He cut and pierced the cigar with an appreciation touching to watch. 'You ought to take to these,' he said. 'Great help in times of stress and strain. What did you do on Saturday, by the way?'

'Spent most of the day at the London Library, took my family to Covent Garden in the evening.'

'What d'you see?'

'Coq d'Or.'

'I like that. All that clash of wills and cymbals. Reminds me of this place, apart from our general penchant for turquoise blue on the walls. We need more gold leaf. What d'you do Sunday?'

'Stayed in the family circle.'

'You'll be back in the fold yet.'

'I doubt it. I hadn't seen my wife or daughter for a week. Did the Baker piece go in all editions, by the way?'

'No, I kept it out of the first, brooding over it. Then, when I got the first edition of the Sunday Times and read the titbit about West and his antics, I thought it time to let him have it right between the eyes. I enjoyed that. I hope to enjoy it still more. Time to go, buster.'

'Which one are you really after?' I asked as we left his room. 'West or Baker?'

'A good shot would bring 'em both down.'

'You'll need a better gun than the one you've got now.'

'Go find me another. I'm in the market.'

We went up to the top floor, through the outer office with the three typists, into Miss Moore's room. She stood up and showed us into West's office, followed us in, took a chair by West's desk and opened her notebook.

West was seated at his desk, talking to a grey-haired man sitting upright in a side chair like somebody being given the sack. West was balancing his ivory-and-silver paper-knife in one hand. He looked through narrowed eyes at Spurway's cigar. Spurway, through equally narrowed eyes, also considered the cigar, but more appreciatively. Then, as if to see the cigar and West more clearly, he put on his horn-rim specs, as if he were about to address the General Assembly at UNO.

West stabbed in the direction of the armchairs. We both sat down.

'I should like to introduce Mr Henry Crossthwaite of Crossthwaite, Howell and Nixon, the company's legal advisers,' he said.

The man with grey hair and grey military moustache, horn-rimmed spectacles and a gold pencil beautifully poised in one hand, half-stood from his chair and bowed as far as the briefcase and notebook on his lap would let him.

West didn't beat about the bush. He said: 'An unforgiveably scurrilous piece of innuendo in last Sunday's paper has had sharp and understandable reactions from both Professor Frensham Baker and Doctor David Gregory of Oxford University. I have here two letters, in similar terms, from the two legal firms representing these two distinguished academics.'

We were both silent.

West seemed surprised by the silence. After a long pause he turned towards Spurway. 'Have you nothing to say, Mike?'

'Not before I've seen the letters.'

'Presumably you wrote the paragraph, Mr Mortimer,' West said, turning to me without further reference to the letters.

Spurway cut in. 'I wrote it. Mortimer did write one version at my request. I thought mine better and exercised an editor's privilege.'

'And Mortimer allowed your paragraph to be published without protest.'

'He had no alternative. For one thing he wasn't here and, for another, I'm the editor.'

'I'm not so certain about the tense you use,' West said coldly. 'It presumes a good deal.'

Spurway shrugged his shoulders, relaxed in his armchair,

211

took the cigar from his mouth and said: 'Let's get this matter over, shall we? We can then discuss private matters in private.' He had the supreme arrogance of a man who knows that three other jobs are waiting for him if this one blows up in his face.

'Might I ask what induced you to write such a paragraph?' West went on, still staring belligerently at Spurway.

'Because I believe it to be based on fact.'

'Did you or any of your staff interview Professor Baker?'

'I did. Mortimer and myself went to Oxford.'

'And he denied your accusations?'

'Of course.'

'You also saw Doctor Gregory?' Crossthwaite put in.

'At the same meeting.'

'What proof have you of these intolerable accusations?' West demanded.

'Enough, I think.'

'Would you care to give me some idea of your evidence of proof, Mr Spurway?' Crossthwaite said, leaning forward. He had one of those deep-toned, self-caressing, legal voices, cultivated since cradle-days.

Spurway outlined his evidence succinctly and quietly. Considering his paucity of material I thought it a fairly persuasive performance. I could see that both West and Crossthwaite were grudgingly impressed as the tale progressed.

'Unfortunately,' Spurway concluded, 'young Mr Storey and his girl-friend were killed in a car accident over the weekend.'

'Which means that you have no evidence of any kind in black-and-white, no documentary verification of any of the statements you made in New Sunday?' Crossthwaite said. Despite the legal habit of never showing emotion of any kind, he could scarcely keep genuine horror out of his voice.

'I have a fairly ropey tape-recording of the interview Mr Mortimer and myself had with Baker and Gregory, but it's pretty dodgy.'

'Tape recordings are only allowed to be heard in court at

the judge's discretion,' Crossthwaite said primly. 'I very much doubt whether he would permit such a version as the one you describe. Apart from that?'

'Nothing of any consequence. An hotel entry in Venice on which we're working. A skilful counsel might make some use of that, but I can't help thinking he'd have to be very skilled and very much on our side.'

'But these are shreds of shreds,' Crossthwaite protested, ignoring Spurway's jibe.

'They seemed enough on Saturday morning,' Spurway said. 'The death of my two young would-have-been-witnesses certainly changes the balance of things, especially as one of them was the son of the senior partner of Gregory's legal advisers. I take it his letter comes from Storey, Storey and Morant.'

Crossthwaite nodded.

'But we haven't a leg to stand on,' West said. 'Or am I wrong, Crossthwaite?'

'I don't think the case would even come to trial, sir.'

'What course of action would you advise in the circumstances?'

'A full apology, payment to each of the two gentlemen of sums to be arranged—they will certainly not be low—and payment in full of costs so far incurred, of course.'

'Would you care to hazard a guess as to the sums involved?'

'It is a difficult off-the-cuff question. If it were to come into court a judge might well award quite crushingly punitive sums, thanks to the standing of the two men and to the fact that judges are notoriously swingeing in their views of newspaper proprietors' ability to pay. I would say that Professor Baker might well be awarded a sum well in excess of one hundred thousand pounds and Mr Gregory something well above half that amount.'

'Plus costs?'

'Plus costs, which would not be insignificant.'

'And if we settle, as you seemed to suggest, out of court . . .'

'We might not have the good fortune to be allowed to.'

'But if we were?'

'Say somewhere between half and two-thirds of the sums I have mentioned, inclining towards the latter.'

'So it could cost us between one hundred thousand and two hundred thousand pounds.'

'At a conservative estimate and my figures to be regarded as strictly tentative at this stage.'

My blood had drained away whilst listening to Crossthwaite's dry and careful recital, Spurway said quietly, 'An interesting legal point would surely arise, Mr Crossthwaite, would it not, if Mr West should decide to settle out of court and Mr Mortimer and myself were to persist in the case and make our accusations in another place—or cause them to be made?'

Crossthwaite swallowed, licked his lips, clutched his briefcase with his left hand and ran his gold pencil nervously over his notes with the other. 'It is not the kind of situation one normally envisages in these matters. Such a course would be regarded as severe aggravation of an offence. It is something I would wish to discuss with Mr West and my partners.'

'You wouldn't dare!' West said, turning to Spurway.

'I think that what I wrote is the truth,' Spurway said coolly. 'So does Mortimer. We'd prefer to fight it out. I think we can get other backers if you want to quit.'

'That's true,' I said, hoping my voice didn't sound as thin to them as it sounded to me.

'Are you mad?' West said. He stood up. 'You have the audacity to sit here, outline a case as thin as rice paper and then expect me to allow you to go ahead, drag my name through the mud and probably stand your costs, too. I'd rather see you in gaol first.'

'That possibility I've also already considered,' Spurway said calmly.

'And consider your editorship suspended as from now!' West almost shouted.

'That may well come under the heading of wrongful dismissal at a later date,' Spurway said. 'Why don't you sit down? I'm just starting, so you'd better. Supposing I fight this case, supposing I win, where will you be then? I shall come after you, T.J., and in a very big way indeed. Make no mistake about that. There are three witnesses here. I shan't hesitate to have them called. They've heard your threats.'

West sat down. He stared at Spurway with puzzled yet watchful eyes.

'I think I should be getting back to my offices now, Mr West,' Crossthwaite said hurriedly. 'There is a great deal to discuss.'

'Stay where you are, Crossthwaite,' West said shortly. 'I am not to be dictated to by one of my employees.'

' "Editorial advisor" is the phrase in my contract,' Spurway said.

I envied Spurway his aggressive *sang-froid*. He was still enjoying his cigar.

'Whatever you may call yourself, you are an employee to me,' West snarled.

'You own too many businesses that have never answered back, T.J.,' Spurway said, almost confidentially. 'A newspaper exists to inform and enlighten. Part of the job is to cast a little light into murky places. I think Frensham Baker's private—and now his public—life are fairly murky places. I shall go on saying so. Others think so, too. I shall have their help. You will finally be known as the man who quit.'

'This is my paper, and what I say goes.'

'It's my position that I'm now discussing,' Spurway said. 'And the position of the paper and its current proprietor.'

'I refuse to have anything more to do with you and your preposterous opinions,' West snapped back.

'I give you forty-eight hours,' Spurway said. 'I shall then give the whole story of Baker, Gregory, you and me to the world. I shall call a press conference and give every other newspaper the story as I see it. A number of M.P.s will be interested, especially Opposition members. Mr Mortimer is with me in this.'

'I have neither suspended nor sacked Mr Mortimer.'

'He is under contract,' Spurway said.

West turned to Crossthwaite. 'Perhaps you'd better go

now,' he said curtly. 'You, to, Miss Moore. And perhaps Mr Mortimer need not stay on.'

'I think he should,' Spurway said flatly. He gazed at the lengthening ash of his cigar. A useful piece of oneupmanship, I thought. Well worth cultivation.

Crossthwaite and Miss Moore left.

'This is an untidy spot to put me in at this particular moment in time, Mike,' West began in a firm-but-willing-to-be-conciliatory tone. 'I'm sorry for what I said just now; let's put that aside. You must know I'm involved in certain negotiations concerning the use of our colour machines.'

Spurway laughed. '*Our* colour machines! Since when? And how should I know? Who told me?'

'You've doubtless read the garbled version the Sunday Times has got hold of. That doesn't make things any easier for me.'

'How garbled?'

'They've got only half the story.'

'Why not tell me the other half and let me decide how garbled it is? Anyway, why do I have to learn these things through the Sunday Times and my own City editor? Was I brought in here as a colleague or a stooge?'

'Take it easy, Mike. As I see it, these matters are strictly managerial. You were running the editorial side. Running it extremely well. I've no complaints. But . . .'

'Thanks for the unsolicited testimonial,' Spurway interrupted. 'I was also your stooge, was I not?'

'Certainly not. You were a partner in all I planned.'

'Phooey!' Spurway scoffed.

For a moment I thought West would call off his attempts at mollifying his editor, but he made a big effort and said:

'That's not fair, Mike, and you know it. I gave you full editorial freedom, but these negotiations involve millions of pounds, and they're pretty delicate. I was playing my cards pretty close to my chest. I had to. Part of the deal is that New Sunday goes over to the new tenants of our machines as I might call them. I am not selling anything but the capacity of our machines in exactly the same way that Thomson sells the capacity of his machines to print the

London end of the Guardian and the Northern editions of the Mirror. But this is far bigger, of course. All contracts will be honoured to the letter. All jobs are guaranteed. But this Baker débâcle is inevitably going to make the final stages of negotiations much more difficult. It suggests editorial immaturity. It's a grave liability to have thrown into discussions at this late stage. Can't you see that?'

'Of course I can see it,' Spurway barked. 'My simple answer is: serve you bloody right. Another time, if you ever start another newspaper, take your editor into your confidence from square one on. The hell with you and your negotiations!' He stood up. 'If you're sacking me today send down a formal letter, will you? But look at my contract first. Carefully. There are one or two items in that I fought for good and hard. And they're going to cost you real folding money—even by your standards.'

'Now look, Mike. Sit down, please. Isn't there a way out of this mess? The heads of the new group are very respectful of what you and your team have done here. They recognize the notable new ideas you've brought into Fleet Street. They need the same kind of fresh wind blowing through their own musty corridors.'

Spurway sat down again: 'Why didn't you have the guts to go on with New Sunday?' he asked quietly as if settling down for a club gossip.

'I'm not a newspaper man, Mike. You know that. I'm a financier. I've no views to put across. I like the way this country is run. It suits me. These machines were ludicrous for the New Sunday project. You must have realized that. They were never intended for any paper of mine. They were brought into this country in great secrecy, one by one, ordered by nominees, installed with the utmost circumspection, in order that I could increase the scale of the West Publishing Corporation's activities, not to air my views on international economics or foreign policy. They were intended for other paying users from the very beginning.'

'And New Sunday was the sprat to catch the mackerel?'

'If you must use such phrases, yes. I had to show the quality and capabilities of the machines. What better way than to produce the finest prototype newspaper in the world?'

'I'm off,' Spurway said, getting up again.

'Try to see my side of things as well as your own, Mike,' West pleaded. 'There would be a great future for you here under the new régime. A very great future. Far greater than anything I can offer you. My colleagues are figure-men, accountants, marketing-men. There is no place here for a creative man of your talents.'

'That's why I'm off.'

'Think, seriously, Mike,' West said, standing up again. 'I can see that I have perhaps acted too secretively in these matters. One cannot easily change the habits of a lifetime and I should have known that the reactions of someone like yourself would be different from those of the kind of men I have always had working for me. Think about what I've said and for God's sake do what you can to clear up this Professor Baker mess if it's humanly possible. Act quickly.'

'I doubt whether it's clear-uppable,' Spurway said. 'It's true and we have to fight it.'

'I don't wish to fight it,' West almost whined. 'Negotiations like those I'm currently involved in are difficult enough without taking such bombshells into the conference-room.'

'It won't wreck your deal,' Spurway sneered.

'Of course it won't,' West said brusquely as if his financial genius were being denigrated.

'Then learn to live with the bomb. Put an extra quarter million on your price if your machines are what they want. Come on, Paul, there's nothing here for us. It's a different world and a different language.'

I got up, nodded to West and went from the room, Spurway holding the door open.

Waiting for the lift I said: 'What's so different about your world and West's? You've been a stooge for West, Robbins was a stoge for you, I'm a stooge for both of you.'

'That's a point I hadn't thought of,' Spurway said, taking a final loving draw at his cigar. He smiled as he ground the stub into the ashtray by the lift. 'Amusing,' he said, ruminating. 'But not very flattering.'

Later that afternoon, Miss Moore rang down to Elspeth to say that in view of recent developments Mr West had decided to postpone his dinner-party. I wasn't surprised.

61

About half-past two the following afternoon, Wednesday, the house phone rang. 'Reception. One of the Commission-aires wants you,' Elspeth said.

Car trouble, I thought. Bloody wardens in Old Bailey, and took up my extension, but the voice said: 'Mr Mortimer, a gentleman here would like a word with you.'

Why the hell can't he ring for an appointment? I thought, but an uncertain voice said: 'Mr Mortimer, my name is Walter Storey. I believe you knew my son.'

'I did indeed.'

'I was wondering whether you could spare me a few minutes in order to discuss one or two matters of possible consequence to us both.'

The voice and the words had a curiously old-fashioned formality. I said I'd come down: or would he rather come up?

'I'd rather we went elsewhere if you can think of a place where we can talk. Would you care to come to my Club? Shall we say the Reform Club?'

'That's perfectly agreeable to me.'

'Then shall we say that we should meet there in half an hour's time?'

'But now you're here I can come down straightaway.'

'No, thank you, Mr Mortimer, I'd rather meet you there. . . . All right then. I'll wait here. Thank you. Yes, I'll wait here.' He sounded lost and uncertain and about ninety. I rang off.

'Ring back to reception and tell 'em to keep an eye on the old boy who just rang up,' I told Elspeth. 'They're not to let him go even if it means tying him up.'

I grabbed my coat from the peg and rushed out to the lift. Yet Storey wasn't all that old, I discovered, when I got down to the ground floor. Somewhere in his late sixties, I judged. In fact, Tim Storey had said that.

Storey père was a small, compact man, square-shouldered, square-jawed, grey-eyed, white-haired and with a grizzled grey moustache. He looked like one of those temporary boy majors of the First War who'd never afterwards been able to demilitarize himself. Even his old-fashioned blue Melton fly-fronted overcoat and bowler were touches from an earlier age.

'Come to my Club, the Garrick,' I said quickly, thinking he'd probably talk more freely away from the background of his own Club.

He agreed. We went out into an unseasonably sunny but chilly afternoon. A train rumbled across the bridge. Men and women climbed Ludgate Hill with heavy slothful steps, their overcoats heavy on their backs. I got a taxi coming down the hill. Neither of us spoke, as if in agreement to keep our words until we could talk without interruption. Fleet Street and the Strand were oddly clear of traffic. We were at the Club in five minutes.

Fortunately the Smoking Room was empty. I ordered tea. Until the steward reappeared neither of us spoke.

I poured tea, trying to feel sorrow for him in his loss, but only a sense of the waste of young Storey's life came through.

At last Storey spoke. He talked without looking at me, staring down into his cup as if in a trance. 'You doubtless know of my son's death,' he said slowly.

I said I'd read of it.

'You had had recent discussions with him, I gather?'

Surprised, I admitted I had.

'I only learned of them last Sunday,' Storey said. 'He came down to my house at Cookham Dean and told me, amongst other things, of his two meetings with you and of their purport.' He paused. 'He also showed me a paragraph which appeared in your feature article.' He paused again. 'All this is very difficult for me, you will understand, Mr Mortimer.'

'I can understand that,' I murmured.

He began to stir the tea slowly, intently considering the

cup. 'I was very fond of my son, Mr Mortimer. Love is the word, I suppose. It is a word I have not used in a personal sense for over forty years. Extraordinary. The trouble is that I suffered from this ghastly English disease of being unable to let him know this simple fact. Have you any children?'

'A young daughter.'

He was silent for several seconds. Then, as if revealing a great truth, he said: 'If you love her, tell her so. And, of course, others you love. What a curious thing for me to be telling anyone at my age on a winter's afternoon.'

A dry sound came from his throat: whether a choked cackle or would-be laughter I could not judge.

'I was also very fond of Miss Munro,' he added as an afterthought.

'She was charming and beautiful.'

'And very efficient,' he added, completing the joint testimonial. 'One of the purposes my son travelled to Cookham was to tell me that he wished to marry Miss Munro.'

'They made a handsome pair. They seemed to be very much in love.'

He nodded slowly, although he seemed not to hear. He had his own tale to tell. At last he said slowly, 'I see that now.' After another long pause he said: 'I utterly condemned the match, Mr Mortimer.' He sounded like a Victorian rector recalling an unsuitable pairing.

'But why?' I asked, surprised.

'I cannot think. No, that is not true. It is only too clear. It is a strange thing, but Miss Munro meant the world to me. I treated her as if she were my own daughter—we have no daughter. Tim was our only child. But only in office hours, Mr Mortimer. Outside the office hours her life was a mystery to me, although I knew her father was a postman, which, of course, made her, in my eyes, a somewhat unsuitable, even undesirable match for my son. At least, it did on Saturday. I told Tim so. In unforgiveable terms.

'We all say these things we can never forget or forgive in ourselves,' I said. Scarcely the happiest contribution to the monologue, I thought, hearing the words, but I doubt whether he even heard me, for he went on:

'In his turn, Tim told me, in equally forceful terms, what he thought of my generation, my views, my snobbery, and, finally, what he thought of my conduct in connection with my client, Mr Gregory. He called me a liar, a hypocrite, a legal crook, and so on. Many of the things he said were, alas, only too true or verging on unpalatable truth.'

I wondered where the tale would end. Storey put his cup and saucer down. I refilled the cup. He thanked me and, like an idiot child, took cup and saucer up again and continued to stir.

'You can perhaps imagine, Mr Mortimer, that since I was telephoned by the police on Sunday evening I have suffered the tortures of the damned. My wife, who was in agreement with me in condemning the marriage, is loyal to me, but it is plain that she thinks our refusal to condone the match and Tim's death are in some way related. Perhaps they are. Who can tell? An excessively overpowered car for our English roads, the memories of a recent bitter quarrel, so young a driver . . . who knows?'

I muttered my own brief thoughts on the matter. Storey did not hear them. He was coming to a point.

'I shall never forgive myself. I can never forget my son's contempt for my conduct on two counts: one social, the other moral. I can do nothing to atone for the one, but the other I must do something about—I owe it to the memory of my son. My wife knows nothing about our quarrel over Gregory. Frankly, Mr Mortimer, I am utterly incapable of knowing what to do and that is why I have come to you. I need your advice.'

I was dumbfounded by this unexpected appeal. For the first time since we had entered the Club he looked up. He also stopped stirring his tea. He put the cup and saucer down and drew his left hand wearily across his head. I offered him a cigarette. He took one and held it between his finger-tips in an oddly fastidious Edwardian manner. I lit it for him and he drew, considering the tip of the cigarette as if it were an exceptional brand, which it certainly wasn't.

'In what way?' I asked.

'You know all the details. Doctor Gregory is my client. I owe him certain obligations, including secrecy, but I gathered from my son that Gregory had told you something of his marital problems. He confessed as much to me when he came to see me, first about instituting divorce proceedings and again when he decided not to go ahead with the matter. He then told me that he had been offered a life peerage. He did not link the two occurrences. Who was I to link them for him? A solicitor may have his own views on many matters that pass through his offices, but gradually discovers that his main task is to listen and then advise. My son saw things differently, and now, perhaps, I do, too.'

'But to back your son now would be to violate your client's confidence in you.'

He nodded his head slowly.

'And you wish me to make up your mind for you in that?' I asked.

The brutality of my remark either escaped him or he was too anaesthetized by sorrow and self-pity to sort out verbal distinctions. He merely said, 'I am afraid so. I find myself in circumstances in which, I am ashamed to confess, I am at a loss.'

'Do you want me to suggest that you should tell Gregory merely to take his business elsewhere? Or would you be prepared to tell Gregory that he must decline the peerage which has been offered him, because you believe certain irregularities are involved, otherwise you must inform the appropriate authorities of your knowledge?'

'Obviously I would prefer the former course. All solicitors are moral cowards, Mr Mortimer, whether acting for themselves or their clients. Compromise is at the very heart of any day-to-day application of the law.'

'Would you be prepared to act as witness for me if I were to be involved in a libel action resulting from stating these things? Arising, in fact, from the paragraph your son showed you?'

Again he passed his hand across his brow. 'If my son was prepared to do this, then I must be prepared to do so, too. It is the least I can do for him.'

The old boy sounded very weary indeed, almost at breaking-point, but I had two more questions.

'It was your firm, I imagine, Mr Storey, that sent the letter on behalf of Gregory, accusing me of libelling him. How would you cope with that?'

'I only returned to the office late this morning. I heard that the letter had gone from one of my junior partners. I should have to repudiate the letter, of course. It will not appear very professional conduct, but there it is. Mr Gregory must get another solicitor to act for him.'

Then my last question, brutal, perhaps, but it had to be. I said: 'You are saying these things now, Mr Storey, partly, no doubt, under the stress of your great sorrow. Would you be as ready to repeat what you have said to me today in a month's time? And in a court of law?'

Storey, sitting back in the leather armchair, his arms limply resting along the arms, his eyes closed, said slowly: 'I shall see Doctor Gregory tomorrow, Mr Mortimer. I have already asked him to come to London. I now see these things in a different light. And my memory of my son is unlikely to fade. I have too short a time left for memories to fade.'

'Let me think over these things tonight,' I said. 'Could I possibly see you tomorrow? Shall I come to your office?'

'I wonder if that would be altogether a wise thing, Mr Mortimer. Would you care to ring me in the morning, if you please? I am invariably at my desk by ten o'clock.'

I said I would.

We sat in silence for another five minutes. Perhaps more. At last Storey said: 'Perhaps I should go now. Would one of your stewards be kind enough to get me a taxi-cab? My train goes from Paddington.'

We got up. He seemed very frail. He seemed, I thought, to have aged ten years since I had first seen him in the hall at West House.

I put him in the taxi, sent him on his way and then went back into the Club and rang Elspeth from the hallway kiosk to say I wouldn't be back: any messages?

'The editor said he would like to see you if you came

back, but said it wasn't all that urgent and could wait until tomorrow morning. I suppose you'll be in then, sometime?'

'Sometime,' I said, wondering how much time thinking really took. I had done so little in recent months.

62

Where is the best place, what is the best time to think a real problem through? might be an interesting subject for a sob-sister's Q and A column in a popular daily. I'd like to read her A.

Mine is a hot bath at the beginning of the problem. Then I fall asleep. Then I have supper, putting off the problem. Then I sleep again. In bed this time. I face my drowsy brain with the problem, hoping the uncanny, unfathomable, computer-like ways of the unsleeping sub-conscious, so clear to the medical scientists, will solve all. When I wake in the morning the problem is emphatically unsolved. I have a good breakfast, hoping that somebody else has come up with a winner.

Perhaps the method is too universal to be personal. And in a curious way I knew that I had to work this one out, not Storey, not Spurway.

That day I tried a different course. I left the Garrick and walked slowly through Leicester Square, along Piccadilly, into Knightsbridge. The sun was persisting, in defiance of Nature and the English way of life. A lot of pretty women seemed to be walking around carrying big boxes labelled Bazaar, Marion and so forth. Christmas as usual, was starting early.

I walked under the Bowater Arch, across Rotten Row, on towards the Serpentine until I found a bench. I sat down to think the thing through, but promptly began to doze, despite a chill in the air. I awoke some minutes later to no solutions but to a problem splintered into a score of segments.

The obvious course was to do nothing. But would that mean letting the libel case go ahead? Not if Gregory knew that Storey would testify against him. And that would mean that Baker would also retreat. He might go ahead on his own, of course, but I doubted it.

Simple. I dozed again, but when I woke I knew that solutions are never that simple.

If, via myself, old man Storey insisted that Gregory relinquish his life peerage, the gossips would undoubtedly link the *New Sunday* piece and the refusal. Questions would be asked in the House. There would be a storm. Baker's Ministry would be finished before it started. Baker, too. I set myself a questionnaire. Roughly along these lines:

Q: Do you believe in the Prof as Minister of Social Welfare?
A: None better.

Q: Do you hate him?
A: Genial dislike rather than hatred in any form.

Q: Does this new job need doing, anyway?
A: Of course it does.

Q: Do you hate Gregory?
A: Just feel sorry for him. Not very deeply, but enough. Who wouldn't?

Q: What do you want out of the whole dreary business
A: The end of it and a quiet life. A stab at West *en route* if that's safely possible.

Q: Why West?
A: No logical reason at all. Just don't like him.

Q: What would be the quickest way of doing that?
A: God knows. Can't think.

Q: What is your personal inclination?
A: To let the whole thing drift.

Q: But what does that mean? Letting the case go ahead or telling old man Storey to polish off Gregory?
A: Can't you see that's what I'm trying to sort out?

Q: What should you do as a so-called journalist of integrity?
A: That's simple: expose the whole damn thing, of course.

The so-called journalist of integrity was momentarily ousted by the sensationalist. God what a story it would make! What a killing! What a scoop!

But I kept coming back to the Ministry. Given a reasonable send-off, it might still prove to be one of the few truly beneficial innovations in British politics since Lloyd George's National Insurance Act or Bevan's National Health Service, and I ranked those two welfare ventures above all others in modern Britain. In fifty years' time, Baker would be dead. Yet all that he would get going in his bull-dozing, egomaniacal way might still be alive and kicking hard.

But to let Baker get away with this was to condone his contempt for probity, politics, the public. I would be an accessory before and after the offence.

Come 'orf it, Mortimer, I told myself. Hadn't some of the appointments made by every Prime Minister since Walpole reeked of complete and utter contempt for the public? And the tradition certainly hadn't faded, even in my own time.

Life peerages for old has-beens stepping down to make way for new whizz kids; baronetcies for time-servers; viscountcies for lickspittles; baronies for trimmers. What was so different about Baker's manipulation of the body politic in order to get on with his job? Somebody, something, had got in his way and he'd bought himself clearance by exploiting the British way of life.

Why not go through the list of probable results on the characters concerned? I asked myself. Name by name. So, sitting there, in the enclosing dusk, I moved on from my questionnaire to a game of Consequences.

Thus:

WHAT WOULD HAPPEN TO BAKER AND THE REST OF THE BAKERS? Complete downfall, resignation from his Ministry, Mastership, clubs, the rest, followed by a stooge advisory job to some do-gooding outfit. Perhaps more books, probably not. ANTHEA BAKER: Well, she'd just go on growing apples: her life would be least affected, if at all, apart from neighbourly condolences. THE BAKER CHILDREN: Scarcely children, but scarcely yet equipped to deal with this kind of scandal, especially the 20-year-old twins, Aminta at U.C.H., and Joshua at Cambridge. It would be a tough day for them when the story broke.

WHAT WOULD HAPPEN TO THE GREGORYS? For him, complete annihilation. Resignation of a tutor cuckolded by the Master of his College, a joke for every undergraduate in Oxford. Resignation followed by a stooge job: tutor with a Correspondence College, perhaps, offering a B.A. in three epistolary years? NAN GREGORY: A journey through the Oxford muck-heap. Divorce? Possible, not certain. Return to Australia? Probable. THE GREGORY CHILDREN: Upheaval. Probably no lasting scars and they'd probably change their names, anyway. Or emigrate, with their mother, to Australia. No extra heart-wringings for them.

WHAT WOULD HAPPEN TO STOREY? Ignominy of a low order. His son's violent disagreement with himself aired in public. Party to an attempt to deceive the State. Probable rebuke by the Law Society. Some kind of break-up in his firm, no doubt. What a finale for a respectable career!

I moved on to consideration of others:

WHAT WOULD HAPPEN TO SPURWAY? Triumph. Hailed as a brand-new version of the old-style nineteenth-century editor, exposing graft, corruption and all the rest. Another rung up the gold-plated ladder.

Then WHAT ABOUT MYSELF? The dedicated, worthy henchman of the above.

And WEST? Apologies all round, a hatchet-burying dinner. Sale of *New Sunday*. Hailed as a financial genius who had kept to his last.

Gregory was clearly the most vulnerable and pitiful. All the others, at a pinch, could look after themselves. But the image of Gregory persisted. The lifelong butt and buffoon. The clever simpleton, good in the lecture-room but a goon in the world, cuckolded, used, abused and finally forsaken. As Spurway had said: Gregory was the one we should try to crack. Go for him! Poor old Gregory!

I sat there, until half-past four. By then dusk enshrouded the park. The lights of Knightsbridge glowed like early Christmas decorations. I walked back to Knightsbridge and told the taxi-driver Swan Court. As I sank back I thought: As usual, Mortimer, you've decided what not to do. What positive action have you in mind?

But that was the part I had decided to leave to a hot bath,

followed by a quiet, solitary, self-indulgent supper and the awe-inspiring activities of the sleeping brain.

I might even ring Helen, I decided, and let her help me work it out.

Instead, I thought, I'd go back and tell Spurway about Storey père. That was the least I could do. I gave fresh instructions to the driver.

63

Spurway wasn't in, but I had some reward for good intentions.

Soon after six o'clock, just as I was about to leave, Marzotti rang from Venice. In the intensity of reflection I had almost forgotten his existence and mission.

'I now have all details,' he said. 'Will you write them down? There are numerous lines and it will take a little time. Or will I cable you?'

'You'll tell me.'

'There are two entries. In Italy we have a long list of entries which are copied from the passport by the proprietor of the hotel or his reception clerk.'

'I know that. I've been around.'

He laughed and went on: 'But all this is strictly between the police and the hotel proprietor. That accounts for my delay in these matters. It was a slow enquiry, exasperating in many ways, but I now can tell you. It needed much persuasion as well as lira.'

'Well done. I'll take down the details.'

'Let me give you the Professor's details first.'

'Take it easy,' I said hurriedly, 'and dictate slowly. My secretary's here. Here she is.'

Elspeth took down the details as Marzotti read them out, repeating words carefully in English and Italian. At the end I glanced at the list and took the telephone again, thanked him heartily, asked him to let me have his expenses. He was taking the overnight train back to Rome, he said. He would be glad to be on his way. Venice in November was a very sad city. We said our fond farewells.

The details he dictated were as follows:

COGNOME	BAKER
NOME	Andrew Frensham
LUOGO DI NASCITA	Heaton, Lancashire, England
DATA DI NASCITA	23.6.1902
NAZIONALITA	British
DOMICILIO	Winch Mill House, Lower Lecon, Herefordshire, England
DOCUMENTO D'IDENTIFICAZIONE	Passport
AUTORITA E LUOGO RILASCIO	Foreign Office
DATA RILASCIO	19.6.57 NUMERO 21579
COGNOME	GREGORY
NOME	Nancy Janet
LUOGO DI NASCITA	Brisbane, Queensland, Australia
DATA DI NASCITA	2.4.1937
NAZIONALITA	British
DOMICILIO	'St Elmo,' Reading Road, Headington, Oxford, England
DOCUMENTO D'IDENTIFICAZIONE	Passport
AUTORITA E LUOGO RILASCIO	Australian Foreign Ministry
DATA RILASCIO	10.12.58 NUMERO 10672

Then followed details of their room number, dates of arrival and departure, even the total of their bill for their six-day stay at the Bellini. Marzotti had certainly done a good job.

So that clinched that, I thought. I now held most of the worthwhile cards in the pack, including at least three of the aces. I could make my decision unclouded by doubts and reservations. Yet it still wasn't a prospect I fancied.

I stuffed Elspeth's typed details in my pocket. I would let Spurway know tomorrow. Fortunately, he was still out, and I left. I had no sense of elation. That I could break Baker and Gregory into a thousand little pieces was beside the point. I hated the whole damn business of being forced to be a man of action. It wasn't my line.

230

64

Before I ran my bath that evening I rang Helen to ask if she were free. She was. I suggested supper. She said she'd given Erika the evening off, couldn't leave Marion. Would I care to join the two of them for supper in half an hour? 'Actually, it's only me,' she added. 'Marion's had hers, but she'll be around, no doubt, nibbling at the edge of your omelette.'

I said I might be a bit late: could I have a boiled egg?

'Don't be so self-sacrificial. You can have an omelette. You know I'm good at them.'

So I took a more leisurely bath, deferring decision whilst I went on reading the *Evening Standard* until my arms got weary and the paper got wet. By then I knew, without any complicated processes of thought, my course of action.

I got up and towelled myself down, mildly resentful that the inevitability of the plan had arrived in my mind ready-made, without due processes of grave reflection. I would have preferred a period of agonizing gestation and reappraisal which others seemed to enjoy: cogitation, analysis, and the rest of the intellectual processes. Instead, I'd got a packaged job. On the other hand, it made the prospect of outlining to Helen the pros and cons of the problem, as I knew I would after supper, that much simpler. And possibly more interesting.

Yet, curiously enough, I didn't tell her a damn thing. Half-way through supper I knew I had to do the whole job alone, make or break. Any discussion, however supposedly hypothetical, would have been seen through by Helen, and would also be an off-loading of my own responsibilities, such as they were, in much the same way that Storey père had off-loaded his on to me.

We had a pleasant evening. One of those evenings when, for the thousandth time, I wondered why the hell we couldn't make a go of it. Yet if we were the kind of couple who could make a go of it, I thought later, I should, as a matter of course, have been discussing the whole affair with my wife without any of this ducking and weaving about off-loading responsibility and all the rest of the intellectual hairsplitting that takes the place of old-fashioned domestic nattering about this and that and the rest. What a hell of a complicated existence two so-called intelligent people can get themselves into.

I stayed overnight at Milner Street, but I slept badly. I had too much on my mind. Around six o'clock I got up, muttered my farewells and wandered back to Swan Court. The remnants of the wintry Indian Summer of the past few days had gone. A heavy drizzle soaked me before I was half-way back.

At eight o'clock I got Storey's Cookham number from Directory Enquiries, and rang him. The maid said he was at breakfast but she'd get him if it was urgent. I said it was.

I told Storey that the best course would be for him to see Gregory as he had arranged to do and to tell him that he could no longer act for him and explain the reasons behind this decision. I wished to see Gregory immediately afterwards. Would he care to ring me at my Flaxman number as soon as he got to his office and let me know the time Gregory proposed to arrive? I didn't want to be around and run into Gregory before he, Storey, had explained his decision.

Storey asked me to repeat my proposals more slowly. This I did. 'Perhaps I can save you the bother of waiting around at home, Mr Mortimer, if you have work to do. I can telephone Mr Gregory now at Oxford. Let us arrange the meeting for midday. I will let you know in any case. Or my wife will if I am pressed, although my train is not for another half an hour.'

'Pray don't let Gregory know, however inadvertently, that I shall be there.'

'But of course. I understand your feelings,' Storey said in his faint old voice.

I went into the kitchen and began to make coffee and toast. Within ten minutes Storey had rung back to say that Gregory would be early. He proposed to arrive at Bedford Row about eleven-thirty. I said I'd be there about midday, probably before.

Meanwhile, I set out two cups, two saucers and two plates.

65

An hour later, I rang Elspeth. I doubted whether I'd be in before lunch, I told her. I had a lot to do. She made suitable sympathetic noises.

I got to Bedford Row at about a quarter before midday.

I gave my name to a tall and pimply youth and told him I'd wait until Mr Storey was free. I had an appointment, I said. He nodded and blushed violently and then returned to his desk alongside a pretty young girl. Both seemed too young to be ekeing out their days as prisoners of massed black deed-boxes, old wooden filing-cabinets, rows of box files and foolscap folders. I couldn't quite see young Storey enjoying life in such a Dickensian dump.

Meantime, I sat puzzling over the out-of-character rôle I had undertaken, grinning idiotically to myself as I considered the untoward way ahead. Could I, for once, make men and events work the way I wanted and needed them to work? It was a tightrope walk and I was unskilled in the technique. But it was my own decision, at least and at last.

I hadn't long to wait before a buzzer buzzed three times and the boy stood up and, blushing again, said in a conspiratorial whisper: 'That was a prearranged signal from Mr Storey, sir, that you were to be shown immediately into his office.'

'Good for him,' I said, and got up to follow the youth.

He led the way through a wicket-gate, out of that office, along a short dark corridor to a door at the far end. The legend WALTER STOREY MA (OXON) was painted in antique black lettering in one of the panels of the door, which the youth held open for me.

As I entered the room, Gregory stood up. He seemed ill-at-ease and my entry undoubtedly added further confusion to his manner. He said: 'Might I ask what on earth this all means, Mr Storey? I have been subjected to enough indignity this morning without this insufferable intrusion.'

I cut across anything Storey might have been preparing to say.

'You're in too tough a spot to bluff,' I said. 'Sit down, as I propose to do. I assume that Mr Storey has told you that he's not prepared to stomach your double-dealing.'

'Not in quite such appalling journalese,' Gregory said.

I laughed and said, 'Not bad. Well, at least, you now begin to know something of the full extent of the spot you're in. I don't know whether you're proposing to be foolhardy enough to take your affairs, including the libel action, elsewhere, but if you do, you're cooked.'

'Of course I propose to go elsewhere.'

'Then there's nothing more for me to say. Goodbye.'

'And if I don't?' he said hesitantly.

'You're also cooked. Frankly, David, it's the end of the road for you. And for Baker. And you know it.' On the spur of the moment I took a chance and said, 'What time are you meeting Baker to report on this meeting?'

'This afternoon at three o'clock,' he said gloomily. His face was almost the colour of his dark grey suit.

'Where?'

'Why should I tell you?'

'Just because I need to see him and it would simplify things to see you both together, that's all.'

My apparent eagerness to get to grips with Baker was even more disconcerting to Gregory. He said limply: 'In his room at the Department of Education and Science.'

'Where's that?'

'In Curzon Street.'

'Good, I'll come and join you and talk it over with the pair of you.'

'You'll do nothing of the kind,' he said, a slave rebelling at the prospect of his master's fury.

'Look,' I said, 'in this matter I can do exactly what I like and you know it. I could even pick up that telephone, get through to one of the P.M.'s press officers and tell him that far from soft-pedalling on the Baker-Gregory story we're going to lead the paper with the whole grimy tale on Sunday.'

'You wouldn't!' he said, aghast.

What the hell had Nan Gregory ever seen in him? I

wondered, looking at the round silly face, the eager-beaver eyes behind the enormous horn-rimmed specs; the high bald pate with the tiny tufts of hair sticking out above his ears. Fortunately, women had a genius for spotting the gent beneath the goon, the man within the mouse. I knew I was being unfair. Physical appearances ain't everything, as Molly frequently opined.

'What is your final arrangement with Mr Storey?'

'Nothing. I'm proposing to leave things as they are until I've made other arrangements.'

'Until you get back and consult Baker, I suppose. You can't leave things as they are, and I'll explain why. Things are going too fast. If you don't write a letter to Mr Storey now, instructing him not to go ahead with the libel action, I shall print everything I know—and I now know a lot more than I did last week.'

'You're bluffing,' he said, defiantly, plaintively.

I took a chance. 'I'll start with a Venetian holiday at the Hotel Bellini of which I now have full details.'

He was finished. I was almost sorry for him.

'Let's begin!' I said. In a ghastly kind of way I was enjoying my brief spell of positive action. Why weren't all other problems as simple as this bullying procedure made them seem? And why weren't other opponents all as weak as Gregory? But what else could he do?

'Write this note on an unheaded sheet of paper,' I commanded.

Storey opened his desk drawer and took out a plain quarto sheet. Gregory took out a ball-point pen with the slow deliberation of a surly but cornered schoolboy hating the guts of his master. 'First write your home address,' I instructed. Gregory wrote. I then began to dictate and Gregory continued writing:

'Dear Mr Storey: On reflection I have come to the conclusion that, although the words in *New Sunday* about which I gave you instructions in my letter'—'Was it a letter?' I asked. Gregory nodded and went on writing—'of last Monday's date, were far removed from what I would have wished to read, they do not warrant the action I was then considering. In the circumstances I suggest that you inform the editor of *New Sunday* that you are taking no further action. Yours faithfully, David Gregory.'

'Good!' I said. 'Mr Storey will keep that. And now, Mr Storey, could I ask you to dictate a letter to the editor of New Sunday carrying out those instructions?'

I took Gregory's letter, read it through, folded it and handed it to Storey. He, putting a brave face on the strange events which had enveloped his office, pressed a buzzer on his desk. When the boy came he asked for Miss Goulden to come in with her notebook.

This was presumably Clare Munro's successor, I judged, watching a tall, young woman with horn-rimmed specs, a long nose and straight brown hair come hesitantly and awkwardly into the room. Storey senior, too belatedly, was taking no more chances around the office.

Storey began dictating: 'To the Editor, New Sunday, West House, Ludgate Circus, London E.C.4. Dear Sir: I am instructed by my client, Doctor David Gregory, that he now wishes me to take no further action in the matter which I wrote to you about earlier this week. I regret any inconvenience which you may have been caused by my letter, but I am sure that you will be relieved that my client has made this decision . . .' Storey looked at me.

'Which, he wishes me to emphasize, should be taken as final and irrevocable,' I said.

'Very well. As you wish. It is unnecessary, but I see something of your point,' Storey said, a slightly tetchy note moving into his weary voice. 'Pray type that letter, Miss Goulden, with two copies, and let me have the original as soon as you can for signature.'

We sat in eerie silence around Storey's desk until Miss Goulden returned with the letter. Storey said she could go, signed the letter, folded it carefully, placed it within the envelope and, turning to me, said: 'Am I right in assuming, Mr Mortimer, that you wish to retain this letter? Or should I send it in the mail?'

'No, thanks, I'll keep this one. You keep a copy.'

We were done. I stood up.

'Goodbye and many thanks, Mr Storey. It may be possible that I shall be seeing you again, but not, I hope, in connection with this matter.'

'That is my sincere hope,' he said, 'but if necessary . . .'

'And I hope to God I shall never be seeing you again. Either of you!' Gregory cried, standing up, tugging his overcoat from an old leather-seated chair. He pulled on the coat, blushed furiously, looked defiantly at the ceiling, and stalked from the room, slamming the door.

'It is sad, but understandable,' Storey said sadly. 'In many ways, I hold myself wholly to blame. Weakness, as in so many unhappy cases, has caused all this. I should have been much firmer, much earlier. Well, goodbye, Mr Mortimer. I trust this unhappy business is at an end.'

Should I ask about the memorial service for young Storey, or let it go? I wondered. Perhaps he had been buried the day before. Perhaps the funeral was to be the following day, Friday. Had there been an inquest? But all such questions would reopen the unhealing wounds, I thought. Best to leave the old boy alone with his sorrows. But what an office full of memories this place would be for this father from now on.

So I left the poor old tragic snob alone in his office full of shadows, weeping dry and yearning tears, no doubt, for his gay, rebellious son. Well, up to a point he had atoned— at least to himself—for the deadly disservice he had done his son. I was also grateful and relieved for myself. Above all, I was relieved to be out in the wide, post-war, neo-Georgian stretch of Bedford Row, despite the continuing drizzle.

To my surprise, my watch stood at only half-past twelve. I walked towards Theobald's Road, to the telephone kiosks at the end of Bedford Row. Gregory was already inside one of them, mouthing and dialling away like a madman, trying, no doubt, to get through to Baker.

I went into the other box, dialled the West House number and asked for my office. Elspeth said: 'Things are hotting up here for you. The editor's after you. So is Mr Morgan. So is Mr Hilton. And there's three outside people to ring. It's all getting rather hot for an unversed girl.'

'Things are fairly hot where I am, too,' I said unfeelingly. 'You'll get more versed as the day goes on.'

'I'll be in the ladies' rest room long before that.'

'I'm coming back for ten minutes, then I'm off again. You'll have to hold the fort, after that. My copy's almost ready, anyway.'

I took a taxi to Ludgate Circus, went up to my office, reassured Elspeth, skimmed through messages, looked through the post, dictated two letters and then rang through to the editor's secretary, Miss Francis, to ask if he was free. He was. I went across to his room. He greeted me: 'I hope your continued absence from the office doesn't denote cowardice in the face of the enemy.'

'The enemy being?'

'A multi-faceted beast, as I see it.' He reeled them off with gloomy glee: 'Baker. Gregory. West. Crossthwaite. The threat of prison. The certainty of bankruptcy.'

'I'm bearing up.'

'West has called another meeting, first thing tomorrow morning. Crossthwaite and his senior partner will be there. I gather T.J.'s feeling less charitable towards me today. He's after blood. It'll be quite a session. Miss Moore and notebook, no doubt. The end of the road for me, I suppose. Will you be there? You don't have to be.'

'Why not? I wouldn't want to miss it.'

'It's a pretty hot spot young Storey put me in and I've put you in.'

He got up from his desk and walked through into the conference-room. I followed. We sat down. 'I'm sorry, Paul. I know you were against it from the beginning and I can see I overstepped the mark.'

'But how? You're the editor. I knew you were going to. I didn't resign.'

'I took the easy way out. I should have put it somewhere else in the paper. Your feature seemed the logical place, that's all.'

'Forget it,' I said yet again.

He smiled, but his thoughts were way off. He jutted his

238

lips, took a cigar from his case, a clipper from his ticket pocket. As if musing, he said, 'I think I'm for the big jump. A pity. I'd have liked another year here. It was entertaining and I was learning. Fast.'

'But you could stay on. West more than hinted that the new lot would want you.'

'That was Tuesday. I gather he's got other ideas by now.'

'Hence this premature obit.'

He nodded. 'West has sewn up the biggest printing deal anybody's ever pulled off in this country. New Sunday will be enlarged, adapted, incorporated, absorbed, debilitated or killed-off. What about you?'

'I'm in much the same boat as you, surely?'

He lit up, drew, got the cigar going. 'I doubt it. It's my blood he's after. What's your drill for the rest of the day?'

'I'm out and about on Faces and Places. I'll be back later to finish it.'

'Well, look in here before the meeting tomorrow. Starts at ten-thirty, we might as well go in together.' He smiled. 'You look pretty cheerful for a man with his head on the block.'

'I like change. I've been with West over two years. That's a long time to be outside television. I've got to get back there. Things happen fast in that gritty world.'

'This hasn't exactly been an old steam job.'

'That's true. Look, what will you do? I gather part of the deal—*pace* questions in the House and all that—is that everybody's job is guaranteed. And it's not window-dressing or West's soft soap. It's part of the deal. The new owners need new talent as well as new machines. I know it's stating the obvious, but there it is.'

'Are you doing Miss Moore to get your information?'

He smiled. 'It's a thought. Finest pair of legs this side of Temple Bar. But you're way off-beam this time, buster.'

'I've a friend who contends a bird in the inner office is worth six in the general office.'

'Generally speaking, I'd agree with your soothsaying friend. No, I got it from Alan Pettiford. He's got his spies.

I'll keep you in touch. May see you later. Otherwise tomorrow here at ten, shall we?'

I nodded. We both stood up. I left him to his future and his spies.

Back in my office I wondered why he hadn't asked about Marzotti. His mind was probably well into the future. Even more to the point, I wondered why I hadn't mentioned Marzotti. I knew then I'd never intended to tell Spurway. At least, not yet. This one I needed to work out in my own way.

66

I lunched alone in the canteen.

Sitting there, trying to read a propped-up copy of *The Times* beyond my bacon and eggs, I also tried to oust the apprehension that was chiselling away at self-confidence.

You're way outside your league, Mortimer, an insistent gremlin's voice began to whisper. This could take you to the cleaners. Even to clink if you go on with it. It's a dicey game and you're not built for it. You haven't the nerve or the stamina. And what about the pursuit of truth, freedom of the press, exposure and the rest of the lingo of the Fourth Estate?

But I countered the gremlin's voice with a few personal facts.

With my own marriage a mess and an active share in another man's wife, who was I to climb up on the rostrum, clad in armour shining bright, and shout the odds in the market-place? And all for whom? For Spurway? For West? For myself? For the Great British Public? Did a journalist have to take a Hippocratic oath in reverse? To tell the whole truth, all the truth, all the time, every time?

Not a chance.

Then why not just drop it?

But the usual toxic lure to go on had got me. I needed to see whether I could get away with my very own notion.

And where would that get me?

Nowhere.

So why go on?

No reason at all. At least, none that made sense.

I finished my coffee, damned Spurway and Baker equally and went out and down to Ludgate Circus and got a taxi to Curzon Street.

67

Of all bureaucratic buildings, that fortress of the Department of Education and Science in Curzon Street must be the grimmest.

I entered the ugly block just before three and asked for Baker. To my surprise I was sent straight up to the fourth floor, Room 703. I made my way along a wide grey corridor. Room 703 held four typists. One took my name, went into the adjoining office, came back and said the Minister could see me.

She showed me into a small office, then into a larger room with a desk and a chair by one of the three windows. A very large table with a dozen chairs set around it straddled the middle of the room.

Baker was seated at the head of the table with Gregory next to him, back to the window. Baker was plainly set upon making a new kind of ministerial image. He had substituted a fairly smart dark grey herringbone for his more usual hairy Harris tweeds. Even his collar seemed under control.

'Come in, Paul,' he boomed. 'Take a pew.'

Whatever grim news Gregory had brought with him, he had failed to dampen Baker, who looked a formidable oak of a man, sitting there with his grey eyes gleaming, his shoulders squared, a long way off defeat. I had to admire the sheer nerve of the old monster on the edge of a scandal that could blow him sky-high.

I took a chair, swung it round so that I faced him. He said: 'David's been telling me his tale of woe. It seems there was a joker in the pack.'

'More than one. It was a rogue pack.'

He smiled. 'I thought you had a much weaker case,' he began conversationally. 'I still think you had. I gather it's stronger now. When I read that young Storey had got himself killed, I thought it was time to act and sent my letter. Wouldn't you have done the same?'

'There was still old man Storey,' I pointed out.

'David thought he would make no trouble. After all, thousands set about divorce actions and then have second thoughts within a day or so. And the offer of the peerage wasn't to be connected. Why should it be?'

'Not even by a solicitor putting two and two together?'

'If solicitors always acted on simple sums like that, the law would be in a bigger mess than it is. And even more behind with its time-tables. No, I think David's mistake—understandable enough—was to take his peerage business to the same firm. He might even have got away with that if young Storey had been less of a busybody or more of a man of the world. I don't think he would have made much of a solicitor.'

'Young Storey had the same idea—for different reasons.'

'And you think you've got us absolutely clobbered.'

'That Venice business seems to have clinched it. I've got all the details.'

He nodded.

We were like a couple of antique dons sitting round a Senior Common Room table discussing a scabrous piece of undergraduate delinquency, I thought; the hapless culprit closeted unwillingly with us, awaiting our judgment on his villainy.

Poor Gregory! He sat looking from Baker to myself like a furtive voyeur, plainly puzzled and wondering what kind of bomb lay beneath the apparent amiability of his two tormentors.

'I suppose you want a letter from me along the lines of the one you've got from David?'

'Similar. But I'd like yours direct to Spurway. I'll also want another from your solicitor.'

'I'll dictate it to him over the phone in a minute. I'd like a minute or so for reflection. I still think there ought to be a way out.'

'Only by shooting me.'

'The wish is there,' he said genially. 'For once, action doesn't follow.'

'So let's start.'

'Why not?' he said. He stood up, full of life, down but far from out. I watched him in grudging admiration as he crossed to the desk. From a small attaché case he took out some of the College writing-paper and came back to the table. He sat down and began to write. 'How will this do?' he asked, declaiming the words as he wrote: 'My dear Spurway: I think I was too hasty in putting my solicitors on to that paragraph Paul Mortimer wrote in his column last week. I don't think his words were in the best of taste . . .'

He looked up. 'Does that seem a reasonable reservation? After all, one can't absolutely crawl, can one?'

I grinned. 'Go on. I'm agog to know how your mealy-mouthed apologia continues.'

'. . . and they could have had, for some of your less well-intentioned readers and my more ill-intentioned opponents, certain implications which could still cause me a degree of embarrassment. I trust not.

'I have decided, however, in view of our long acquaintance, to instruct my legal advisers, Pollit and Muntz, to write you a note killing the whole matter stone dead.

'I hope a similar fate awaits the unfortunate paragraph, although I should be glad to have a correction to the words which implied that my wife and I live apart. We don't often live together, but that is quite a different matter. Yours etc, Frensham Baker.'

'How's that?' he asked at the end, handing me the letter.

'Not bad. Now would you care to ring Pollit and Muntz?'

'Not even a pause for breath or refreshment? We have a terrible tea and/or coffee contraption here which I find thirst-quenching in a real crisis. Comes out of a machine and tastes like it. Any good to you?'

'Too early.'

'You're very sensible. You're damnably single-minded.'

He got up again and crossed to his desk and the telephone. 'Get me Pollit and Muntz,' he commanded one of the girls in the outer office. 'Mr Muntz junior. Peter Muntz.'

We sat silent until the call came through. Baker took the call, and said: 'Hello, Peter. About that New Sunday thing. I've decided to can it. No, nothing radical, but I think I was being a bit hasty in view of my current commitments. And the editor's by way of being an ex-student of mine. So was the blasted columnist himself, too, for that matter. Moral: never trust one's cast-offs. All vipers. Well, see you soon. Will you get an appropriately phrased letter round to the New Sunday offices by hand this afternoon? Good. Hold on, wait a minute . . .'

'Addressed to me,' I said.

'Mark the letter Confidential, of course, and address it to Paul Mortimer, will you? Good. Ring me back here at this Mayfair number if you've any query. How much? Hm . . . you really think so. Could have founded a chair for Social Welfare with that. . . . Well, well. Must be big-hearted about these things. Bye.'

He came back to the table. 'Peter Muntz thinks that, based on the precedents he's been dipping into, I could have probably bounced your group for a hundred thousand smackers, at least—if I'd won the case, that is.' He laughed. 'Peter said it was an open-and-shut job. Couldn't lose. And now this. It's heart-breaking.'

'I ought to be getting back,' Gregory said, almost plaintively. 'We have a dinner party.'

'Not celebrating anything in particular, I hope,' Baker said heartily and brutally.

Gregory blushed pathetically. We knew the answer. Baker spoke for him. 'Yes, indeed,' he said, turning to me. As if Gregory were no longer there, he went on: 'What we haven't considered in all this letter-writing is what happens now? What about David and his life peerage? How do we hand that back? It's going to be very awkward indeed after your beastly paragraphs.'

'What d'you suggest?'

'Dunno, exactly.' He chuckled. 'Rum go, what?' He chuckled again. I wanted to join in, but Gregory's pathos was so complete I kept as stiff a lip as I could.

'How does one set about handing these honours back?' Gregory stammered.

'God knows,' Baker said. 'Has been done, of course. A chap who got involved in some extra-mural anti-social activities in a boys' club handed one back a year or so back. Remember? Pleaded overwork or something. You'd have trouble pleading that, old boy. But you'd better think up something pretty quick.'

What an unmitigated swine you really are, I thought. Yet, as always, I still found a kind of unholy joy in listening to his insufferable remarks. In a way, I suppose he usually said what few of us ever have the nerve to say. He turned to me: 'What happens after David's handed his peerage back? He was due to have the whole thing sewn up by next week. Am I to take it that you're dropping the whole business once this peerage business is dropped?'

'There's nothing else that concerns us,' I said. 'The rest is between you and David. I hope other people will drop it. David may wish to start his divorce action again.'

Baker looked sharply from me to Gregory, but his sudden qualm—even if there were one—was unnecessary.

'How could I?' Gregory said. 'How would it look after this ghastly and juvenile piece of collusion? We'd all be in the mud deeper than ever before, especially Nan. The Public Prosecutor might even want to take a hand in the matter. D'you think I haven't been through all this a thousand times in the past few days? God, what a fool I've been!'

He was utterly outwitted and defeated, a man at the extreme limits of none-too-bountiful reserves.

'Why hand it back then?' I asked in malice aforethought.

They both looked round sharply. 'What the hell d'you mean?' Baker said. 'Is this another little gambit? Fifteen years of stored-up venom bursting the dyke, eh?'

'Shut up!' I said with enormous relish. 'And try to stay shut up for five minutes. You landed David in this shambles and if he tries to hand back his peerage, everything I wrote in my piece last week will seem confirmed. Hasn't that occurred to you, you unholy bloody egomaniac?'

'Take it easy,' Baker protested.

'It had—to me,' Gregory said feelingly.

'I'd overlooked that aspect of things in the rush of setting-up this new Ministry,' Baker said easily.

'What a God-given gift your outsize complacency really is,' I said.

All Baker did was grin appreciatively and say, 'Man-made, my boy. Nothing God-given about it.'

'Well then,' I said. 'David keeps his peerage. Is that settled? Everything will be simpler that way.'

The Lord High Chamberlain at Queen Elizabeth the First's Court must have felt much as I did that November afternoon, thoroughly enjoying my moment of infinite patronage.

'If you say so,' Baker said with a huge grin. He, too, was enjoying himself. 'Arise Lord Gregory.'

I laughed. Gregory, blushing deeply, giggled nervously.

Once again I began to experience some of the feelings vis à vis Baker that I had known as an undergraduate all those years before. I remembered Nan Gregory's words: that the Prof had the gift of making everything seem so simple. I saw once again his grandiloquent contempt of all life's ills, ironies and inconveniences, living his life to the full on two planes: a teeming, minute-by-minute physical existence that would have crushed any normal human being, allied with a planned programme for twenty years ahead. 'In half a century at Oxford,' an ancient don at Oxford had said the week before on a *Panorama* programme, 'I've only known two men with this extraordinary power for subduing the slings and arrows and so forth: F. E. Smith and Frensham Baker. Adventurers in life, I call them. In the same way it seems to me that these astronaut fellows are adventurers in space.'

I turned to Gregory: 'Oughtn't you to be going if you're to catch that train?'

He agreed, stood up and turned to me: 'Do I take this as final, then? I've had as much as my nervous system can stand. I'm not made of the same stuff as you and the Prof.'

'The most dubious compliment I've ever been paid,' I

said. 'Take it as final. I wish you well, and I look forward to hearing and seeing Lord Gregory, the eminent classicist, discussing Greek drama on the telly. My salutations to your wife.'

Gregory blushed.

Less fulsomely, Baker said, 'Probably see you at the week-end, David.'

Gregory left, edging his way out of the room like a schoolboy let off the hook of authority.

'What a fascinating interplay of personality and circumstance this has been,' Baker said as the door closed. He might have been starting on a peroration after a discussion on *Madame Bovary* or *Moby Dick*.

'Balls,' I said.

'I beg your pardon?'

I repeated my view of his truism. 'Perhaps you're right,' he said agreeably. 'Nevertheless, you must agree it's been a most curious story all round. I suppose old man Storey's last-minute call to grace really cooked my goose.'

'A last-minute confirmation from Venice with all the details of your stay there with Nan Gregory cooked it even crisper.'

He nodded. 'To change your metaphor, I knew I was on very thin ice when I realized you were on to that. It was the kind of slip one overlooks at one's peril.'

'Peril!' I scoffed. 'You've never been in peril in your life.'

'Near enough today,' he said.

'You'll have to do better next time.'

He grinned.

68

I now had two letters in my pocket. A third should be awaiting me at West House soon after I returned. I began to wonder whether it was worth trying to get the fourth that had been needling at my imagination for the past twenty-four hours. It would be a dangerous game, no doubt, but I was enjoying myself. The day's events had been heady stuff. Perhaps I was getting above myself, but I went on.

'Would a Chair of Social Welfare really prove of any use to this country?' I asked.

'Don't be an ass, Paul. Of course it would. You heard what I said at my press conference. We need a unit that will abstract the essential meaning from the facts and figures that are available. Not merely collate them, but set them up as signposts for action. Obviously it's something that will have to come some day. Sooner rather than later, I hope. We have Chairs of Social Psychology and God knows what else, but nothing that does this job. But it'll be a long haul. Now what I'd like to see is a small unit, not more than four or five idealistic and energetic young graduates . . .'

I interrupted. 'This isn't a tutorial.'

'Sorry. I get carried away.'

'Why don't we get T. J. West to found it?'

'After all this? Are you mad?'

'We can try. Take another letter.'

He shrugged his shoulders as he again crossed to his attaché case. 'I find a dictatorial note creeping into your approach to fellow-men, Paul. I think you should guard against it.'

'You've done pretty well on it. I'm beginning to get a taste for it. To tell the truth, I'm increasingly astonished by the ease of it all. People seem to be yearning to be told what to do. I'm appalled and fascinated.'

'It's the first great secret of self-expression,' he said, smiled and sat down again. 'I'm all agog in my turn,' he said. 'I'm assuming you'll do this one *in toto*. No help needed from me. Fire away.'

'Head it Strictly Confidential,' I said and began to dictate very slowly: 'My dear Spurway, As you are doubtless aware, Doctor Gregory and myself take the most serious view of the references made to us in your issue of last Sunday. As you well know, our respective legal advisers have the matter in hand. I am told, off the record, that they will press for exceedingly heavy damages, and I am sure that your own advisers have told you the same thing. Yet I am loth to go ahead with so harsh a prospect for you and your colleague,

248

Paul Mortimer, for I well remember you both as former luminaries of this college. Full point. . . .'

'Must I?' Baker pleaded with a grin. 'Apart from that outrageous lie I'm intrigued by the way the letter is going.'

'Continue,' I commanded. He went on: '. . . I could have wished for any other course. Strictly between ourselves, and well behind the backs of my legal advisers, I am prepared to make the following settlement: that Mr T. J. West, proprietor of the West Publishing Corporation and New Sunday, should found a Chair of Studies in Social Welfare in this University to be known as the T. J. West Foundation. I have the sum of £100,000 in mind. New paragraph.'

'More than ever I like the way the letter is going,' Baker interjected. 'But whose side are you on, Paul? This is one of the most spectacular and altruistic gambles I've ever heard of. Quite fantastic. D'you think we'll get away with it? What rate of commission d'you have in mind?'

'Not so much "we".'

'Of course not,' he said hurriedly.

'And there's more to come.'

'That's the part that scares me,' he said, smiling.

I went on dictating: he went back to writing. 'As you can well imagine, neither my legal advisers nor the University authorities know anything of this suggestion. I should be banished from the University forthwith and for ever if it were to become known. On the other hand, I am also equally certain that the offer to found such a Chair would be most sympathetically considered by the University authorities: the Hebdomadal Council and so forth. . . .'

'I can guarantee that,' Baker said.

'I'm still dictating,' I said. He nodded. I went on:

'There is one further proviso for this suggestion . . .'

'The inevitable fly in the ointment now follows, I suppose,' Baker said gloomily.

'Carry on!' I said. '. . . and that is that a strong recommendation should be made by Mr West—which I should strongly support—that Doctor Gregory . . .'

'I can't,' Baker said. 'I know and dread what's coming.'

249

'You're in no position to query a damn thing,' I said. 'Proceed.'

'. . . or Lord Gregory, as he will soon he known, should be the first occupant of this Chair. New paragraph.'

'Oh, no!' Baker groaned.

'Oh, yes!' I said. 'Go on!' and went on: 'I trust that what I regard as a sensible, civilized and what I hope will be seen as an unselfish attempt to clear up this dreary mess will be considered in the same light. None of us, ultimately, wants these matters dragged through the Courts. Of that I am certain. New paragraph. I should be grateful if you let me have some equally off-the-record word of Mr West's reactions to this suggestion. New paragraph. I realize that I am to some degree placing myself dangerously in your hands by writing this letter, but I hope that the sense of magnanimity which prompts its despatch will be shown by you in its receipt and in your proprietorial response.'

'Quite a good eighteenth-century touch, that last sentence,' Baker said approvingly.

'I thought so, too.'

'Why are you doing this for Gregory, by the way?'

'In a curious kind of way I feel sorry for him. Not very, but enough. The way you've treated him like dirt. The way you've used his wife and used him. That kind of thing.'

Baker showed no contrition. 'He'll be unbearable, of course. Preposterously so. You realize that. He'll be quite impossible to work with. Why have you done this to me, Paul?'

'Sheer interest. It'll be fascinating to watch. He may even be your successor as Minister. Outside the House, of course.'

'Once he gets over his recent upsetting experiences and sees the whole thing moving his way he'll be insufferable,' Baker went on reflectively. 'He's a university bore now. In a year's time he'll be a political bore. And five years from now, if your scheme comes off, he'll be the universal bore. He'll opine on the air, dogmatize on the television, stupefy in committee rooms. Lord Gregory of Slumberland, God help us.'

I laughed at his outburst. 'You're speaking of the husband of your mistress,' I pointed out. 'And your colleague, possibly, in a great enterprise.'

Baker smiled thinly, and slowly shook his head. 'One doesn't sleep with women on account of the quality of their husbands,' he said, logically enough. 'One of the larger mysteries of the twentieth century is how she ever came to marry him.'

'She once explained that fact to my satisfaction,' I said. 'David took the place of her father.'

'On that basis, I presumably take the place of her grandfather. You're poor comfort to an old man's ego.'

'Old man!' I scoffed. 'I'll believe that when I see you down on your kneecaps acting like an old man. Anyway, enough theorizing. Action's the thing. Positive action. Put that letter in another envelope, address it to Michael Spurway, New Sunday, West House, E.C.4, and write By Hand of Messenger across the top of the envelope.'

'Your attention to detail suggests latent criminal tendencies at last finding appropriate outlet,' Baker said, dutifully following the instructions. 'But aren't you collecting a somewhat contradictory set of letters?' he asked gently and genially. 'I'm a crawling lickspittle in one, a contemptible defeatist in another, a beneficent dictator in this. If you're not careful, you'll find yourself like a bridge player with hands from two packs. Don't get 'em mixed, for God's sake. I shall, as you might imagine, be especially interested to hear of the reception given to this latest effort. Will you ring me?'

'Where?'

'I'll leave a message here.'

'Should I reverse the charges?'

'Why not?'

'Where will you be in the morning?'

'Here until midday. But only ring me if the answer is agreeable. I hate any kind of setback before lunch. Always been a weakness. Now, dear boy, although it may sound a most unforgiveable piece of pomposity on my part, especially after this entertaining interlude, I do have to see the Chancellor in half an hour's time. I also need to winkle some money out of *him*.'

I got up to go. He stood up, too.

'In an odd kind of way, Paul, I take rather a tutorial pride in your performance today. It has a touch of Regency bravado about it which I always tried to inculcate, as a side-effect, as it were, into the outlook and conduct of my students. Life should be seized by the throat and shaken.'

'Some are born with the technique,' I said slowly, thinking aloud. 'Others have to learn slowly. With enormous trepidation. Step by faltering step. Perhaps I've started at last.'

'Indeed you have. And to some purpose, I hope. Starting is the main thing. Faltering is unforgiveable. I sincerely trust that you will be ringing me.'

At the door I said, 'There's one point in all this that particularly interests me. Have you had any awkward moments as a result of my paragraph last week? Has your reputation suffered? Have you been embarrassed in any degree?'

'Nothing unendurable. On Monday five newspapers were after me. A few Civil Servants were inclined to be distant. The P.M. also sent a polite but icy note. That was the worst. But all were answered and silenced by the explanation that the matter was in the hands of solicitors.'

'But what about your reputation in Oxford?'

'My dear boy. You know my reputation. It is the tittle-tattle of Oxford. I have nothing to lose, as far as reputation is concerned. But I did feel rather sorry for poor David. And his wife. And more particularly my wife, although I happen to know she never saw the offending words. But if the whole thing had blown up and gone against me—as I now realize it would have done—this job of mine would have been finished. At least as far as I'm concerned. And that would have been a national tragedy.'

'You don't underrate your impact.'

'A fatal error for anyone. The world is full of self-doubters. We'll never have another Elizabethan Age until we breed a race of self-believers.'

'Hrumph!' I said, and then: 'Goodbye.'

'Goodbye, Paul. I hope for my sake—and for David's, of course—that your plan comes off.'

'Magnanimity is your middle name.'

'As you so aptly pointed out in my letter.'

I went down by the lift, out into Curzon Street and walked, in a curious half-real daze, along to Heywood Hill's. I needed half an hour amongst the reality of books. So much more logical, predictable, comprehensible than life. I was there an hour. By the time I came out I decided it was too late to go back to West House. I walked round to the Post Office in Queen Street and rang Elspeth to say I wouldn't be back. She groaned in self-pity, but I told her to leave, too. She sounded more cheerful after that.

69

The letter from Pollit & Muntz duly awaited me the next morning, Friday. After putting the finishing touches to *Faces & Places* with Hilton, I went across to Spurway's office.

He sat talking about the paper, as if without a care in the world and no prospect of a stormy meeting ahead. He had seen an early first proof of *Faces & Places* and had one or two suggested revisions to make, not especially important. 'Take 'em or leave 'em,' he said. 'We'd better be getting ready to go along and meet T.J. and all his legal ghouls. I'm half-dreading, half-looking forward to it. My instinct is always to hit back. I must curb it, especially now I'm knackered. Damn young Storey. Did Marzotti come up with anything?'

'Nothing of consequence,' I lied.

I took out Baker's second letter in the envelope addressed to Spurway. 'By Hand of Messenger', and handed it to him. He took out the letter and read it through, frowning in furrowed astonishment. Watching his eyes, I saw him read it again, still in disbelief.

'When did this come?' he asked sharply, looking up. 'Why didn't it come direct to me? Why isn't it sealed? How did you get hold of it? Why are you sitting there grinning like a Chinese executioner?'

'Because it's funny. Because I was the messenger. Because it's a long story and would take too long to tell. Because I'll probably never tell it anyway.'

'But this alters the whole thing,' he almost shouted. 'This will be meat and drink to West. Instead of a terrible bloody court case, he'll be half-way to a barony. Might even give the old bastard a hobby for his last few years; a new way to spend his shekels. I'd better try to see him now, alone, before the meeting starts.'

Spurway crossed to the house telephone and dialled. 'T.J.? Mike Spurway here. I've had a confidential note from Professor Baker which vastly changes the background of this morning's meeting. No, I'll come up.'

'Stay here, Paul,' he said, passing me like a rocket. 'I won't be more than ten minutes.'

He was away for half an hour. When he came back he walked, almost floated, through the door into his editorial room. 'Made for the job!' he said. 'You'd think he'd thought the whole crazy idea up by himself. He's mad for it. Can't wait to start. Who did it? You did, I know. But how?'

'It's a long story.'

'So you keep on saying. Well, keep it. Tell me when it suits you. Over lunch next week. We'll put three hours aside for the job. All I know, it's a natural. What a relief! I know I started it, that it was all my own doing, but it's still a bloody business to have hanging over our heads. I met Crossthwaite going in as I was coming out. He looked like the hanging judge. He'll look worse still coming out, after he's learned he's lost the business.'

'D'you mind if I ring the Prof?'

'Ring the old crook, by all means. I suppose I'll hear the tale one day. Promise me that, at least. I know there's no chance of getting it out of you now.'

'Next time we lunch as you suggested,' I promised. 'But let's wait until it's all signed and settled.'

'Within a week, the way things were going upstairs.'

I asked the operator to get the Department of Education

and Science, to ask for Professor Baker personally. No intervening minions. When the call came through I said: 'It looks as if there will be a Chair of Studies in Social Welfare after all. And very soon. You'll be hearing.'

'A notable effort all round, Paul. Very exciting. I think we all come out of it with honour, wouldn't you say?'

'Depends what *you* mean by honour.'

'Only a skilled sophist could answer that one.'

'Shall I tell David or will you?' I asked.

'Let's leave it to Mike, shall we?' he said. 'After all, I wrote to him, didn't I?'

I laughed. 'Don't work too hard. All these details have got to be worked out, don't forget. You'll have to square the authorities, you'll have to meet West, you'll have to co-opt David. . . .'

'Quite a programme. Thankfully, I know most of the drill. Give Mike my regards. Must go now, dear boy.'

I turned to Spurway. 'You're right,' I said. 'An old crook.'

'And he'd like you to tell Gregory the good news.'

'Willingly.'

70

That afternoon I wrote a final paragraph for that week's *Faces & Places*, now buried in the files of the first and last dozen numbers of *New Sunday*, before the paper was merged, as a weekend supplement, to that new version of that old favourite family newspaper, once upon a time selling three million copies a day in black-and-white and now five millions in colour.

The files reside in the Newspaper Records Office of the British Museum out at Colindale, but nobody apart from thesis-writers will ever read them again.

Under the heading of DEPARTMENT OF CORRECTION, the footnote ran: In last week's *Faces & Places*, reference was made to the friendship of Professor Frensham Baker, the newly appointed Minister of Social Welfare, and Doctor David Gregory, the new life peer. It has been pointed out to me that the paragraph might easily have unintentional

255

implications read into it. My apologies to both the Professor and the Doctor, who receives his peerage this week, I understand. Also to Mrs Baker, who, far from living apart from her husband, is busily helping him in his new Ministerial tasks. *Faces & Places* wishes the Baker and Gregory families only strength and success in their brave new worlds.

Paul Mortimer.

'More than either of 'em deserves,' Spurway said.

He couldn't have cared less. He was already on his way: out of journalism back to colour television. Initial soundings had been made that morning, he said.

71

Early in the New Year the pundits on Granada's ITV programme, *What the Papers Say*, named Michael Spurway as *Journalist of the Year*, and *New Sunday* as *Newspaper of the Year*. 'There could be no doubt,' opined the spokesman for the sponsors of the awards, 'who was the Journalist of the Year, who did most for journalism: Mike Spurway, the man who moves between television and journalism as if born to both media—as he probably was. Spurway's imaginative and revolutionary editing of the short-lived, now-absorbed colour tabloid, *New Sunday*, made newspaper history, technically and journalistically. All those with the future of journalism at heart must regret the passing of this newspaper, which promised to bring fresh and much-needed new talent and techniques into Fleet Street.

'We had hoped to see these qualities reflected in the group which asborbed *New Sunday*, and in the supplement which was supposedly to be based on the *New Sunday* formula. So far, alas, few signs are to be seen. *New Sunday* died and has, it seems, been buried quickly by the new owners.

'Mike Spurway has now returned to television, but his brief and dramatic impact on journalism will not soon be forgotten, and there is always the chance that he may return to Fleet Street.'

And so on. Promise or threat? I wondered.